Try Your WORST

Also by Chatham Greenfield

Time and Time Again

Try Your WORST

Chatham Greenfield

BLOOMSBURY
NEW YORK LONDON OXFORD NEW DELHI SYDNEY

BLOOMSBURY YA
Bloomsbury Publishing Inc., part of Bloomsbury Publishing Plc
1359 Broadway, New York, NY 10018
50 Bedford Square, London, WC1B 3DP, UK
Bloomsbury Publishing Ireland Limited, 29 Earlsfort Terrace, Dublin 2, D02 AY28, Ireland

First published in the United States of America in September 2025 by Bloomsbury YA

Library of Congress Cataloging-in-Publication Data
available upon request
ISBN 978-1-5476-1393-9 (hardcover) • ISBN 978-1-5476-1394-6 (e-book)

Book design by John Candell
Typeset by Westchester Publishing Services
Printed in the United States by Lakeside Book Company, Harrisonburg, VA
2 4 6 8 10 9 7 5 3 1

To my parents, for getting me on medication and into therapy. Good call!

AUTHOR'S NOTE

Try Your Worst is a rom-com that's silly, sappy, and joyous. I wrote it to make you laugh, squeal, and scribble down theories as Sadie and Cleo work together to solve a mystery. But it also follows Sadie's struggles with depression and her withdrawal from antidepressants when she stops taking them abruptly.

Please make sure to consult a medical professional if you feel you need to stop taking your medication for whatever reason. While this book isn't a tragedy, quitting antidepressants suddenly can have tragic consequences, and should only be done with the guidance and supervision of an expert.

Try Your WORST

Sadie and Cleo

SADIE KATZ AND CLEO Chapman were, quite literally, born to hate each other.

They were due a week apart: Sadie, on December 25th, Cleo, on January 3rd.

Sadie's mom willed her body to wait—she could not, in good conscience, give birth to her Jewish daughter on Christmas Day. Imagine the off-color jokes, comparing her to Jesus. Imagine her deserted birthday parties, all of her Christian friends (which would be most of them, growing up in Florida) busy with their families.

Sadie would be doomed to a lifetime of lonely celebrations with her parents. Absolutely not. Mrs. Katz knew she needed to hold out for a day, maybe two. But then she met Mrs. Chapman in Lamaze class.

Mrs. Chapman was trying to induce labor early to score the status of having the first baby born in the new year. Local news stations loved a cheery puff piece, and her second born would be the talk of the town. Of course, it wouldn't hurt that Mrs. Chapman herself would be the talk of the town too. She packed a travel makeup kit and a hairbrush in her hospital bag, in the event she could pull it off.

Mrs. Katz was inspired. That year's hurricane season had been brutal, tearing parts of their bed-and-breakfast to shreds. They rebuilt stronger, but they were ready for this year to end, for their daughter to never see it. Instead, her baby girl would grow up knowing that her first breath heralded a fresh start.

Their doctors warned them that they couldn't control when they'd give birth, that the babies would come when they were ready. But they tried anyway. Mrs. Katz scoured the internet for tips on how to delay labor. Mrs. Chapman ate thick wedges of pineapple, went on long walks, anything to help her daughter join the world a little bit sooner.

Despite all odds, they both started having contractions on December 31. On a blustery New Year's Eve, the sky ripe with a storm too strong for fireworks, they competed to give their children a chance to nab the sacred title.

Both women looked upward, toward the small TVs mounted on sterile hospital walls, blaring warnings of a hurricane on the horizon. They looked outward, toward the storm steadily picking up speed, the black of night fading into ashy gray, the rain cascading down the windows in waves. They looked toward their Gods. One who speaks to his people directly, one through a vessel—both being called upon in Flagler Hospital's maternity ward.

In the end, Cleo was delivered three minutes into the new year, at 12:03 a.m.

Sadie, on the other hand, was born at 11:58 p.m., on December 31.

Mrs. Chapman got the attention and acclaim she was after—the first baby of the new year *and* she was born during a hurricane. It was better than she could have imagined.

Mrs. Katz got a hell of a story to tell her daughter. She recites it often, always with tenderness. *I love you so much that I put up with being pregnant for an extra week, just so your birthday would never be lonely. You may not have started off a new year, but you were born a finale, that last, perfect moment before everyone bursts into raucous applause.*

Sadie, however, comes away with a different message every time she hears this story: that she was born to lose—and Cleo, by some absurd miracle, was born to win.

I DON'T REALIZE MY tire's slashed until there's a stream of angry honking behind me.

Sure, I saw the little yellow exclamation mark lighting up my dashboard. I studied extensively for my driver's test, so I knew immediately that the symbol meant my tire pressure was low.

I thought it could wait until I got home though. The inn is only ten minutes away. After mere minutes cruising on a slightly low tire, I'd ask my parents for help. Then I'd curl up in bed with a cat on my lap, a mug of tea in hand, and the yearbook layout aglow on my tablet.

Instead, I'm jammed between a pickup truck and an SUV, the imbalance of my tires now very glaring. *Shit.* The honking starts immediately after the SUV in front of me inches forward and I don't. The design of our parking lot is deeply flawed—the single-lane exit is flanked by a concrete wall on one side and a metaphorical wall of cars on the other. There's nowhere for me to pull over and no room for people to drive around, so my flat is now everyone's problem.

I don't have time for this. On top of sorting out the yearbook layout, I have an AP Bio test to stress over and a pop quiz in Calc

BC that I'm *convinced* will be sprung on me by the end of the week.

Out of options, I reluctantly put my car in park. As I open my door, the driver of the pickup truck lays on his horn. "I GET IT, I GET IT," I call back, the cars behind him honking along in an excruciating chorus.

"WHAT'S THE HOLDUP?" Jason Hayes, the shining star of the football team, pops his head out of his car window. He thinks he's entitled to all the air in town since he's the player with the strongest chance of making it "to state," whatever that means.

"TIRE'S FLAT," I yell. Then I hear it. Cutting through the loud wail of honks is Cleo Chapman's laugh, loud and nauseating as ever. I whip around, my eyes finding hers immediately. We have a habit of doing that, like we're always ready for a standoff.

She's leaning against the bike rack with her friends. Bria takes a hit of her weed pen, enveloping them in a cloud of smoke. They're all watching me, laughing like we're in on some big joke. I should have known. *Of course* Cleo slashed my tire. She rides her bike to school, so it's not like she cares about the chaos she's created, especially when her main goal in life is ruining mine.

With the end of second quarter creeping up, she's probably feeling her grip on valedictorian slipping. I'm still second in the ranks, but I could overtake her any day. I bet she wants to cut down on my studying time, bit by bit.

"REALLY?" I shout, arms folded.

"What?" she calls back innocently—but that smug smirk gives her away. "Need some help?"

"Oh, I see," Jason yells. "Nice one, Chapman!" His voice is drowned out by a mix of laughter and more honking.

It's November, and she had yet to pull a prank this year, so I naively thought maybe we'd outgrown them. We're seniors now. Can't we keep it classy and just exchange the occasional death glare?

"Get a move on!" a voice behind Jason shouts. "Some of us have to get to work, asshole!"

Shit, shit, shit. I can barely hear my own thoughts over the sound of honking and yelling. I take three weak attempts at a deep breath, trying to remember the exercises my therapist taught me, before I stopped seeing her in favor of SAT prep classes. When my lungs inevitably fail me, I pull out my phone and call Mel.

"Hey, hey."

Two syllables and I can breathe again. "Hey."

"What's wrong?" One syllable and Mel knows the answer is *everything*. "And what's all that noise?"

"My tire's flat. Cleo slashed it as an early happy Thanksgiving or something." I roll my eyes so heavily she can probably hear them over the phone. For some reason, Cleo always pranks me around holidays. Like last year, on Valentine's Day.

The Aca-Ducts, the school's acapella group, were taking donations in exchange for a singing telegram sent to your classroom. Cleo paid for a telegram to be sent to every. Single. One of my classes. Not only was it humiliating to be endlessly serenaded in front of twenty-five sets of eyes, but their singing was *terrible*. And they only knew one outdated song: "All of Me" by John Legend.

Ever since, I've had to stop myself from punching a wall whenever it comes on. I want to punch a wall now, but Cleo would only win if I injure my hand on the concrete. I consider giving my Toyota Camry a swift kick, but it's been through enough today.

"Deep breaths. I can skip out on chem tutoring and help

you change it," Mel says. "Do you have a spare? Wait, you do, I made sure before we road-tripped to the Keys. I'll be there in a minute."

"No, I'm okay," I huff, pushing back a ringlet of hair. My curls can only stand a few more minutes in this humidity before becoming fluffy beyond recognition. "I know how to change a tire."

"Yeah, but your voice is shaky, which means your hands are shaky too. Hang tight, we'll fix it. I'll fix it."

"Okay, thanks. See you soon."

When I slide my phone back into my pocket, I look up, mentally asking one word: *why?* I'm not the type to curse God, but it's well within my right as a Jew to question him. And it's certainly worth questioning why Cleo Chapman of all people was put on this planet at the same time, in the same city as me.

"Hey." Mel's voice comes out of nowhere, making me jump. She's been on the track team for years, but I still get surprised by how fast she is. Without another word, she pops the trunk and starts changing the tire. It still isn't enough to stop the incessant honking. "EVERYONE SHUT THE HELL UP, WE'RE ON IT!" she calls back. "What do they think that's going to change, honestly?! You okay? You need your antianxiety meds?"

"I'm good," I say faintly. She gives me a look, like *bullshit*, so I head over to the passenger side where my backpack sits. By the time I've fished out my daisy-shaped pill case and water bottle, she's finishing up. "You're my hero."

She waves a hand, sliding into the passenger seat. "Mind if I tag along? I carpooled with Logan, and he's helping out the JV team today."

"Sure." Even after six months, I can't believe Mel's dating a football player. Like, she's on friendly terms with Jason, who's currently honking like his life depends on it.

"I'M GOING!" I shout, pressing hard on the gas. Now that the antianxiety med has settled and I'm driving full speed ahead, I can finally breathe. "Thank you, seriously. I'm sorry you had to skip tutoring."

"Eh, it wasn't clicking for those sophomores anyways. I'm just sorry you had to deal with Cleo's nonsense yet again. You should report her."

"I can't. I don't have any hard proof that she did it."

"Maybe take it to Mr. Simmons? He'll listen."

I laugh. "Yeah, to *you*. He'd never give me the time of day." Our principal notoriously plays favorites. He already loved Mel since her dad's an old college buddy of his *and* she's an athlete. But now that she's dating the Sea Turtles' prized offensive lineman? Someone like her is practically untouchable.

Someone like me on the other hand? A lesbian who once accidentally started a food fight thanks to Cleo? My high GPA gives me some credibility, but not as much as an athlete in his eyes. He would laugh me out of his office—if I could actually get in for a meeting.

"I hate that he's like that." Mel sighs. "Well, if Mr. Simmons won't handle it, at least karma will."

"Definitely. It's fine. I'm fine." I take breaths. In, out. In, out. It's okay. I'm going to be okay.

After a few minutes of Lamaze-level breathing, I'm home, in my happy place. The Katz Meow Bed-and-Breakfast was created for relaxation. Inside the pale-pink historic mansion are inviting suites, spreads of homemade pastries, and views of the water out every window. It's the perfect escape from the chaos of downtown and the stress of school.

My parents and I used to live in the inn, but two years ago, they remodeled the adjacent guest cottage for us. They felt bad about how small it is, but I prefer it that way. It's cozy, and even cozier in the attic, which I turned into my bedroom. On top of my soft rug and beneath many string lights, I try yet again to banish all thoughts of Cleo. Inevitably, I fail. "She's going to ruin my life."

"She doesn't have the power," Mel says. "Is she trying to? Absolutely. But she's not organized enough to succeed. Just ignore her. Attention is exactly what she wants—no, expects, since she thinks she's *famous*."

I groan. As if holding the top spot in our class wasn't enough of an ego boost, Cleo's now an *influencer* because of hands. Like, literal hands that she sketches and posts. There's variety— some have wrinkles or whatever—but they're literally all hands. Yet she's amassed a ton of followers, 71.4K the last time I checked, which, admittedly, was two days ago.

I'm not proud of how often I hate-scroll through her account, glaring at every glowing comment. I just can't stand that this one gimmick has garnered *fans* for the least deserving person.

And sure, I also hate that this account is the perfect subject for a Common App essay. I've worked so hard to get into Tufts, but if she applies, I'm screwed. She's a legacy thanks to her mom, *and* she's on the verge of social media stardom—no amount of straight As can compete with that.

Boston has always been the plan. Me, conquering the premed program, Mel, a short T ride away studying communications at Emerson. On Sundays, we'll meet up at the Common to do homework together. But if Cleo applies too? If she already applied early decision like I did? My dream will never become reality.

"You're hate spiraling, aren't you?" Mel asks. Whenever my

mind goes to dark, spiteful corners, she sees it in my eyes and pulls me out. She reaches a hand out of the soft gray hoodie she wears 24/7, regardless of how hot it is, and puts it over mine. She's one of those thin girls who's somehow cold all the time, so the fabric is worn in, familiar enough to bring me back to earth.

"No. Well, yes, I was. But not anymore." *She has no power over you*, I remind myself. A slashed tire means nothing in the grand scheme of things. If I get into Tufts—*when* I get into Tufts—she'll become a memory of that girl who used to get on my nerves sometimes. *What was her name?* I'll think as I laugh with my new friends about old high school stories. *Theo?*

"Want me to beat her up?" Mel jokes.

"Ha, yeah, you could totally take her."

She pokes my shoulder. "Seriously though . . . are you okay?"

"I'm fine, I swear."

"How's the new antidepressant? Are you doing okay on it?"

My body tenses up. I kind of regret telling her that I started a new one when it's too soon to know if it will work. But the last time she held me while I was sobbing, she had this fear in her eyes that I was desperate to make go away. I confided in her about my new medication (one of many that I've tried since freshman year) and made a promise that I may not be able to keep: that I'll be better soon.

"I'm good." I reach for my backpack and pull out my tablet. "I gotta sort out the yearbook layout, wanna co-work?" She nods and we fall into companionable silence. We stay that way until an alarm goes off, letting me know that it's 7:30 p.m. Without a word, I pull myself off the carpet and jog downstairs, Mel hot on my heels.

It's teatime, my favorite time of day, when guests mingle, compare trip notes, and enjoy complimentary pastries. For all eight years of our friendship, Mel and I have tagged along, pretending to be tourists while people-watching actual tourists.

I wonder who I'll be today. A British twenty-year-old considering a semester abroad at Flagler? A whiny fifteen-year-old whose parents dragged her here to marvel at old cannons and forts? A flight attendant splurging on the authentic B and B experience during a long layover? This is what I love about teatime. I can be anybody. When I walk into the inn's sitting room, I accept a cup of chamomile from my mom and slip out of my skin.

"First time in town?" an older woman asks, the scent of peppermint wafting from her cup.

"Third." After years of this game, the lie slips out easily. "I'm being considered for a marine biologist position, and they're throwing me through the ringer with interviews." When the woman's eyes widen in surprise, I add, "I'm fresh out of grad school. Don't let the baby face fool you."

Liesl, my cat, chooses this exact moment to wander up, nipping at my ankle. My parents indulge in my charades, but the cats give me away. I reach down, scratch her ear, and offer the woman a sheepish smile. "Animals love me—aquatic and otherwise."

"Hi, I'm Hannah, her sister," Mel pipes up with one of our go-to stories. When we were younger, we'd get so mad when people didn't believe it. If us looking nothing alike didn't give it away, our giggling definitely did. We've gotten better at fibbing since. "I'm a senior at UCF, just here for the free vacation and moral support."

"You two must have sipped from the Fountain of Youth on your last trip! I'm Margaret, this is Harold." She taps her husband, who's nodding off in a heart-shaped, pink cushioned chair beside her. "We came from Oregon to visit the fountain."

"It's a marvel." This lie doesn't come as easily. The Fountain of Youth is a sulfur-scented tourist trap that snatches its jaws around every visitor to St. Augustine.

The truth is, St. Augustine is a city of maybes. *Dine in the Alcazar Café, which used to be, perhaps, the world's largest indoor swimming pool. Sip from the spring where Juan Ponce de León may have done the same. Ignore the fact that there's no actual historical evidence he was here.*

I hate all these half-truths that, strung together, make up my hometown. Of the many cheap attempts to get money from tourists, the Fountain of Youth is my least favorite. What about it is worth marveling at? That someone may have stopped there briefly for a sip of water, while tearing the world apart for an impossible dream?

It doesn't help that that fountain is where my loathing for Cleo was cemented. I didn't like her much before, since she beat me to becoming the first New Year's baby. I hate losing, so I hated her by default, but we stayed out of each other's way. As a third grader, I wasn't exactly seeking a mortal enemy.

That changed the day we went to the Fountain of Youth on a field trip. Someone spread a rumor around the bus that if you drank the water, you'd stop aging. Maybe for someone Margaret's age, that's a tempting prospect, but for a bunch of eight-year-olds, it was straight out of an R. L. Stine novel.

When we got to the fountain, the only person brave enough to fill up a cup was Cleo. "This smells funky." She wrinkled her nose. Curious, I walked up to try it too.

At that exact moment, Cleo pressed the cup to her lips and, upon finding it not up to Brita filter standards, spat it out—directly on my face. It was a mistake . . . but when she laughed at me and everyone else joined in? That was on purpose. So I filled up my own cup and dumped it on her head.

The next week, she put a whoopee cushion on my chair. The week after, I stole all her pencils. As ridiculous as it sounds, that one field trip sparked a decade-long feud.

"You're doing it again, aren't you?" Mel whispers. "Don't give her any of your energy."

I mutter that I won't, knowing deep down that that's easier said than done. After all, hating Cleo Chapman is my birthright.

MY BIG, FAT, GINORMOUS crush on Sadie Katz is becoming a problem.

I don't know when exactly it started, but it needs to go the hell away. She's crawled into my brain and set up a permanent camp there. It's one of those pretty camps, with an air mattress and twinkle lights, but it still needs to be torn down.

I literally lost sleep because I kept beating myself up for not helping her in the parking lot yesterday. But helping would have made it worse. When it comes to Sadie, I always make things worse. There's a reason I can't seem to put an end to our pointless feud. My foot lives in my mouth around her.

Like, last spring, I told her that if she needed a tutor ahead of the AP Lit exam, I was there. I meant it, but she assumed I was being an asshole. She lost it, then I lost it, and in five minutes flat, we were screaming at each other in the middle of the courtyard. A circle formed around us, egging us on to fight. They were pretty disappointed when the most physical it got was Mel dragging Sadie away.

Yesterday didn't seem like a great time to have a do-over of that, so I stayed away. I did go up to her this morning, though, to tell her that I didn't slash her tire. I have no idea why she thinks I did. I've pranked her before, but vehicular vandalism? Not my style.

"Cleo." Ms. Blum snaps her fingers. "Are you still with me?"

I blink, shifting on my stool. "Yeah, of course."

"I need you to think seriously about what you want—not what your parents want. It's your future, not theirs."

"Uh-huh." Right now, what I want is to go home and sleep off the major headache that's creeping in. But Ms. Blum insisted I stay after school to talk art school options. *The clock is ticking*, she said dramatically.

"Tufts isn't the only option," she says. I don't have the heart to tell her that, despite my mom's begging, Tufts is barely an option to begin with. I have no interest in her stuffy, pretentious *alma mater*. "There's SCAD, RISD, even MIT, believe it or not . . ." She rattles off more letters, and I go back to tuning her out.

Ms. Blum is an amazing art teacher. She's like if Ms. Frizzle fell out of a screen, down to the curly red hair and eccentric wardrobe. But, like literally everyone else in my life, she cares too much about college. I don't get the hype. I'm supposed to make one decision that apparently determines the rest of my life? It's absurd.

I rub a hand into one of the many knots on my neck. Ms. Blum clocks it immediately, frowning sympathetically. She's the only teacher who noticed that my pain stuck around long after I fell out of that tree sophomore year. "All right, I've lectured you enough for one day. You should head home."

"Thanks." I grab my backpack and scramble to the door before she can change her mind.

"Cleo," she calls after me, "just think about it. Your future's bright, but that won't matter if you refuse to see it. You need to face it head-on, no matter how scared you are."

I nod solemnly, because I don't know what to say to that. Finally, I make my way to the parking lot. Thunder rolls overhead, rain falling in sheets. Just dandy. By the time I reach my bike, I'm already soaked.

When I go to undo my lock, I spot a gash in the back tire. It's completely flat. "Seriously, Katz?" I groan, looking around the empty parking lot. She didn't even stick around to see her handiwork—what's the point?! And worse, there's no one left to give me a ride home. Maybe one of my friends would swing back to pick me up, but I don't want to wait around in this storm to find out. I definitely don't want to go back to Ms. Blum when she's in lecture mode.

I resignedly start rolling my bike home in the pouring rain, Ms. Blum's voice in my head cutting through the thunder. *Scared.* What the hell did she mean, *scared*? What, it makes me a scaredy cat because I'm not naive enough to buy into the idea that college is the end-all, be-all of my life?

I'm so annoyed that I don't notice I've stepped ankle-deep into a puddle until it's too late. Great. This day isn't just bad, it's pitiful. Not only am I lugging my bike through cracks in cobblestone, the rain's now coming down harder and there's a concerningly brown substance coating my Vans.

When I finally reach my house forty-five minutes later, I park my bike by the garage and try to wipe myself off before heading inside. My mom will kill me if I track anything in. I open the door as quietly as I can, slipping off my shoes without so much as a squeak. Somehow, she still hears me and materializes like Casper the damn ghost.

"What's going on, Cleo?" Her perpetual frown deepens at the sight of me. "Why do you look like a drowned rat?"

"I got a flat tire," I say dully. "Had to walk home."

"You could have called me." Her voice echoes as she walks back into the living room. I follow her, because I know she expects me to. "What if someone saw you? What would they think of me, letting my kid walk home in a storm?"

Of course her response isn't *I'm sorry that happened, Cleo. Let's get you into some dry clothes!* It's the age-old *What would they think of me?*

That's always the question on the tip of my mom's tongue. It's the question that sent my sister, Lily, all the way to New York, wishing Columbia was even farther. It's the reason our house looks like a model home, so gray and sterile it's more move-in ready than actually lived in.

The outside of the house is gorgeous. It was built in the second iteration of St. Augustine, after the Spaniards who colonized the city got their wooden forts torched to the ground by the British. When it was time to try again, they wised up and used coquina, these shells strong enough to rebuild the city and keep it standing. Our house is a tiny bit of history that clashes with the horrendously modern and showroom-esque interior.

The only source of mess to be found on the entire first floor is the formal dining table. We never use it, but come September, Mom takes it over to prep for her precious New Year's Eve gala.

"Go wash your hands, then sit down." She places a towel over the chair beside her, like she does after Chester, our corgi, goes out to pee in the rain. He pants at my ankles now, blissfully unaware of my misery. "Want to fold some pamphlets? Ann's coming by to pick these up in an hour, I need help finishing."

What I *want* is to take a hot shower, slather Biofreeze on my aching shoulders, crawl into bed, and never emerge. But she's not actually asking. I wash my hands, sit down, and pick up a pamphlet, pressing it neatly along each crease.

I learned to fold pamphlets before I could walk, probably. As much as I hate the gala and its stuffy showboating, I don't mind this part. It's soothing, and it gets my mom to shut up—for a minute, at least. "Look at our big-ticket item this year. Beautiful, right?" She opens a pamphlet, pointing to a gaudy diamond bracelet.

"That's the big one? Not the weekend on a yacht?"

"This bracelet is one of a kind. It's priceless. Well, not really, it's estimated at around ninety thousand dollars."

"Wow."

"It's for a good cause!"

"What even is the cause this year?"

"It's a surprise. All I can say now is it's a big one." She purses her lips and goes back to folding, but I know she's not done. I can feel it. "Maybe if you took the time to understand delicate pieces like this, you'd appreciate them more. Fashion isn't *only* intended to be functional, you know."

There it is. The inevitable jab at my wardrobe of muscle tees and cargo shorts. I don't let it get to me that much. I mean, I can't stand her weirdly large collection of black turtlenecks, so I guess we're even. Still, I pull my phone out of my pocket and text Lily: mom's being Aggressively Mom rn. helppp

She responds thirty seconds later: lol, when is she not?

Then, btw, wanna talk soon? You still have time to apply early action some places. I can help you with your supplementary essays!

It takes everything in me not to bang my head against the table. Why not throw in a lecture from my sister, like an after-dinner mint to finish off this awful day? A slashed tire and a long, muddy walk weren't torture enough, apparently.

I still can't believe Sadie messed with my bike. The thought of it makes my fingers tighten around a pamphlet. I just wish she would understand that, yes, we've had our fair share of fights, feuds, and one messy incident involving a hard-boiled egg . . . but I'm not out to get her.

Have I stooped low before? Absolutely. I've put caterpillars in her hair, left a whoopee cushion on her seat, smiled mockingly when I scored higher than her on a quiz. But I was younger then. I hadn't noticed the way her eyes brighten when she gets an idea, how she fiddles with her glasses when she gets nervous. Today, though, none of that matters to me. I kinda wish that I *was* the one who'd slashed her damn tire.

"Cleo." My head snaps up at the sound of my mom's voice. I can feel every knot in my shoulders now, the pain going from a light spark to a bonfire. "Stop folding so aggressively. You're going to rip it."

"Oh, right. Sorry." I take a deep breath, steady my fingers, and move on to the next one.

Sadie

TEARING MYSELF OUT OF bed is torture. It's hard enough on a good day, but even worse when I have to get up early for an appointment with Dr. Milonas.

I've been on Cymbalta for two months, so we're checking in on my progress. Or, wait, am I on Wellbutrin now? After three years of cycling through antidepressants, I can't keep track. I rub a hand over my forehead, willing myself to be clearheaded. I can't give Dr. Milonas any indication that I'm off my game. If I do, she'll push me to try yet another medication that will mess with my brain in new, inventive ways.

My sneakers press firmly onto the carpet of her office, the leather couch creaking as I steady myself. Mom casts me a harrowing look, like she sees right through my faux cool demeanor.

"How have you been lately?" Dr. Milonas asks. The question is as loaded as the omelets Dad serves up at the inn every Tuesday.

"I'm fine," I reply at the same time that Mom says, "She's been sleeping a lot." I add her to the running list of traitors in my life, beneath Cleo and the woman at the inn yesterday who said she didn't believe I'm in a Benjamin Button–esque nightmare and came to St. Augustine to enjoy my last days.

"So she's been more tired on the Zoloft then?" Dr. Milonas always defers to Mom, as if I'm not in the room.

Right, Zoloft. Cymbalta was last year. That was the one that made my depression a thousand times worse, which ironically is something antidepressants can do. "I'm sleeping about the same. Maybe an extra nap here or there, but it's senior year. I'm busy." I shrug, hoping this is enough to appease her.

I just can't do it. I can't go off yet another medication and on to a new one. Switching meds is like being asked if you'd rather have your house flood or be set on fire. There's only wrong answers. I'll stick with Zoloft, the devil I know, rather than risking trying something that could be even worse.

I'll be fine, really. I got a 98 on my last AP Calc BC test. Mr. Hart is sure this is going to be the best yearbook yet. I'm killing it. I'm not totally happy, but happiness isn't what matters right now. Keeping my grades up so I can get to Tufts and finally thrive is the priority.

"Busier than usual?" Dr. Milonas charges onward, tapping her pen against her clipboard like she has better places to be. She probably does. There must be patients who are worse off than me that she should be getting to. "Are you facing any new stressors lately?"

"Nope," I say without thinking twice. The thing is, the cottage is small. Mom tried to conceal the noise, but I heard her sobs freshman year when my depression was at its worst. I saw her face when, through sobs of my own, I wondered out loud if my life would be easier if it was over. I didn't mean it. It just felt nice to have a break-in-case-of-emergency escape route. Well, nice for scared, fourteen-year-old me—not for my parents, who rushed me to the nearest inpatient program.

I spent three days failing to sleep in a bed that wasn't mine, wondering what it would be like to be able to cure a bad day with ice cream. When I got home, my mom was a wreck. I never want to make her feel that way again, especially not when I'm at my regular, baseline level of sadness and rage. Which, sure, is high, but I can manage. I *am* managing.

Do I sometimes, occasionally, fantasize about saying screw it, deferring for a year, and stay home instead of heading to Tufts? Sure. But that's only on bad days, days when the hustle and bustle of downtown St. Augustine overwhelms me and I can't imagine living in *Boston* of all places. I can do it though, I know I can. I haven't made it this far to give up before college even starts.

"Really?" Dr. Milonas asks. "Senior year hasn't been too tough on you?"

I make eye contact with the abstract portrait of a cockatoo above her head to avoid her skeptical eyebrow scrunching. "Nothing out of the ordinary. I applied to Tufts a few weeks ago, I'm waiting to hear back. But nothing else is new."

"She's taking four AP courses," Mom says, and I can't tell if she's proud or concerned. Probably both?

"Wow, good for you. I can imagine that's stressful. If you find you're struggling to handle the pressure, we could consider upping your dosage. Or switching medications altogether. You shouldn't be sleeping all the time. And maybe you should get back into therap—"

"I'm not sleeping *all the time*. I'm fine." Sometimes it feels like *I'm fine* is all I say.

"Are you sure?" She turns to Mom. "It's normal for her to nap sometimes, of course. Especially if she has a packed schedule."

"She *is* a busy girl," Mom relents, squeezing my shoulder. "I had to practically beg her to take a library aide class just so she'd have one break from the constant tests and homework."

"All right, let's leave it be for now. But I want you back in a month to see if your fatigue's any worse."

I breathe a sigh of relief, thanking her as she gives me a wary side-eye and a Zoloft refill.

Afterward, I sit in the passenger seat of Mom's car, sucking a Life Savers mint I snagged from the waiting room, pointedly ignoring a similar side-eye from the driver's seat. "You know you can talk to me, right?" Mom says, like she always does. "About the small stuff and the big stuff and the stuff in between."

"I'm fine," I repeat what's basically my catchphrase, looking out toward the water. We're nearing the Bridge of Lions, which connects the island where I have my appointments to downtown St. Augustine. I'm anxious to get to school in time for second period, so of course the drawbridge opens. We sit on one side, waiting for a boat to make its slow maneuver through.

"You don't have to be fine. Katz women are historically terrible at being fine. You know your bubbe—"

"I know." My eyes squeeze shut. I don't want to hear her long speech about how everyone in my family is as messed up as I am. It makes me feel like I was born to be broken, like sadness is my destiny. I roll my head back against the seat, doing my best to ignore the blaring boat horn below us. "I promise I'm okay."

For now, thankfully, she nods and pretends to believe me.

"DRAW FOUR." I DROP a wild card onto the sticky cafeteria table. "And the color is red."

"I hate you," Bria says around a bite of her burger, grabbing four UNO cards.

"You could never." I blow her a kiss. She mimes catching it with her hand and throwing it over her shoulder.

"Do you still want to swap Common App essays, Zeke?" Manuela asks, pointedly ignoring us.

"That would be great! I'm hoping to get all of my applications out next week. Do you want us to read your essay for Tufts, Cleo? How's your application coming along?" Zeke says it in that same curious but *totally not prying* tone that everyone and their mother uses. Especially my own mother . . . As if Lily's lecture last night wasn't enough, Mom greeted me this morning with, *Let me know when you submit your application so I can set up that alumni interview.*

The day Lily got rejected from Tufts was the most disappointed I've ever seen our mom. That's saying a lot because disappointment is basically her default. Now the pressure's on me to be the one to "continue the family legacy." Apparently Lily getting into four other prestigious schools wasn't enough.

I bristle so visibly that Zeke mutters, "Never mind," casting his eyes down like a wounded puppy. My stomach sinks with guilt. Unlike my mom, he's probably only asking because he cares about me.

"It's fine. I just don't know if I want to go to Tufts. My mom's on my case to apply early decision two, but I'll probably apply regular, if at all." I shrug like it's no big deal—because honestly, it isn't. My mom was pissed when I didn't apply ED I, but it's just one deadline. Letting it pass me by won't be the end of the world. Actually, I think applying now would be, considering ED apps are "binding." Like, if you get in, you *have* to go.

The thought of signing myself over for the next four years makes my skin itch with the force of a thousand mosquito bites. I'll figure out where I'm going during regular decision—if I'm going anywhere. Who knows if college is even the right move for me? I could go to community college and sell my art through my Instagram, maybe. Just because I'm naturally good at school doesn't mean I *have* to get a degree. My options are limitless, no matter how much my mom tries to convince me otherwise.

"I still don't know if college is for me," I say.

"Our valedictorian, ladies and gentlemen." Bria laughs.

I thrust my middle finger in the air. "I need more time to figure it out. Is that so wrong?"

"Not at all," Manuela says. The reassuring smile on her face reminds me why I dated her last year—and why I dumped her after a month. We're too similar. She's calm in the same ways that I am, so laid-back that she's practically falling over. It makes for a great friendship, but not for a great relationship. I'm more of an opposites attract kind of gal.

My gaze casts across the cafeteria, toward Sadie. For once, she doesn't meet my eyes. She was absent first period, which is weird for her, and then she avoided me in second period when I asked her about slashing my tire. Not only that, but she had the audacity to act mad at *me*.

Her eyes finally make contact with mine right as a voice booms, "SADIE KATZ AND CLEO CHAPMAN, PLEASE REPORT TO PRINCIPAL SIMMONS'S OFFICE."

My stomach churns, the terrible cafeteria burger threatening to come right back up. I do a 180 in time to see Matthew Pierce slip a light-blue note into the hand of the administrator overseeing lunch. The smug smirk that's permanently attached to his face is even smugger than usual. Ugh.

"Good luck with the mega bitch," Bria calls as I stand up. She uses *bitch* as a gender-neutral term, so I have no clue if she means Sadie or Mr. Simmons. I'm leaning toward the latter.

I've only been called to the office once, when Bria and I got caught with a joint sophomore year. Even then, it was left to an assistant principal who gave me a lecture on not "succumbing to peer pressure." Having a meeting with Mr. Simmons himself is a big deal.

"Do you know what this is about?" I ask Sadie nervously as she brushes past me through the double doors. We have the same lunch period on even days, so I guess we'll be making the trek together.

"He's probably going to tell us our valedictorian and salutatorian standings," she says nonchalantly. Seriously? I wanna grab her by the shoulders, shake her, and tell her she doesn't have to know everything all the time. Then, I want to keep holding her shoulders and kiss the hell out of her.

I shake my head, pushing the daydream far from my mind. "In November? Isn't that early?"

"Not if you're applying early decision, which I assume we both did. It'll be nice information for Tufts to have—or wherever you're applying." Geez, is this all anyone can talk about?

"Maybe it has something to do with the fact that both our tires were slashed." I speed walk to catch up to her. It's hard for me to believe we're the same height, with how quickly she walks.

"Both? When did you become a victim?"

"Uh, yesterday, when *someone* slashed my bike's tire. I had to walk home in the rain. My Vans got all muddy, see." I kick a foot out.

"I didn't slash your tire. You slashed *my* tire."

"No, I didn't!" I throw my hands in the air, staring her down. She stares right back. Brown eyes to brown eyes, we wait for the other to fess up—and I wait for my heart to slow to a bearable speed.

In the end, neither of us cave. She keeps walking, back to her quick pace. She always walks like she has somewhere better to be than me, even when we're headed in the same direction.

"Will you listen to me? I didn't slash your tire," I shout at the back of her head. She ignores me, not even turning around. "Wow, real mature, Honey Bee, giving me the silent treatment."

"Honey Bee?"

"Ha! I knew that would get you to talk."

"Seriously? Now who's the immature one?"

"Look." I run ahead, walking backward a few steps to maintain eye contact. "My tire was slashed. Really, it was, I can show you a picture. And if your tire was slashed and it wasn't by me—which it wasn't, I swear—then—"

"Who else would have slashed it? You're telling me you, the girl who sent a singing telegram to every one of my classes last year, isn't at fault here?"

I chuckle. "To be fair, I only did that because *you* signed me up for the talent show." I didn't know she'd done it until they called me up to perform. I ended up drawing live portraits of some teachers and winning second place. "But neither of those are the same as slashing a tire."

Her eyebrows furrow in thought. "No," she finally admits, "they aren't." Her face is dazed, as if considering. I open my mouth to respond, when she gasps. "What the hell?"

I follow her gaze to her locker, taking in the hypnotic circles spray-painted across it. They're weirdly blurry. *Huh*. Sadie's eyebrows narrow, in confusion or hurt, I'm not sure. Whatever the emotion is, I feel terrible watching it surface. I drop my own eyes to the ground—where a single red-stained paper towel lies. Did someone try to clean it off?

"Wow," Sadie says. When I look back up, it's immediately clear that she's *pissed*. My burger threatens to make another comeback. I should really start packing a lunch. "Now you can't pretend you didn't slash my tire. Who else would mess with me like this?"

"I didn't!" I hold up three fingers. "Scout's honor. Wait, is that scout's honor or the resistance symbol from *Hunger Games*? Whatever. The point is, I didn't slash your tire. Someone's framing me or something."

"Yeah right." She marches the rest of the way to the front office. I stay hot on her heels, shouting that I'm not the tire-slashing type, but she doesn't listen. Of course she doesn't. She settles into one of the plush turquoise chairs outside Mr. Simmons's office, turning her whole body away when I sit beside her.

“Excuse me.” Matthew makes a show of striding past us, equipped with another blue note and that signature smirk. He veers to avoid coming near my messenger bag on the floor, like it’s catatonic.

I ignore him in favor of Ms. Adams, the receptionist on duty, who gives me a friendly wave. I may have only been in trouble once, but I’m a frequent visitor to the office. Ever since the accident sophomore year, I find myself here every month or so, waiting to go home early.

I call it *the accident*, because it makes it sound much cooler and mysterious than it really was. My friends and I were at Anastasia State Park watching the sunset. It was a gorgeous one—the type where burnt oranges make way for deep purples in an instant. I wanted to memorize every color so I could try to paint them later, even though no palette could re-create it. So I climbed a tree for a better view.

The fall happened quickly. I lost my footing and found myself on my back, in the dirt. I was born with hypermobile joints, which I’ve always known. I thought it just meant that I’m flexible, that my joints sometimes bend far past the point they’re supposed to. But I learned something new in the hospital that day: hypermobile joints don’t heal right. Whiplash made a home in my shoulders and never left.

Now they’re perpetually aching, and there are days where the pain’s so bad I can’t think. I either stay home or, if it hits me midday, beg my mom to pick me up. She always rushes over, thankfully. How bad would it look if she kept her poor daughter waiting?

I bring a hand up to my neck now, pressing my fingers into it. The pain’s always worse when I’m stressed. Out of the corner of my eye, I spot Sadie watching me. Immediately, I drop my hand, poking her in the shoulder. "I didn't do it," I whisper. "I didn't, I didn't. I'm gonna keep saying it until you believe me. I didn't, I didn't slash your tire—" Her fingers fly up, plugging her ears. And she calls me childish?!

"Cleo." Ms. Adams's voice cuts through our spat. "Mr. Simmons is ready for you and your friend."

"*Sadie*," she says with a grimace, like being referred to as my friend makes her physically ill. I ignore her, leading the way into Mr. Simmons's office. It's my first time seeing him up close. He's bald, with a mustache so thick you'd think he's overcompensating. He sits in a huge leather chair, while Sadie and I are stuck in hard plastic ones. Apparently, the luxury of cushions is reserved for parents waiting to pick their kids up.

Mr. Simmons clears his throat. "I assume you know why you're here." Sadie nods eagerly, while I remain blank faced. What a suck-up. "This may be our first time meeting, but I know what happens in every hallway of this school. I'm well aware of your little rivalry. I've never bothered putting a stop to it, because you both have strong academic standings and I have no issue with spirited competition. I'm sure you can glean as much from our astounding football team." There's a glint in his eye as he says it, like he's talking about a great love.

"However," he continues after a dramatic pause, "today's escalation was not appropriate. I know vandalizing a locker may feel like a personal attack, but it's an attack on the school. Your lockers are not yours, they're school property. Therefore, vandalism of a locker is considered vandalism of San Marcos."

"Of course." Sadie nods somberly. "I agree completely. Appropriate action must be taken." She shoots me a hardened look, and I quickly shift my gaze away.

Mr. Simmons frowns, or at least he appears to. His lips narrow in a way that I thought only eyebrows were capable of. "Ms. Katz," he says slowly, "I'm confused. If you agree, why did you vandalize Ms. Chapman's locker?"

Sadie

WAIT . . . *what*? Vandalize *who*? *When*? *Where*?

I'm certain I've misheard—until Cleo starts laughing hysterically. "And you're over here lecturing me? What did you do to my locker?"

"What did I do? What did *you* do? I bet . . . sir, Mr. Simmons, she must have messed with her own locker to look innocent. She did the same thing after slashing my tire."

"How many hours in a day do you think I have?" Cleo interrupts. "What do you think I am, an evil mastermind? Like I'm Mufasa's cousin, circling a rock, debating when to push you off?"

"Scar was his brother. Why would they make a *Hamlet* retelling about his cousin?"

"I—"

"Girls!" Mr. Simmons shakes his head. I let out a tiny gasp. I can't believe I'm on the receiving end of a *disapproving headshake*. Am I dreaming? This has to be a nightmare. "This is exactly why I called you in here. I should have never let that courtyard screaming spat slide, not to mention the food fight. That's right, I may have chastised everyone, but I know it started with an errant hard-boiled egg from you, Cleo. This rivalry has gone too far. You're good kids. Your test scores are probably single-handedly maintaining our status as an A school. Don't tell anyone I said that."

"So don't you think—"

"*Because of that*, I won't put this on your permanent record and I'll refrain from alerting your parents." Cleo audibly exhales, muttering a quiet thank-you. Of course she doesn't want anyone to know; she's actually guilty! How does Mr. Simmons not see that? "However, if these pranks continue to escalate further, I'll have no choice but to consider serious consequences. I'll certainly have to notify the colleges you're applying to. You're both considering Tufts, aren't you?"

My blood runs so cold it nearly freezes. I might vomit. No, wait, I'm definitely going to vomit. I eye the trash can beside the table. Would it reflect well or poorly on me if I spew my guts right now?

"Simms!" A bellowing voice cuts through my rising panic. I whip around, coming face-to-face with Jason Hayes. He has a football under his arm, as if he's trying to look like a stereotypical jock. "Still down for that one-on-one about recruiters?"

"Of course." Mr. Simmons lights up at the sight of him. "You girls can head back to the cafeteria. And remember, treat this school with respect. Leave it cleaner than you found it from now on."

"But—" we both shout, in sync for once.

"Ah. Get back to the lunchroom, or I might change my mind and consider consequences *now*."

I stand slowly as Jason shuffles past me, giving Mr. Simmons a fist bump. I've never understood the stereotype that kids like me, who ace every assignment and answer every question, are teachers' pets. Half of my teachers roll their eyes when I raise my hand. They ignore me in favor of gossiping with cheerleaders, regaining some semblance of seventeen.

If Jason had vandalized a locker—*been wrongfully accused of vandalizing a locker*—Mr. Simmons would never believe he was involved. If I was a football player, or even dating a football player like Mel, I wouldn't be storming out of the principal's office right now, trying to figure out how to prove my innocence.

Cleo storms beside me, seeming actually upset, rather than her typical state of nonchalance. We're both silent as we head back to the cafeteria, until she makes a hard left. "Where are you going?" I call after her. The last thing I need is to get in more trouble for not being in the cafeteria during lunch.

"To see what happened to my locker."

I follow close behind, so frantic that I almost run into her when she stops in front of her locker. The word *lazy* is spray-painted across it, along with some nondescript scribbles. Cleo's face falls at the sight—no, that's too mild of a word. Every one of her features collapses. This isn't the expression of someone who vandalized her own locker in a contrived revenge plot . . . is it?

I'm not quick to believe that Cleo played no role in this, but I've seen her act. We had to write and perform an antidrug PSA together once, and she was *awful*. She can't lie to save her life. This isn't the face of a girl who's looking at her own work of vandalism. At least, I don't think it is?

"You didn't do this. Did you do this?" I search for any chips in her armor, any hint that yes, she could do something so absurd, then lie to my face about it.

"No! Of course I didn't vandalize my own locker. That's what I've been trying to tell you. Why would I do . . . this?" She points below the word *lazy*. I lean closer, toward what I first thought was a weird pink blob, like the drawings on my locker, but no. It's a pig.

Cleo, like me, is fat. It's one in a small handful of things we have in common (along with being lesbians, a good GPA, and nearly a birthday). In our many, many years of despising each other, we've never made fun of each other's appearances. It's too low of a blow. With this pig, the unspoken line we haven't crossed has been run through and battered.

Before I can second-guess myself—or Cleo—I snap a picture of the locker, for evidence. Then I pull my backpack to the front of my chest, rooting around until I find my makeup kit. I dab makeup remover onto a cotton swab and start scrubbing the pig.

"Well, that's not going to work," Cleo mutters. She feels around in her own (far messier) backpack, until she emerges with a crumpled-up napkin and hand sanitizer. She squeezes out a healthy dose. Together, we scrub in silence, until the pig disappears completely.

"There." I admire our work, satisfied. It's even cleaner than we found it, just like Mr. Simmons requested. Or demanded, I should say.

"Thanks for helping," Cleo says quietly. "You know what's funny? I've always thought this locker was unnecessary. I mean, it's never cold enough for jackets, and half our textbooks are online. I barely use it. But it still feels awful, seeing it messed with like that." She looks down, a pained expression contorting her face that I can't quite read. "Who do you think did this?"

I bite my lip, forcing out the five words I hate saying most in this world: "I have absolutely no clue."

Cleo

SADIE, LIKE ALWAYS, WORKS fast. By the end of sixth period, she has a list of potential suspects and a lengthy email drafted to Mr. Simmons. I know because I'm sitting diagonally behind her, drawing a sweat-drenched hand gripping a can of spray paint. The sight of the finished drawing makes my heart rate climb higher. I rip it to shreds without another look.

I don't know what her plan is, exactly. Mr. Simmons notoriously isn't on the side of justice. He nearly expelled Manuela last year because a racist teacher swore she stole from him. Her name only got cleared because the real culprit was caught stealing in the background of some girl's outfit of the day video. If we're going to prove we're innocent, we need hard evidence.

The bell rings, and Sadie startles to her feet, shoving papers in her backpack haphazardly. Well, that's new. Usually, she's already packed up and ready to go. If whoever's pranking us is doing it to throw us off our game, mission accomplished.

She still manages to scurry out the door faster than me. Curse her long legs. I follow her through the heavy flow of traffic headed toward the parking lot. It's starting to feel like all I've done today is chase after her. "Hey!"

She whips around, her tin lunchbox lightly whacking my arm. "What do you want?"

"What do I want? Hmm." I tap my chin as the crowd splits around us, forming two streams, some people occasionally yelling at us to get out of the way. "I want better funding for the art department. I want a UFO from Burrito Works. And I want to know who slashed my tire and made me walk home in the rain. We need to get to the bottom of this."

"The bottom of what?" Mel materializes beside Sadie, seemingly out of thin air, like she teleported here.

"What I was texting you about in fourth period."

"You mean the lockers?"

"And tires," I chime in.

Mel frowns. "Uh, didn't *you* do that?"

"Why does everyone assume I vandalize *cars*? Don't you think better of me?"

"No," they say in sync, before turning to each other and exchanging a pointed look. Rude.

A group of guys wearing salmon-colored shirts pummel by, knocking into Sadie. One shouts a rather impassioned, "Watch it!" in her direction.

She shoots back a half-hearted, "No, you watch it!" She must be really off her game; she never does anything half-heartedly.

"Well," I say, "regardless of what you think of me, it's the truth. It's, like, illegal to slash someone's tire. I would never take it that far. We need to figure out who's doing this."

Sadie sighs, leading me toward the old, empty fountain in the middle of the courtyard, away from the crowds. "I'll email Mr. Simmons tomorrow and ask him if we can review the campus security cameras. That will clear everything up, easy-peasy," she says cheerily, like she didn't spend the last hour scrawling serial killer–esque maps.

"After our conversation today, do you honestly think he'll

hand over the footage? That he'll be, like, 'Yes, I trust you implicitly, here's access to the school's security network'?" The thought of even making the request gives me anxiety. I doubt it would end well.

"It's worth asking. If he doesn't let us look at them, that's where you can lend a hand. Your sister's a bigshot lawyer, right? Maybe she could threaten to sue the school or something."

I see what she's doing. It's the same way she runs group projects. She delegates her partners one simple task while completing the majority herself, convinced that anyone who's not her will ruin her perfect GPA. "She's a sophomore studying prelaw."

"But at Harvard, right?"

"Columbia." I rub my neck. The more agitated I get, the more it tenses up, and the more I'll be paying for it tonight.

"Well, there ya go. She can assist with the legal side if the need arises. That would be a big help."

She has to be kidding me. "Golly gee! What an honor, to be your backup option."

"Don't put words in my mouth—"

"Uh, sorry to interrupt . . . but it doesn't really matter," Mel interjects, startling me. I'd kind of forgotten she was here. "The security cameras don't work."

"What?"

"The school keeps it quiet, for obvious reasons. I overheard Mr. Simmons talking to my dad about it at one of his poker nights. The system malfunctioned a few years ago, and they can't afford to replace them. They keep them up to try to scare people into following the rules, but they don't actually do anything."

"What the hell?" Sadie's jaw drops. "There's, like, six shootings in Florida a week. They can't *not* have cameras."

"They have one or two functioning cameras on the entrances

to see who's coming in and out, but that's it. Mr. Simmons said it was their next fundraising priority, but then they sprung for new turf for the football field instead. Typical. I mean, look at this fountain. It's been broken, empty, and covered in bird shit for *years*. If it doesn't help a team, it's not worth the money to him."

"But . . . how can they . . . ?" Sadie's eyes go wide with panic. "The security footage is the hard proof we need. Without it, we're screwed."

"Not if you let me help you—"

"I've got this. Go get high and skip rocks in the intercoastal, or whatever you and your friends do after school."

"Homework. We do homework." It should be illegal for someone to be as infuriating as they are hot.

"Do that then." She pats me on the shoulder and walks away, her curls smacking me in the face as she goes.

"SHE'S RIDICULOUS," MEL SAYS once Cleo's out of earshot. I spare a glance back to see her still standing by the fountain, looking pissed. "How could she even help you?"

"No clue, but I'm not gonna wait around to find out." There's no way I can investigate this side by side with the person who may very well be suspect number one. And I'm certainly not going to spend a second outside school with her. I can do this on my own—I *will* do this on my own.

"She did have one good idea . . . Burrito Works? Wanna get it to go and eat at my place?" Mel asks. "My mom's been freaking out if I'm not home or at your place right after school. You're so lucky your parents don't make you share your location with them."

"That's tempting, but I need to focus on figuring this out."

"Really? I think it's pretty clear that Cleo's the culprit."

"Yeah, she probably is, but I need to figure out some other suspects just in case. Mr. Simmons said he might tell Tufts. *Tufts*, Mel." I say it like it's a revelation, as if I didn't text her every horrible word Mr. Simmons uttered during that meeting as soon as it was over. Saying it out loud makes it a thousand times more terrifying. "I gotta head home and start brainstorming, sorry. Can you go with Logan?"

"When he's out of practice, yeah. But it won't be the same without you." She smiles. It's unreal to me now, how scared I was when she and Logan started dating. I was terrified she'd ditch me for him, but she's proved me wrong time after time.

"I'm sorry. Raincheck?"

"I'm holding you to that!"

"Good! Add it to our Google Calendar, okay?" I wave and make a beeline to my car, heading home at top speed. First things first: a power nap. As much as I'm ready to figure this out, my body's desperate for sleep.

I set my alarm for 3:50 p.m. Forty-five minutes should be enough.

When I wake up, it's pitch-black in my room.

I rummage around for my phone to check the time: 12:06 a.m. Shit, shit, shit.

Lately, I've been sleeping through my alarms so much they're practically ornamental. I swipe out of a text from Dad letting me know dinner's in the fridge, and get to work, equipped with the lavender notebook I use for Yearbook, a ballpoint pen, and my phone.

Initial panic aside, I don't think we're *totally* screwed. We don't need cameras to figure this out, not when I have my brain. First, I take my jumbled, anxious notes and transform them into a neat, bulleted list of suspects. Cleo's name, surrounded by a bunch of question marks, sits at the top. Her crestfallen face after seeing "lazy" smeared on her locker seemed genuine to me, but maybe that's what she wants me to think. Maybe it's all an elaborate act of reverse psychology so I'll look in the wrong direction.

If I'm being honest, it's easier to assume this is all Cleo's convoluted scheme. If it's not her doing—and that's a big *if*—that means somebody hates us both enough to not just pray for our downfall, but manufacture it.

I know I'm not the most likable person. I speak too rashly and have a bad habit of rubbing people the wrong way. What's tripping me up is that whoever's doing this is coming after Cleo too. For reasons I'll never understand, she's pretty well liked. Her social media following gives her a big boost, socially speaking. And whenever she passes by anyone, literally anyone, she flashes them this big, contagious smile.

So if (*if*, *if*, *if*) Cleo didn't do it, who hates both of us enough to get us sent to the principal's office? I look at my current suspects—eight in total. I know what issues they have with me, but I need to cross-reference to figure out who has issues with Cleo too.

I open up her Instagram, scouring for hints of resentment in her comments. Maybe a jealous artist, bitter that her follower count has reached an inscrutable 72K. Or a homophobe, annoyed at the emoji of two girls kissing in her bio. Or maybe someone who, like me, sees right through that "chill" persona and knows she's vain and obnoxious. There has to be *someone*.

But after scrolling for a solid thirty minutes, I find . . . nothing. Just hands, compliments, spam bots promoting T-shirts, and more hands. It's the kindest corner of the internet I've ever seen. I glare down at the comments, annoyed as I always get when I spend too long on her page.

ZahirA99: Wow, this is stunning. Do you take commissions?

banjobabezz: This one's as gorgeous as you are 😉

puppybear666: I love what this represents. The string that threads us to the world around us. So deep.

I can't help but audibly laugh at the last comment. I don't totally understand art, as evidenced by my A-minus in AP history, which is basically failing in my book. (Taking the class to impress the admissions office at Tufts was probably not my best idea.) But it's clear even to me there's no deeper meaning to Cleo's art. She nailed this one thing, so she draws it over and over, somehow provoking constant oohs and aahs. What are people seeing that I'm not?

I push closer on some absurdly realistic veins, as if magnification will magically evoke the same emotion in me that it did in puppybear666. It doesn't—so I pinch tighter, move my fingers wider.

And then, I make a colossal mistake. In all my desperate pinching, I accidentally double tap . . . on a post made two and a half years ago.

"SHIT."

I frantically unlike it, tossing down my phone like it's hot enough to warrant a stop, drop, and roll. *Okay, okay. This is fine*, I tell myself. It's past midnight. I unliked it immediately. What are the odds that Cleo saw the notification in that split second? Maybe 5 percent? Or is even that too high? A notification pops up just as I'm beginning to talk myself down via percentage calculations.

hands_off: late night lurking?

I groan, sinking into the purple throw pillow behind me. Anyone else would have laughed, maybe sent a screenshot to their friends, but ultimately had the dignity to pretend it never happened. Only Cleo would have the *audacity* to message about it. It's like she lives to humiliate me.

skatz29: I'm trying to figure out who dislikes both of us enough to vandalize our lockers. I was looking for hate comments.

hands_off: uh huh. Sureee

hands_off: you could have just asked me. I told you, this will be easier if u swallow ur pride and talk to me

I stare at the message for far too long, tapping my fingers against my thigh. One question won't hurt, right? It's probably a good idea to talk to my top suspect anyway. She may start yammering and accidentally give herself away. I wouldn't put it past her.

skatz29: Okay, fine. Who hates you?

hands_off: lol idk

I drop my phone again and scream into a pillow. Once I've (somewhat) gathered my bearings, I exit out of Instagram and fire off a text to Mel: Okay, seriously, Cleo Chapman is going to kill me

She responds within thirty seconds: You know I won't let her. I'll buy you a bulletproof vest!! 🖤 But remember not to give her too much headspace. She's not worth it!

I take a deep breath that comes easier than the last one. *She's not worth it*, I echo, half Mel's voice, half mine. *This vape pen of a human being is not worth any of my stress, time, or energy.*

After five more exhales, I reopen Instagram, using all my willpower to keep my response short and sweet, rather than typing out an angry paragraph.

skatz29: and this is why i didn't ask

hands_off: lmao relax

hands_off: I'll think on it & get back to ya

I stare at the screen, waiting for more dots that never come. I'm pulled away by the sound of floorboards creaking—Mom coming up to the attic. I've memorized the sound of her footsteps, quicker than Dad's. She doesn't check on me as much nowadays, but freshman year it was constant.

"Hey, kiddo. I had to deal with a leak in room six, and I figured I'd come check on you before I head back to bed. How was school today?" she asks.

I avoided her when I got home, precisely so I wouldn't face this question. I want to tell her the truth so badly—but I can't stand worrying her. "It was fine. Just typical Cleo nonsense."

She doesn't know the extent of my hatred, but she knows that Cleo drives me up a wall, all the way to the ceiling. "Oh, yeah? I bet you two have more in common than you think, ya know."

"Yeah, sure." This is her go-to line whenever I complain about Cleo.

"I'm serious! Have I ever told you how your aunt Suzanne and I met?" *Only one hundred times.* I don't bother saying this, because I know she'll tell me anyway. "We played softball together, and something about her just got under my skin. We couldn't stand each other. Then one day, I went to an anniversary showing of *Planet of the Apes* and who was one of three people in the audience? Suzanne. We shared popcorn, and now we're so close that she gets an *aunt* title."

"I highly doubt that me and Cleo will ever reach that point." I laugh at the thought. "But it's fine, I guess. I don't care that she's the most annoying person on earth. Well, I do. I just wish I didn't have to lose to her all the time. She's gonna be valedictorian, you know." It's so painful, losing that spot to someone who sleeps through nearly all her classes.

"And you'll be salutatorian. I wish you wouldn't see that as losing. Do you realize how impressive it is to be ranked *second* out of two hundred kids?!"

She doesn't get it. Every 99 Cleo gets to my 94 is a slap in the face. It's a reminder of how much better I could be, if only I didn't spend half my time fighting the chemicals in my own brain.

MY MOM SITS ACROSS from me, peeling a hard-boiled egg, and all I can think about is Sadie. She'd be insulted if I told her, but the smell of them reminds me of her. Specifically, it reminds me of sophomore year, when her hair was frizzier and she was going through a purple eyeshadow phase.

We were working on a project together for chem, and I had made the fatal mistake of doing more than the allotted task she assigned me. The *horror*. Okay, maybe I also questioned how knowledgeable she was and tried to turn the rest of the group against her. In return, she spilled some dye for the experiment on my lap "by accident."

At lunch that day, I threw a hard-boiled egg at her "by accident." I didn't mean to start a food fight, but she lobbed a handful of *spaghetti* at me, and she has awful aim. It missed and hit a sophomore on the football team, who threw spaghetti back. In an obnoxiously cliched move, someone shouted, "FOOD FIGHT," and soon, marinara streaked the walls.

I dove under a table; my mom would kill me if I came home with another pair of stained pants. Sadie crouched across from me, digging egg out of her hair. When she withdrew her finger to flip me off, I weirdly got butterflies.

"I was talking to Janice yesterday," my mom says, snapping

me back to the present, "and she thinks you have a really good shot."

As chaotic as it was, I wish I was squatting under that table now, instead of sitting across from my mom. I hate when she starts a conversation by forcing me to ask a question. I think it's a habit she picked up from talking to Lily, who barely engages with her. As annoyed as I am, I still humor her. "Who's Janice?"

"My friend who works at Tufts. She's not an admissions officer, but she may be able to put in a good word. Isn't that great, Steve?" My dad grunts in assent. He seems to dislike meals with her as much as I do, which is probably why he travels for work so often. "She thinks your social media is an asset. Budding artist achieving Instagram fame? That's sure to set your application apart."

I bite back a laugh. My guidance counselor said the same thing, but I don't get it. Instagram is such a joke. Like, I literally started my account as a joke.

Sophomore year, Ms. Blum had us draw the human body, warning that we'd likely struggle with the eyes and hands. My eyes were, as promised, wonky, but the hands? I'd nailed them. Ms. Blum gasped when she saw them, said I was a "natural talent." After that, I drew them constantly.

Zeke saw me drawing one and grabbed it, gushing. I told him to get his hands off my hands. We were all high, and that "hands off my hands" joke was the funniest shit I'd ever said. I wasn't exactly "with it" most of that year. For a while after the accident, I was high more than I was sober. Weed was the only thing that helped with my newfound chronic pain, so it became as much a part of my life as the ache in my neck and shoulders.

Somehow, our inside joke spiraled, and I made an account with the username "hands_off" and posted a drawing. With time,

I eased off the weed, only using it every once in a while when the pain—or my mom—gets unbearable. But I kept posting, and somewhere along the way, the bit became real, popular.

People gush in the comments all the time, saying my art means something to them. I can't see why; it really is just hands. But I'm drawing them anyway, so I keep posting, despite the fact that I barely scroll myself.

"Isn't that great?" my mom repeats. "Unlike Lily, you'll stand out." Dad grunts again.

"So great." I grin, but I can't bear to make it genuine. Chester scurries under the table and curls up beside me, like he can sense the discomfort in my voice.

She frowns. "You have to start taking this seriously. Some of the best years of my life were at Tufts. I know you'll love it."

And you'll love bragging to your alumni friends that your daughter's going, I think. But I don't say that, because the fight's not worth it. It never is. I've seen Lily pick and lose enough battles. "I'll apply soon," I mutter.

"Great. Let me know when you do so I can tell Janice."

"Okay." I push my bowl of cereal forward, unable to stomach another bite. It's this terrible, sugar-free Fiber One knockoff, like most of the food Mom stocks in the kitchen.

"Cleo," she says, because she always has to get the last word in, "I promise you'll love it there. You'll meet people who are actually, you know, your *caliber*."

"Uh-huh." I crack my knuckles nervously, anticipating her typical rant about how my friends are *lowlifes*. I remember too late that the movement is a mistake in itself.

"Honey, don't crack your knuckles at the table. You'll make me lose my appetite," my mom groans. She hates the way my fingers bend back, all the way to the top of my hand. It's not like

I'm doing it on purpose, it's just how my hypermobile body naturally moves. But to her, it's a glaring reminder that I'm imperfect. This is why I have whatever the opposite of an Oedipus complex is. Well, minus the wanting to sleep with my dad bit.

"I gotta get going." I stand up and skirt away from the table, unable to take another second. When I'm at the front door, pulling on my Vans, her phone rings. She has this annoying, loud wind chime that goes off when she gets calls. And she gets calls, like, twenty times a day.

"Maureen, hi! No, no trouble at all. I'm finishing up breakfast with my lovely daughter." Her voice echoes through the entryway. "Cleo, yes. Elizabeth's up at Columbia. I know, can you believe it? Yes, we miss her so much. We're hoping to visit soon, but she's *so* busy with her course load."

I head out the door and stumble toward my bike before I have to hear her practiced speech about how *close* we are as a family. In a weird way, this is why I could never hate Sadie.

My mom's so fake. She'll scold me all night, then spend the next day gushing to her friends about how amazing I am. It's constant whiplash, so it's refreshing to have someone who always tells me the truth. Sadie's blunt, but at least she's real. Most people can't say the same.

Like, when I get to first period and slap a piece of paper on her desk, she glares at me, not hiding her disdain. Granted, she makes this face every morning. Ms. Thomas let us choose our seats for the year, and I chose the one right next to Sadie. First period is the only class we have every day since San Marcos runs on an even/odd block schedule, so I start each morning by her side. I naively thought we could use this time to get to know each other beyond our rivalry, but no luck so far.

"Ta-da," I say. Last night, after she made my heart drop three stories by liking my old Instagram post, I took the liberty of whipping up my own suspect list.

People who (maybe) hate my guts:
Kasey Porter
Buzz ???
Ms. Skittles

"This is the whole list?" She squints at it. "Did you write it while high?"

"No!" There she goes again with the high stuff. She makes more stoner jokes than Seth Rogen. "I'm just not a very hateable person."

"Half of these aren't real names."

"Rude. Kasey Porter's literally right there." I point to Kasey, who's two rows over swinging around the keys to her brand-new truck, probably to remind everyone of the existence of said truck. She's still pissed at Zeke for rear-ending her old one, and at me for the crime of being in the passenger seat at the time.

"I know, but who the hell is Buzz?"

"My ex. They're homeschooled now, doing Florida Virtual. We ended on okay terms, hence the question marks." Or, at least, we *were* on okay terms, until I got pissed a week after the breakup and TPed their house with Bria. They came out as we were wrapping a tree trunk and were *livid*. In my defense, I had no clue that the tree was planted in honor of their beloved late grandma. Maybe they're finally getting back at me with petty vandalism of their own.

"Is Ms. Skittles another one of your exes?"

"Oh, that's Buzz's pet hamster," I say. Sadie looks close to stabbing me with her pencil. "That was part of the reason we broke up. Ms. Skittles hated me, and Buzz trusted her instincts."

"That's the most ridiculous thing I've ever heard."

"I know, right? Like, give the little furball some time to warm up to me, geez."

"Not that! Why did you put a hamster on the list?" She balls her hands into fists and scrunches her nose. She probably thinks it's intimidating, but she looks like a bunny rabbit. "We're looking for *people* who hate you, not hamsters. A hamster can't vandalize a locker."

"She's a smart hamster! Or *was*. Oh my God, we broke up two years ago. There's no way that hamster's still alive, is she? How long do hamsters live? Poor Ms. Skittles." I lower my head. I really did like her, even if she didn't like me.

"Enough about the hamster!" Sadie shouts loud enough to make half the heads in class swivel in our direction.

One of those heads belongs to Ms. Thomas. "Anything you'd like to share with the class?" Sadie mumbles a no and an apology. I press a hand over my mouth, but it's not enough to mask my laughter. "Wonderful. Let's all *quietly* enjoy watching children pretend they're on *Good Morning America*, then." Ms. Thomas turns on the smart board, where the morning announcement crew is presenting today's lunch menu. Rubbery chicken sandwiches galore.

Sadie folds the paper into a neat square, tucking it into that lavender notebook she always has on her. "Whatever, I can work with this. Kasey's on my list too. She's still mad I told Ms. Gardner that she cheated off my test freshman year."

"*We* can work with this. I'm tired of your lone-wolf routine. Or lone *Katz*, I should say." I give her a look like, *Get it?* She responds with an eye roll, rather than a well-deserved chuckle. "We both stand to lose something if we're framed again."

"And what do you have to lose? Are you even applying to college?" She tries to sound annoyed, but I can tell she's worried. Sadie's desperate to find out if I applied to Tufts. Like, frothing-at-the-mouth desperate. Last month, she tried to bribe Bria into telling her with cookies. Bria told her to fuck off, but she kept the cookies. Unsurprisingly, they tasted heavenly.

"Maybe if you asked me, you'd have the answer. You know you can do that, right? You can say, 'Cleo, please tell me if you're applying to Tufts' instead of shoving baked goods at my friends."

She turns her head, but not quickly enough to hide her reddening cheeks. She's saved by Ms. Thomas clearing her throat and beginning to lecture. Quietly, we both face forward.

I scrawl another note and slide it onto Sadie's desk.

Strategy meeting at your place after school?!

When Sadie looks over, I flash an enthusiastic thumbs-up. She doesn't return it, but she nods, and I'll take that as a win.

Sadie

I CAN'T DECIDE IF I should hang around after school and drive Cleo to the inn. Or should I send her the address? Should I do what I actually want to and message her: *Please don't come?*

I wish it were Friday, not Thursday; then I could use Shabbat as an excuse to get out of this. It doesn't start until sundown, but I doubt Cleo knows that.

In the end, I leave without her, and brainstorm a plan on the drive. Once I'm back, I'll message and ask to meet at a coffee shop instead. We'll have a brief conversation about suspects, thirty minutes max, then I'll crash for my afternoon nap.

I'm yawning at the thought of it. Despite my protests at Dr. Milonas's office, I've developed a bad habit of coming home, falling asleep right away, then working on homework long into the night.

I feel heavy on these antidepressants. That's the only word that can describe it. My body's so weighed down that dragging it to and from school is a feat in itself. Sleep is the only thing that helps, at least temporarily.

As soon as I put my car in park, I start drafting a text. When I walk through the front door of the inn, I'm startled by the voice that haunts my nightmares saying, "Nice of you to finally join us."

I jump. Cleo's sprawled out lazily in the sitting room, her tie-dye muscle tee and fraying jean shorts a harsh contrast to the soft, pink aesthetic of the room. It's like seeing an enemy on the wrong side of the battlefield. Liesl sits purring in her lap, the little traitor.

Reluctantly, I press the backspace button, deleting my unsent plea. Of course Cleo beat me here. This city was built for horses and bikes, not cars. "How'd you know where I live?" I bristle.

"Your name's literally outside." Ah. Right. My last name *is* outside, on a huge sign beneath a silhouette of a cat. "So many years of cat jokes, yet I had no clue you have one."

"I have three." We adopted Liesl a few years ago, and my dad swore we wouldn't get another. Now we have two more and a glaring allergen warning on the inn's website, alongside photos of each cat pretending to enjoy an afternoon scone. I'd never tell Gretl and Kurt, but Liesl, who resembles a ball of fluff more than a cat, is my favorite. I'll have to lecture her later on the betrayal that is lying in Cleo's lap.

"This one's a sweetheart. And I don't say that lightly, I'm more of a dog person. My corgi Chester's basically my best friend." Cleo pats Liesl's head, smiling down at her. "What's her name?"

"Liesl." Before she can ask, I answer, "My family's big *Sound of Music* fans. Every Christmas, we order Chinese food and cheer when the baron rips up the Nazi flag. The baron's the dad."

"Yeah, I know. I've seen *Sound of Music*, I'm not a heathen." Before I can retort with the obvious "Are you sure?" Cleo's eyes get all . . . gooey. "The scene where Rolf spins Liesl around the gazebo . . . Obviously that didn't end well, but it was my gay awakening."

"My sexual awakening was the flag-ripping scene. I think young me pretended he was a butch lesbian." The words spill out before I can stop them. Cleo's eyes go wide, her lips turning up in an amused grin.

Why did I say that? Now she's going to share that very personal anecdote with her friends. I can picture them circled up, laughing at me like they did in the parking lot. *Thirty minutes.* The sooner I cut the small talk, the sooner she'll leave. "Let's get down to business. So far, our shared suspect list is just Kasey?"

"And Buzz. I think you probably know them by their dead name." She pulls out her phone and tosses it to me, their Instagram already open.

"Yeah, I do recognize them. I didn't have many run-ins with them when they went to San Marcos though." This time, I'm careful to conceal the truth: I only remember Buzz in the context of Cleo.

I have this vivid memory of seeing them together in the cafeteria, Cleo with her head against the table, Buzz running their hands through her hair. The motion stopped me in my tracks. As I watched them, this intense *want* consumed me. Then Buzz looked up, we locked eyes, and I made a hard pivot in the opposite direction.

"But you do remember them," Cleo says, taking her phone back. "Maybe you accidentally offended them. Let's add them to the list just in case."

"Right. The list that's one-third hamster."

"Well, where's your list? I know you made one. I saw you writing names down yesterday, but I couldn't make them out."

"You were watching me?"

"You were watching me too," Cleo says, making me flush with embarrassment for the third time today. I remind myself of the plan yet again: get in, get out, take a nap. Resisting would only waste time. I pull out my notebook, flipping to a page where I've written a second version of my list, sans Cleo's name. It's best to hide my suspicions. If she knows I'm keeping an eye on her, she'll be less likely to slip up, give herself away.

I hand the notebook over. My list's much neater and, even without Cleo's name on it, much longer.

<u>People who may hate me:</u>
Olivia Liu
Ella Beakman
Kasey Porter
Ms. Thomas
Willow Fitzgerald
TJ Preston
Jeff Morris
Bria Kinney

I threw a few other names around, but they've all been scratched out. I've narrowed down the list to people who seem to outright despise me, rather than mildly dislike me. The distinction is important. If someone's out to get us, they have to be fueled by pretty intense hatred to go through so much effort.

Cleo pulls out the pen that's tucked into my notebook, crossing out a few names. "Why's Ms. Thomas on here?"

"She hates me. Why else would she give me mid-As when I deserve high ones?"

Cleo laughs, the sound grating. "And Bria? Are you serious? The only people she hates are Fox News commentators and John Stamos. Long story, don't ask."

"She hates me too." I knew Cleo would take offense to her best friend's name being on there, but it's worth considering. I'm about to tell her to keep an open mind when the French doors to the sitting room swing open. Shit. I forgot about afternoon teatime, since lately I've been asleep until the evening session if I'm not at an extracurricular.

"Girls?" Mom calls out. "We have a lot of guests today. Can you take the piano bench? Oh . . . you're not Mel." Mom's eyes widen as she sets down a tray of teacups.

"I'm Cleo Chapman. Pleasure to meet you, ma'am. I'm afraid I'm no good at playing piano. I didn't make it past the recorder stage of music class."

Ma'am? I stifle a laugh. But like everyone else, Mom falls for her fake charm. "*Cleo.*" She throws me a pointed look. "So nice to meet you. Well, remeet you—I met you the day you were born, you know." Cleo chuckles like Mom told a hilarious joke. "We have tea hours in the afternoon and evening. When we have a full house, I ask the girls, usually Sadie and Mel, to sit on the piano bench so the more comfortable seats can be reserved for guests. You're welcome to stay and partake, of course!"

"We can go somewhere else. Wanna do coffee? We could go to Kookaburra if the line's not bad." This is perfect. Now I have a real excuse to get Cleo out of here.

"Actually," she says, smiling like a shark about to eat a guppy, "I prefer tea."

It's like she *knows* that's the last thing I want to hear. I can't think of a good enough rebuttal, so we sit thigh to thigh on the piano bench. It's where I learned to play when I was younger, where I've slumped against Mel's shoulder many afternoons. This is even more sacrilegious than her holding Liesl, who's now hiding under a ruffled chair anticipating the crowd.

Guests trickle into the room, then pour, picking up teacups and homemade cinnamon scones. Cleo slurps her tea (really, she slurps it) and holds her pinkie out, as if this makes up for said slurping. She sets it down and picks up my notebook, making more scribbles before handing it back to me. "I crossed out people I don't know or am absolutely certain don't hate me. And I added a few suspects, I spent most of the day brainstorming."

People who may hate ~~me~~ **US**:
Olivia Liu
~~Ella Beakman~~
Kasey Porter
Ms. Thomas **???**
~~Willow Fitzgerald~~
~~TJ Preston~~
~~Jeff Morris~~
~~Bria Kinney~~
Buzz Fowler
Matthew Pierce
Kermit the Frog

At least everyone falling for Cleo's charm helped narrow down the list. And Matthew's a good addition; he's gunning for the valedictorian spot too. Wait . . . "Why is Kermit the Frog on here?" Can she take nothing seriously?!

"Obviously Kermit wouldn't hurt a fly—except for, ya know, actual flies. But you put Bria down, so I figured joke names were permissible. Seriously, what do you have against her?"

"Why don't you ask her what she has against me? I once overheard her call me"—I drop my voice to a whisper—"a pain in the ass." I had gone to the bathroom after fifth period last May and heard her voice, loud as ever, carrying over the stall.

"That's just Bria being Bria. She talks shit, but she's a Chihuahua. You know, all bark and no bite. She's helped me prank you before, but she wouldn't go rogue like this," Cleo says. An older patron glances at us over her floral cup, tsking disapprovingly.

"No cussing at teatime," I hiss. "You never know where tourists are from. We don't want to offend them."

"Oh, sorry," Cleo says, seeming genuinely apologetic. She's more sorry about offending a stranger than she is about her best friend offending me.

"The bark still bites, you know."

"What?"

"I don't care if she didn't mean anything by it. Hearing her talk about me that way . . . it's not a fun feeling." Granted, I've been called worse. But she sounded so angry, and she's always been Cleo's right-hand man for pranks. It's not outside the realm of possibility that she could have vandalized my locker, slashed my tire. Maybe she finally got sick of Cleo's shtick and decided to throw her under the bus too.

"Are you kidding me?" Cleo laughs, loud enough that the tsking woman shoots her another glare. "Zeke overheard you and Mel laughing about my accident sophomore year. Apparently, Mel said the fall knocked out the few brain cells I had. So, no, I don't have much sympathy for you, and I don't think Bria's evil for calling you a pain in the you-know-where."

I don't remember that conversation, but I do remember the accident. It's bold of her to act like getting so high that she fell out of a tree *isn't* a laughing matter. Besides, it's not like she was seriously injured or anything. She had a bruise or two, but she was fine. She didn't even miss any school because of it.

Maybe I'm just trying to soothe my guilty conscience. But if Cleo's not going to offer me an apology, I won't either. "It doesn't matter. Let's turn the whole list over to Mr. Simmons so we don't have to worry about this anymore, deal?"

"What? No, no deal. What do you think he's gonna do, conduct an investigation and interrogate everyone on our list? No, we need to go full Nancy Drew on this. You're Nancy, I'm Drew."

"Seriously?"

"Yes, seriously." She takes another slurp.

I close my eyes. This one conversation is so tiring. There's no way I'll be able to handle investigating all those suspects with Cleo. Even if I *could* tolerate her, her plan's still ridiculous. "This is absurd. We're probably blowing this out of proportion. Two popped tires and some vandalism and suddenly we're detectives? Who's to say they'll strike again? Shouldn't we ignore it, hope they don't take things any further?"

Cleo lowers her teacup, looking at me like I have three heads and two bodies. "Sadie, you're a lot of things, but you're not someone who sits idly by and hopes things away."

I don't have anything to say to that—because she's right. I'm not a thoughts and prayers kind of girl. I pray *and* I get shit done. But this? I have a yearbook to edit, a secretary position in Key Club to maintain, and a massive, constantly growing load of homework. I'm not sure I can add anything else to my plate without it teetering over. I refuse to be one of those people who lets their grades slip senior year and gets their dream school acceptance revoked.

"Maybe you're right," Cleo says. "Maybe that was it. They pulled a prank or two, had their fun, and called it a day. But what if they *do* strike again? Can you really risk that?"

My mind drifts to Tufts, settling into my dorm, sitting beside a sunny window, knowing I can finally become the person I've been dreaming of for so long. "I . . ."

"Don't do it for me. Do it for Tufts."

It gets under my skin and stays there, that Cleo knew exactly what I was thinking. It's like she reached into my brain and latched on to the right words to win me over. She's a snake who wraps her tendrils around you, squeezes tight, then tries to convince you she's been a butterfly all along.

I stand up, grab a saucer, and set my cup on it atop the piano. Even in my outrage, I can't risk water rings. "I'm not going to let you convince me there's some big conspiracy just because you're panicking and don't want to take the fall for vandalizing my locker and messing with my car."

"I didn't mess with your car—"

"But didn't you?" I demand too loudly over the instrumental music spilling out of the speakers. I hover close and whisper, "This isn't an episode of *Criminal Minds*. There's no big plot out to get us, there's just you. And I'm not going to let you use your charm to convince me otherwise like you do with everyone else."

"My charm?" Cleo grins. I didn't think it was possible to hate her more, but here she is, making it happen.

"You know what I mean." I wave a hand, ignoring the heat rising in my cheeks yet again.

"I don't actually. We need to figure this out."

"*I* will figure it out." I press my fingers to the bridge of my nose. "I'll think on it. And you can too if it'll help you sleep at night. But there's no way we're launching a full-scale investigation, that's absurd."

"You're absurd!" Cleo shoots back. Even her comebacks are sloppy. "We at least need to talk motives. Like, why you put people on the list, why I kept them there."

I shudder at the thought. No way am I explaining to Cleo why each of these people hate my guts. "We have the names, that's enough. You can leave your dishes wherever and see yourself out."

I turn on my heels. Cleo scurries after me and yelps, "You're not a genius, you know!"

"Excuse me?"

"You're smart, obviously, but you're not all-knowing. Everyone needs help sometimes. Don't let your ego cloud your judgment here."

She has some nerve talking about *my* ego. "Okay, wow. This conversation is fucking over."

"No cussing at teatime!"

I gesture to the closed doors behind us. "We're not at teatime anymore. And you're not welcome here!" Without further ado, I walk away, slamming the front door to the inn behind me. When I finally get to the cottage and up to my room, I sleep until the sun sets.

Cleo

THE GOOD NEWS IS it's been four days since our fight and the weirdo prankster hasn't struck again.

The bad news is it's been four days and Sadie hasn't spoken to me. That was the one advantage of all this anxiety-inducing chaos; she was finally talking to me. I put my foot in my mouth down to the ankle around her like always—but she was *talking* to me. She told me about her sexual awakening, she called me charming. By Sadie's standards, that's basically close friendship.

Today, she isn't talking at all. Not just to me—she's not answering any of Ms. Thomas's questions, which is out of character for her. Her note-taking is more haphazard than usual too. Like, she's only writing down half of what we're learning, rather than every word.

I'm doodling, trying and failing to mind my business, when Sadie heads to the front and asks to go to the bathroom. Not to sound like a total stalker, but I can't remember the last time she's gone to the bathroom in class. I'm pretty sure she's one of those weirdos who only pees between classes.

The hand holding her planner shakes as she holds it out. As she leaves, I swear I hear a sniffle. I'm probably making something out of nothing. But just in case . . .

I scurry to the front of the room with my own planner. "Can I go make sure Sadie's okay?"

"Yeah, she seemed a bit upset." Ms. Thomas signs it. "That's very kind of you, Cleo."

I rush out the door and stick my head into the bathroom. "Sadie?" All the stalls are empty. I walk to the courtyard, ignoring a jittery freshman and a scowl from Matthew. Finally, I spot a mass of curly hair sitting by the dingy, broken fountain. "Sadie?" I repeat.

"What?" She doesn't turn around, but I can tell from her voice that she's been crying. I remember the noise well from the time I heard her sobbing in the bathroom because she got an 86 on a test. I wanted to throw the stall door open and tell her she's brilliant, but I knew she wouldn't believe me.

"Ms. Thomas sent me to check on you," I lie, because the truth would piss her off. "She's worried you're sick, or something."

"I'm fine. You can tell her I'll be back soon." She sniffles around the last word. I wish I had a tissue on me.

"Are you okay?" I sit down, careful to leave space between us. "Is this about, like, your locker? Or what I said the other day? I didn't mean to—"

"Not everything is about you!" she snaps, finally turning her tearstained face in my direction. Ouch. Fair, but ouch.

She stands up and walks away. I don't know where she's going, but it's definitely not back to class. Without a second thought, I follow her. She must hear my footsteps, because she starts walking even faster. "Sadie."

"Leave me alone—"

"Sadie."

"Seriously, you don't have to pretend we're friends."

"We may not be friends, but I still want to make sure you're okay."

"I said I'm fine!"

"Except you're clearly not. So what's bothering you? Waiting to hear back from Tufts? Eggshell in your morning scone? No, that can't be it, those scones are perfect. If it's Tufts, you should know that your odds are good. And you don't have any competition from me. I didn't apply ED. I'm not sure I'll apply at all, honestly. Not trying to make it about me, but one less thing to worry about, yeah?"

This stops her in her tracks, like I hoped it would. Tentatively, she walks back to me, until we're face-to-face. "You're not applying?" Her voice rises with hope, and I nearly exhale in relief. In a weird way, it's like I offered her good news on a silver platter.

"Hell no. I was never going to." I grin. "I just like watching you squirm."

"I . . ." She trails off. For once, I've rendered her speechless.

"I'm kidding. I didn't tell you because it's kind of a secret. My family thinks I haven't made my mind up yet."

"Okay . . . so where are you applying?"

"I don't know. Probably nowhere? I may just not do college." I shrug.

A laugh bursts out of her. "You may not 'do' college? Are you kidding me?"

"What?"

"You've been fighting me for that valedictorian spot like it's the last lifeboat on the *Titanic*, all for you to not 'do' college? Absolutely not."

I don't tell her, for fear of breaking her spirit beyond repair, but I haven't been fighting her for the spot. The truth is, when I hear something, it sticks. Simple as that. I don't stay up all night rewriting essays to make every word sing like Sadie does. I'm not a prodigy, I just have a good memory. I wish people understood that so they'd stop expecting so much of me. "Lots of people don't go to college. There's nothing wrong with it."

"Sure, but not you. Not after how hard we've worked. If you don't go to college, I win too easily. I want a fair fight."

"Wait, you really think I should decide my future based on whether or not it gives you a run for your money? That's the most ridiculous thing I've ever heard." She opens her mouth to respond, but I put a finger up. "Hold on. I need to get some water if we're gonna argue. I can't think of good retorts with a dry mouth."

I walk past her, mostly because I know it will get on her nerves. The decibel-breaking scoff behind me proves me right. Just before I reach the water fountain, I spot an unnervingly familiar image on the mildewy brick wall by the girls' locker room. Oh my God . . . is that . . . ? No, it can't be. Can it?

I take a few more steps away from her, closer to the wall to make sure I'm not imagining it. "Hey!" Sadie calls after me. "We're in the middle of a conversation."

I reach a single finger up to my lips. "Shh. Come here."

"Did you just shush me?!" she yelps. I ignore her, waving her over wordlessly. The corridor's tucked away, and she needs to see this for herself. Otherwise, she'll never believe me. *I* can barely believe it. "What's going on—"

As soon as she spots it, she shuts up. Together, our eyes trail upward. In huge, red letters sprayed across brick are the words "MR. SIMMONS SUCKS EGGS."

Beside it is a very recognizable painting of a pig, now eating a hard-boiled egg.

"WHAT THE HELL IS that?" I ask, or rather choke. As I look up at the giant piece of graffiti, oxygen forgets how to enter my lungs. The humidity certainly isn't helping. I strip off my cardigan and tie it around my waist, dress code be damned.

"I think it's a pig."

"I know what it is! I just mean . . . how do we . . . what do we . . . ? We should tell Mr. Simmons. This will prove that we had no involvement, right?"

"Are you kidding me? This"—Cleo says, waving her hand in the direction of the wall—"has our names written all over it. It's the same pig that was drawn on my locker. *And* he brought up the egg that started the food fight in our meeting, which this is clearly referencing. We need to get rid of it."

She's right. We don't have alibis. In fact, we're currently out of class, roaming the halls, and now standing at the scene of the crime. That's the literal opposite of an alibi. Shit, we're gonna get in so much trouble. "How can we get rid of it? I don't think hand sanitizer will cut it this time."

The pig is huge. Like, *the size of a person* huge. In fairness, real pigs are also the size of people, though on four legs, so they don't look it. Except some pigs are smaller, like Kunekune pigs, which are closer in weight to humans but only about two and a half feet long. Wow, all the knowledge I have is about to be wasted. Years spent poring over textbooks for what? To be taken down by an animal I don't even eat?

Okay, truth be told, I snuck a piece of bacon at Mel's house once, but it was too salty for my taste. Is that what did it? Did my small foray into pork piss God off enough to lead me here, teetering on the edge of expulsion?

Two firm hands materialize on my shoulders. I didn't realize I was on the verge of hyperventilating until my breaths became practically nonexistent. Cleo presses me gently until I'm seated on the concrete. I'm too busy trying to breathe to care that she's manhandling me. "It's taken care of."

"What?" I gasp, the single syllable using up a monumental amount of energy.

"I'm taking care of it. Stay here and take deep breaths. I doubt anyone will walk down this hallway, but if they do, pretend you fainted or something." She runs away, leaving me alone with the vandalized wall.

This is a setup, right? She's running to Mr. Simmons so he can catch me red-handed. Who knew someone so ridiculous is capable of being an evil mastermind? Unfortunately, I'm not in any state to flee the scene. My attempts at deep breaths are all shallow. I would kill for one of my as-needed antianxiety pills right now.

Dr. Milonas told me to only take them when absolutely necessary—and this is definitely one of those times. But my pill case is in my backpack in the classroom, buildings away. All I have now is ragged, unhelpful breaths.

And here I was, thinking this shitty day couldn't get any

shittier. Up until now, there hasn't been a reason for it to be a shitty day, it just . . . is. Sometimes, it's like my brain wakes up on the wrong side of the bed. Everything feels off. *I* feel off.

I asked to go to the bathroom, hoping the fresh air might help. But having to miss part of Gov made me feel worse. I hate missing class. It's hard to find anyone who takes notes as thorough as mine.

The only person who came close was the kid who took notes for me freshman year when I missed school for inpatient care. Everyone else takes notes similar to Cleo. No, that's not true, hers are exceptionally bad. I once glanced at her notebook after a hefty APUSH lecture, and she had written one line. All it said was, "Wow, England sucks ass."

I was already on the verge of tears, and struggling to think of who I could get notes from pushed me over the edge. I'm just so frustrated by how much I miss out on because of my depression. I'm frustrated that sleep takes up half of my days lately. I'm frustrated that I keep crashing, then scrambling to finish my homework. Though I guess after today, I may never have homework again.

With shaky hands, I take my glasses off and press my head against my knees. This is it. I finally got to my last year of high school, and I won't make it to graduation. My mental health is so bad that it's grounded me at the scene of a literal crime.

I'm on the verge of blacking out completely when Cleo shouts, "WATCH OUT." I lift my head in time to watch her toss a bucket of soapy water against the wall. A second bucket sits at her feet, waiting for the first to be emptied.

Distantly, I think that I should help, but when I lift a hand, it trembles. Frozen, I watch the steady slosh of water, Cleo occasionally grunting under the weight of the buckets. She eventually pulls out a sponge—from where, I don't know—and scrubs the last remnants of paint off. When she's done, she drops to the ground, breathing heavily. "Did anyone walk by?"

"I don't think so? I'm not sure." I gulp for air, panic rising higher in me. How long did I spend with my face pushed into my legs? A million people could have walked by, and I was too stuck in my head to notice.

"It's fine. I'm sure we're fine. Luckily, the janitor left the supply closet unlocked. Even if someone saw, there's no proof anymore. We're okay." Cleo tilts her head, looking up to admire her work. Admittedly, I'm amazed. The spray paint is gone, replaced by dark, slightly damp brick. Maybe Cleo being obnoxiously perfect at everything has its advantages.

"Thanks for taking care of it." The words feel like a foreign object on my tongue, but she deserves to hear them. She could have taken the out, run screaming to Mr. Simmons's office, and pinned the blame on me. She didn't have to save me—but she did anyway. The realization makes something soft, warm roll over in my stomach.

"Yeah, no problem." She stretches her forearm over her beet-red face nonchalantly, like this is a typical Monday for her. "I knew you couldn't, so . . ."

"Excuse me?" I bristle. It lands like an insult, even if it's true. Just like that, the fuzzy feeling is gone.

"You know what I mean. You were . . . preoccupied." She sizes me up, much like Gretl sizes up lizards that make the mistake of sunbathing on our porch. "Does that, um, happen a lot?"

It's one thing for Mel or my parents to see me during an anxiety attack, but Cleo? It's worse than her being at the inn. Hell, it's worse than her seeing me naked would be. It's a level of vulnerability that only people (and cats) in my innermost circle should be privy to. “It looks like you were right,” I say, ignoring the question. “Someone’s definitely framing us.”

It’s terrifying. Tufts is inches over the horizon, and it feels even closer after Cleo’s confession. Who would try to yank it away from me in the eleventh hour? And how can I make their life as much of a hell as they’re making mine?

“So does that mean you’ll be the Nancy to my Drew?” Cleo asks with that satisfied smirk.

I roll my eyes. “You know Nancy Drew is one person, right?”

“I’ll take that as a yes.”

“Yeah, fine. Let’s . . . investigate.” I have to set aside how I feel about Cleo, at least temporarily. No matter how much it takes out of me, we need to put our heads together and figure this out before it goes any further.

Cleo rubs her neck. “I doubt Ms. Thomas would let us talk to Kasey for more than thirty seconds, but I have gym with her on even days. Fourth period. Wanna start there tomorrow? Since she was on both of our initial lists.”

“Okay, I have Yearbook then. I can make up a piece for it, ask her some questions.”

“Sounds good.” Cleo stands up. “We should get back to class. We’ll tell everyone you had food poisoning and threw up and I held your hair back or something.”

She holds her hand out, waiting for me to take it. Reluctantly, I press my fingers against her calloused palm. It’s the first time I’ve really touched her, unless you count when she walked too fast and scraped the back of my heel with her shoe. I pull my hand away as soon as I’m up, but the shadow of hers lingers.

Cleo

"A HARD-BOILED EGG?" BRIA smiles—or at least I think she does. I can barely see her face since the string lights that illuminate her basement are half-broken.

"Like the one I threw at Sadie sophomore year," I say. "You've gotta admit, it's pointed." I've thought about that pig all afternoon. What does it mean? Is someone really trying to get us expelled? I can't imagine what else the endgame could be. The locker was one thing, but this is a whole other level.

"I know who's doing this to you. Wanna phone a friend?"

"Sure." I hold my hand up in a mock phone, my thumb and pinkie pointed out.

Bria forms her own phone hand and says, "Her name rhymes with *lady*," before miming hanging up.

It takes me an embarrassingly long minute to figure out what she means. "Wait, you think Sadie did it?"

"You don't? She's obviously messing with you as revenge for all the times you've messed with her. Who else is smart enough to pull this off? And annoying enough? How do you know it's *not* her?"

"Because I . . . I know her," I say softly. Manuela's head whips up from where she's scrolling on her phone. She watches me like she's figuring me out. Shit. None of my friends know about my feelings for Sadie, let alone the way they've been festering like those gross balloon-like blisters you get after walking in a new pair of Doc Martens.

I'm not one to hide anything from them, but my feelings for Sadie are different. There's something sacred about this crush that makes me want to keep it close to my chest. I duck my head. "I've known her for years. We've had a million classes together. I can tell when she's lying, and she's not about this."

"After everything, do you really think you can trust each other?" Bria gives me a pointed look. I drop my eyes to avoid it.

"How'd she react when she saw the pig with the scrambled eggs?" Zeke asks. "Did she seem surprised?"

"It was hard-boiled," Bria says. "How would you draw scrambled eggs?"

"I don't know, I'm not an egg vandal!"

"She . . ." Telling the whole truth would feel like betraying her, and we've betrayed each other enough for one lifetime. I don't think I was supposed to see her shoulders shaking, her breaths shortening. "She was really freaked out. It was genuine." There's no way she could fake that.

"I agree, I don't think she'd do it. I like Sadie," Manuela says. Three pairs of eyes turn in her direction, in shock, as if she just said, *I like homework*. "What? She's cool."

"Cool?" Bria honest to God cackles. "She's never been cool in her life. I've been cursed with the last name Kinney, so I've been placed alphabetically next to her for years. She's exhausting." Damn, has Bria always been this rude? Have I just not noticed because I typically share her resentment?

"She's herself," Manuela says. "That's more than most people at this school can say."

"Well, herself is annoying." Bria snaps off another bite of beef jerky. "You know what bothers me most about her? She's greedy. Like, she feels like she's owed the valedictorian spot. Honestly, Cleo, you *should* apply to Tufts. It would be hilarious to watch her freak out when you get in and she doesn't. That would be the only time I've ever rooted for a nepo baby. Except for Gracie Abrams. And Jane Fonda. And that gay guy with the glasses."

"Dan Levy?" Zeke offers.

"No, the other guy."

The conversation moves on to gay celebrities, but I can't bring myself to participate. I'm frozen with the fear that Sadie was right. I mean, Bria's always been eager to help me prank Sadie. Maybe I do need to keep an eye on her.

No. No way. She would mess with Sadie, but she wouldn't mess with me. Eager for a distraction, I pull out my phone. There are texts waiting for me from all the usual suspects.

MOM: Where are you? I need a second opinion on floral arrangements, the board's torn. What do you think, hydrangeas or petunias?

DAD: Text your mother back.

LILY: Okay, I seriously think you should come tour Pratt!! It's near meee and their art program's stellar, look!!

I always open Lily's texts first, but this time, I regret it. She doesn't care whether I go to Tufts or not, but she's still on my ass about college—even more than our mom is some days. At least Mom has the gala to distract her; Lily doesn't let her boatload of homework stand in the way of nagging me.

I respond: looks cool, maybe I'll apply!!

In five seconds flat, she replies: I know you didn't open the link 🙄

Whoever said it's moms who have eyes in the back of their heads must not have had an older sister. Yes I did! I send back, before opening the link. The page she's sent me is of a mixed media student exhibition. I zoom in on a portrait of a school bus that's the size of an actual bus.

She's right. It *is* cool. But I don't need school to make art. And honestly, my art's probably not good enough for a program like this anyway. I exit out of the link, opening my messages with my mom instead, ignoring the Pratt propaganda texts from Lily that keep coming in.

Hydrangeas, I write back, definitely hydrangeas.

SAN MARCOS HAS ALWAYS been a hellish place, but there are bits and pieces I like about it. The always freezing Yearbook classroom, goggles fastened to my face in the lab, the adorable cows on campus that the agriculture class tends to. High on the very short pros list is the fact that the school only requires one year of physical education.

Most students take it freshman year at our guidance counselors' urging. But Cleo insists on going against the grain, so she waited until the last second. It's amusing, watching her and Kasey run amid a crowd of fourteen-year-olds, each shorter than the last. I'm still shaken from yesterday's incident, that pig and its hard-boiled egg ingrained in my brain, but watching the run is a good distraction.

Although, to say Cleo's running isn't entirely accurate. "Come on, Chapman," Coach Graham shouts, "you can do better than that." Based on his exasperation, I get the sense that he says this a lot.

Cleo picks up the pace for a whopping five seconds before slowing back down and wiping sweat from her forehead. I consider letting her run another lap before I pull her, but it's in the high eighties today. It should be illegal to make anyone run in this weather.

"Coach Graham?" I ask in my sweetest can-do-no-wrong voice. He startles, so absorbed in watching the field that he didn't notice me standing beside him. "Can I pull Kasey Porter and Cleo Chapman for a yearbook interview? It's on seniors who put off gym till the last second."

I pitched this idea to Mr. Hart at the beginning of class, and he loved it. He tried to assign an underclassman to it, since it's not my job to be "on the field" as editor in chief. But I insisted on writing this one myself "for old times' sake."

Coach Graham's gaze barely leaves the field as he grunts assent. "Fine."

Cleo practically walks through the end of the lap as Coach Graham gestures, pulling her out. In a terrible display of acting, she pretends to be surprised before collapsing on the bleachers, taking a long chug from her bright orange reusable water bottle.

"Careful, you might drown." I sit beside her, the hot metal creaking as I readjust to avoid it stinging my legs.

"Only in your dreams," she retorts, looking ahead to where Kasey's run has transitioned into a slow trot. "Have you noticed any new pranks today?"

Just the mention of the P-word makes the humid air heavier. Things have really gotten dire if even Cleo's paranoid. "No. Have you?"

"Nope."

I pull my phone out, sending Mel a picture of the field captioned on your home turf!! After my own awful experience with gym freshman year, I only set foot here for her meets.

She responds with question marks, but before I can explain, I'm distracted by Cleo asking, "We weren't that young as freshmen, were we?" She gestures to two kids, their gangly arms dangling from short torsos.

"We were. You literally had braces." Yet again, it's out of my mouth before I can stop it. It feels like a confession that I've been watching Cleo for years, noticing her. I feel my face redden to the same shade as her sweat-drenched cheeks.

She winces, taking another swig of water. Luckily, she's too dehydrated to be smug. "Don't remind me. I got them when I was *eleven*. It takes four years of agony to get these puppies." She flashes an unnervingly straight smile.

"At least you got them." I reach a hand up, covering my teeth self-consciously. My dentist told my parents that they weren't bad enough to justify the cost. At the time, I was thrilled to not go through the hassle of years' worth of metal in my mouth. Now, though, I hate being surrounded by perfect teeth while mine are *slightly* off. Some days, I stand in front of the mirror, pushing my two crooked teeth with my finger, as if force alone will move them into the proper place.

"Oh, please," Cleo says, "as if you need 'em. You only have, like, two crooked teeth."

I drop my hand, eyeing her as she registers the weight of her words. It sends a thrill through me, to know that despite her nonchalant front, she's watching me back. "Have you been memorizing my smile?" I ask, unable to help myself.

"Only in your dreams," she repeats, but the way she says it this time reminds me of that sophomore year antidrug PSA. She's using the same inflection as when she shouted, *Marijuana is called the devil's lettuce for a reason!* while reeking of weed.

"Kasey!" Cleo waves her over with the eagerness of someone desperate to escape a conversation.

"What?" Kasey folds her arms. "You're setting a bad example for the children by giving up."

"Sadie wants to interview us for Yearbook!"

Kasey perks up and jogs off the field, settling onto the bleacher step below us. She pulls her hair down before tying it into an even higher ponytail. "Hi, Sadie. I still think you should take me up on my proposal. After that stunt you pulled freshman year, you owe me that much."

I grimace. In hindsight, I regret turning her in for cheating. I probably should have let it go—but I was struggling so much that year, and I couldn't stand that she was mooching off my sleepless nights studying. "What proposal?"

"A two-page spread about the trials and tribulations of getting kicked off of the cheer team."

"Ah, right." I recall now receiving that email and immediately deleting it. I joined Yearbook freshman year to diversify my extracurriculars for college applications. *Look at me*, my four years and editor in chief position proclaims, *I'm not a robot built to study science, I'm a well-rounded individual.*

Over the years, though, I've come to really enjoy it. April's my favorite month, when everyone scrambles to get the layout perfect, before inevitably failing and begrudgingly accepting it being mostly fine. Then in May, I get to see our finished product scrawled over in Sharpie with sweet (and vulgar) messages. It's rewarding to make something imperfect and watch it be loved anyway.

"So what's this article or whatever about?" Kasey asks.

"People who wait until senior year to take gym." I push my curls behind my ears and try to clear my head. I haven't done this since last March. I'm rusty, but I need to get it together. This might be my most important interview yet. "Mind if I record?" Kasey nods, and I open the voice memos app, pressing the little red button.

"This is actually the perfect tie-in to the spread you're doing about me. It's so unfair." Everyone's heard Kasey's rant about being kicked off the cheer team. Knowing Kasey, the president of the United States has probably heard it. Still, she starts her speech like it's breaking news. "I was so dedicated." Out of the corner of my eye, I see Cleo mouth the opening line along with her. I fight hard to stifle a laugh. "*So* dedicated! Then I miss a few practices—to take care of my boyfriend with a torn ACL, mind you—and they kick me off? If that's not bad enough, they tell me my varsity sports participation no longer counts as PE credit and I have to take gym as a senior. Only weirdos and stoners do that. No offense, Cleo."

"Why would that possibly offend me?" Cleo says dryly.

"So have you taken any action recently?" I ask, giving Cleo a small eyebrow raise, as if to say, *Cut the sarcasm and focus.* "I heard some of your friends were passing out petitions the other day. Are you considering protesting? Maybe with art of some kind?" Cleo rolls her eyes, but I'd like to see her do better at sneaking in a vandalism question.

"Off the record?" Kasey leans forward, pressing the pause button on my recording. Is she about to confess? I hold my breath, cursing myself for not bringing a secret backup recording method, like one of those spy pens. "The petition was my doing."

My chest deflates. Of course she wasn't going to say, *Yes, I vandalized your lockers*. "Why off the record?"

"Because, everyone likes you if you stick up for someone else, but no one likes you if you stick up for yourself. Put down that Robbie organized it, will you?"

"Okay . . . but were you involved with it?" I press the record button again. "Were you passing out petitions when they went around last week?" *Do you have an alibi?*

"Yeah, I've been going door-to-door before school all month, asking teachers to sign it. Half of them won't, they refuse to make a 'statement.' It's so annoying. Even Mrs. Adams won't sign it, which is ridiculous since she runs that little gay club."

"You mean GSA?" Cleo offers, as if Kasey simply forgot the name.

"Yeah, right. Wait, I'm not against it or anything! My cousin's bisexual." She eyes my recording. "Aren't you gonna interview Cleo now? I recommend asking her where she learned to drive."

"Okay, once again, I was in the passenger seat when Zeke hit your car."

"Exactly. Close enough to yell, 'STOP!' "

"Yeah, it's Cleo's turn," I interrupt. We got what we came here for, I suppose. There was no recognition in her eyes at the mention of protest art, no fear of being found out. And to be honest, she seems way too absorbed in her own cause to care about what happens to me and Cleo. "Why did you wait until senior year to take gym?"

"I got kicked off the cheer team too," Cleo says sarcastically. "It was a shame, I made a great bottom."

"Ew! It's called a *base*." Kasey scrunches her nose like she can smell Cleo's lesbianism. "You're the worst. Can you finish without me? I'm gonna go crash Robbie's speech class. If Coach Graham asks, I'm in the bathroom."

I wait until she's out of earshot, her ponytail swishing behind her, to say, "I don't think she did it."

"Of course she didn't. She's an ally, her cousin's bisexual." This time, I can't help but laugh. "Let's discuss more in the locker room. I gotta get changed."

"Into what? You're wearing what you always wear." I gesture at her basketball shorts and muscle tee.

"Yeah, but this is sweaty."

"You don't sweat in your other clothes? It's so hot out." I've already applied deodorant twice today, and even that doesn't feel like enough.

"I only really sweat when I exercise," she says, leading the way to the girls' locker room. I roll my eyes behind her head. Not sweating in this heat is literally impossible. Is she really that obsessed with pretending to be perfect?

I'm considering calling her on her bullshit, but I'm distracted by the brick wall above us. I still can't believe that Cleo saw me break down like that yesterday. It's so embarrassing. I rush past the wall, into the locker room, but the familiar rubbery smell takes me back to freshman year. That's pretty much the last place I want to be transported to.

"What do you think?" Cleo asks, pulling her clothes out of a locker. "Is her alibi solid? Was one of her petition paloozas the same day our lockers got vandalized?" She pulls off her T-shirt with one hand. I've always found it obnoxious when heartthrobs in movies take their shirts off like that. It seems ineffective, not using both hands. Who's she showing off for?

I drop my gaze to the floor. "Uh, it sounds like she's done it every morning this month, but we could double-check her Instagram highlights to corroborate." My eyes flit up, assuming Cleo's dressed, but she's still in her bra, frowning at the tank top in her hand. I swallow so hard I nearly choke.

"Is this inside out?" she asks.

"I . . . What?"

She steps closer, holding the shirt out. "It has one of those seams where you can't really tell which side is the right one. See?"

"Oh." My eyes leap back and forth between the gray of Cleo's sports bra and the blue shirt. Am I supposed to ignore the fact that she's shirtless while we're close enough that I can make out a tiny freckle on her chest? My stomach turns like a salad spinner. I take the world's quietest breath, forcing my gaze on to the shirt and only the shirt. It's very clearly inside out. "Looks fine to me."

Cleo shrugs, finally, mercifully, pulling it on. She changes her shorts (quickly this time, thank goodness) and settles onto the bench. Like, literally, she settles. She sprawls across it, picks up her backpack, and props it behind her neck like a pillow. She does this often, as if the whole world's her bed and she simply needs to lie down.

I should leave. I mean, I *could* leave. We've crossed a suspect off our list, as ridiculous as that sounds. But something implores me to stay—maybe Mr. Hart's voice in the back of my mind, telling me how great the story idea is. Yeah, I'm sure that's it. "So, why *did* you wait till senior year to take gym?"

"What's it to ya?" Cleo asks, her eyes now closed.

"I had to pitch this story to get out of class. I went with the 'seniors taking gym' angle, and my teacher loved it, so now I'm actually writing it."

"Oh, great, I'm gonna be famous." She doesn't open her eyes when she answers, "There were some art classes I wanted to take freshman year."

I steady my pen over my notebook. "Wouldn't it have made sense to get gym out of the way first? Since it's required for graduation and art isn't?" I try my best to follow the first rule of being a reporter: objectivity. I'm doing everything I can to keep the condescension out of my voice, but Cleo makes it so *hard*.

"Maybe. I was fourteen though. I didn't even have boobs yet. I wasn't old enough to think long-term."

It seems impossible, but my face gets even warmer. "I don't think I can include your . . . lack of boobs in the yearbook."

"What a shame." She opens her eyes, squinting at me like I'm an intrusion. This is one of the top five things I can't stand about her: the way she looks at me. Her stares have gotten worse this past year. Something about them makes me feel like a subject underneath a microscope. "Any other questions?"

I keep my pen firmly in place. "Is it hard being one of two seniors in class?"

"Gym's always hard, especially when you're fat. But I'm glad I waited. It's less daunting, running with kids I barely know. The fourteen-year-olds are softer around seniors. They're so scared of high school being as bad as middle school that they haven't realized the truth yet."

I wait for her to elaborate, but she doesn't. Ah, she's pausing for dramatic effect. Reluctantly, I humor her. "Which is?"

"It's worse. High school, I mean. It's worse than middle school."

For what feels like the hundredth time today, she makes me laugh. "Nothing's worse than middle school."

"High school's exactly like middle school but with more homework and more pressure. Like, how many times did you rewrite your Common App essay before submitting it?"

"Once." I'm as bad at lying as she is.

"Bullshit. I know you wrote it at least ten times."

"You don't know a thing about me." My tongue nervously nudges against one of my crooked teeth.

Cleo sits up, straddling the bench, one leg on either side. "I know you love those cats and Melanie Caswell and no one else. I know that every time you write an essay, you rewrite it a bunch of times, because once I printed at the library after you and your file was still up. It was called 'Julius Caesar analysis—draft 8, final—seriously final.' I read the whole thing."

"That is such an invasion of privacy!" I press a hand against my chest, appalled, even though that essay was a far cry from a diary entry.

"It was good. You're a good writer." This alone is proof that Cleo's talking out of her ass. I *hate* writing. Essays are where I most often score low As, instead of high ones. Unlike my preferred subject, chemistry, where you're given equations that follow the same rules, essays begin with a blank page. It's unbelievably daunting. "That's why you do Yearbook, right?"

"What?"

"Because you're a good writer."

Was that a . . . compliment? "I prefer the graphic design element." I lower myself slowly, sitting across from her on the bench. "Getting everything to align on a page is really satisfying."

"That's how I feel about my art. It's satisfying, getting a sketch just right."

"Right? I spent, like, six hours on one page about students' favorite ice cream flavors last year. It was ridiculous, but worth it somehow?"

"I remember that one!" Cleo grins. "Zeke was interviewed for it. He was raving about mint chocolate chip—"

"With chocolate sprinkles. Believe me, I have it memorized." I laugh. It's unsettling, not arguing, not bantering, just talking. But unsettling in a good way, maybe? Before I can make my mind up, Cleo decides this is the perfect moment to pull her weed pen out of her pocket and take a hit. "Seriously? That's so vile. How do you stand it?"

"Easily. Wanna see for yourself?" She holds it out. I shake my head. I've never gotten high, but I did get drunk at a party Mel dragged me to last year. It was *not* for me. I hated how out of control I felt. And, well, it didn't help that I vomited my guts out.

I don't remember much about that night, besides Mel holding my hair, stroking my back, and telling me it would pass.

"All right, suit yourself. I'm not one for peer pressure. Did you get what you need?"

"What?"

"For the interview?"

"Oh! Yup." I shut my notebook, my fingers fiddling with one of the tabs.

"Cool. Now that we've basically ruled Kasey out, why don't we talk to Olivia Liu next? I can message her about meeting up. Maybe after school today?"

The locker room doors open with a clamor, and Cleo slides her pen back into her pocket. The chatter of fourteen-year-old girls fills the room. They lament about the heat, the teachers they hate, and the teachers they love who assigned homework they hate. "Make it tomorrow," I tell Cleo.

After being reminded of the horrors of freshman year, the last thing I want is to come face-to-face with my ex-friend. Olivia's the suspect I'm least looking forward to speaking to. It's good to get it over with, but I need time to prepare.

"Works for me," Cleo says over the sound of the bell ringing. I stand, joining the hordes of anxious kids scrambling for the door.

My walk to last period is slower than usual. I can't shake how odd it is, that when I was talking to Cleo, I had forgotten about the interview—and the investigation—entirely.

Cleo

IF PURGATORY IS REAL, it's folding paper flowers with my mother. Every year, she makes gift baskets for the businesses that donated to the silent auction and tasks me with adding a homemade touch. Every year, I dread the meticulousness and inevitable paper cuts. It makes me miss pamphlet folding.

"How was school today?" she asks.

I wonder how she'd react if I told her the real answer. *Same old, same old. I investigated a disgraced cheerleader, then spent the rest of the day blushing because I swear Sadie checked me out when I was getting changed.* "Good," I say, creasing pink paper. Chester barks, which I'm pretty sure is dog for *You're such a liar.*

"My day was good too. I was running around town meeting with vendors. Can you believe the gala's only a month away? It's going to be the best year yet, I can feel it. We're set to break our fundraising record. The masquerade theme will really elevate it to perfection. Well, almost perfection. It won't be a *perfect* night since Lily can't come again."

"Uh-huh." I'm expected to keep up this lie that Lily can't come because she's too busy at Columbia. In reality, she doesn't *need* to hightail it back to New York on December 28. She chooses to because she's not interested in playing our mom's games.

I don't know how she does it. I can't bring myself to skip out on the gala, even though it's the worst way to spend my birthday eve. It's bad enough that my actual birthday is limited to a brunch with the gala's board and a quiet family dinner since everyone's tired from the night before. On top of that, I have to spend my New Year's mingling with people four times my age in a dress that makes my skin crawl.

There's no sense in asking to skip out though. My mom would say no. She wouldn't be able to handle losing her other shiny trophy to show around the gala. Besides, it's just one night. It's fine. I can muddle through it. I've done it before, I can do it again.

As if aspiring to make me dread it even more, Mom says, "You know, I've been reading about this great workout regimen that helps you lose ten pounds in a month, like that." She snaps her fingers. "If you start now, you'd be done before the gala. Want me to send it to you? I'll send it to you."

"I'm not sure I'll have time," I mutter. "I gotta go call Lily. She's, uh, helping me with my Tufts application." It's another lie, but a good enough one to get out of flower folding with a side of fatphobia. The knots in my neck are deepening and beginning to morph into a headache. I can't take any more of this.

"Let me and your father review your application too, okay? Lily's bright, but her own application wasn't good enough to get accepted. I'm not sure you can trust her judgment."

I wince remembering all the fights Mom and Lily got in when she was rejected. Lily kept explaining that it's a lot harder to get into college these days, but it was like arguing with a brick wall. That's exactly why I don't bother. "Uh-huh."

"And tell her to give me a call soon," she shouts as I head to the pool, Chester hot on my heels.

As soon as I'm outside, I pull up FaceTime. After the

whirlwind of the past few days, I need to see Lily's face, even if it's fuzzy. She picks up after two rings. "Save me," I say as a greeting.

"Mom?"

"I swear the closer we get to the gala, the more she gets on my nerves." I sit down, dipping my feet into the pool. I don't swim often anymore, but Lily and I used to basically live in the chlorine. I miss that. I miss her. A car honks on her end, followed by yelling. I hate hearing the background noise of New York, a reminder that she's so far away.

"I can't relate. She gets on my nerves year-round."

"Ha."

"You should skip the gala. Or at least skip the prep. She doesn't deserve to have you bending to her every whim."

"I'll think about it," I mutter. She's always trying to get me to stand up to Mom, as if it's easy. "How long are you gonna be home for Thanksgiving again?" I ask before she has the chance to lecture me.

"Three days." Damn. I was hoping I'd get four this year. My face must show it, because she rushes to add, "I'm sorry. If it was just you, it would be different. Next year, maybe we can celebrate just the two of us. Pratt's a subway ride away!"

"Can we not go there today?" I groan. "I'm dealing with enough shit."

"What shit?"

"Oh, you know, typical senior year stuff like being framed for petty crimes." When her eyebrows shoot up her forehead, I color in the lines. The tires, the mural, the whole shebang.

"This is so messed up," Lily says, "and I can't believe I'm about to say this, but I think you should tell Mom."

"What?!" I'm so shocked I nearly drop my phone into the pool.

"If you got expelled, she'd lose it. Think about the optics. If you tell her now, she'll go full Karen on Mr. Simmons, put him in his place."

"That's not a bad idea . . . but I can handle it on my own." The last thing I need is for my mom to stick her nose into this; it's stressful enough already. Besides, as pathetic as it sounds, I don't exactly want the investigation to end. I feel like Sadie and I finally got somewhere earlier, somewhere worth pursuing.

Before my pain flared up so badly that I grabbed my weed pen without thinking, we were connecting. She was talking *to* me, instead of at me. It was an actual conversation. Playing it back makes my stomach swarm with both butterflies and regret. Why do I always have to ruin things between us?

"Just consider it, okay?" Lily says. "And consider Pratt too. Or, like, anywhere. I just want you to know that Mom's wrong. The universe doesn't start and end with Tufts."

"Believe me, I'm well aware that Mom's often wrong."

"You mispronounced *always*." She gives me a pitiful frown, like she's talking to a prisoner during their weekly visitation. Mom's annoying, sure, but sometimes Lily gets dramatic about how bad she is. "Are you really okay? This is a lot to deal with."

"I'm fine." I clutch a fistful of Chester's fur, willing it to be true. "What's up with you? You still haven't told me about that awful date you mentioned last week."

"Oh my God, don't get me started," she says, before getting started. As she dives into the sordid tale, I pull my feet out of the pool and head upstairs. I'm in desperate need of some Biofreeze. I lather it on my neck, the minty smell tingling my nose.

It doesn't help. By the time Lily's finished her twenty-minute story about some asshole debating abortion rights with her, the pain has escalated and my head is full-on throbbing. "Sorry, I gotta go," I say.

"Your neck acting up?"

"Yep."

"Go put some heat on it and rest. And when you're feeling better—"

"Look into Pratt, I know." I'm in too much pain to hide the annoyance in my voice.

"It doesn't have to be Pratt," she says. "I just want to make sure you're thinking seriously about your future."

"I am!" I bite back without thinking. "Ease off, *Mom*."

She huffs and hangs up with an annoyed *I love you*, not waiting for me to say it back.

Tomorrow, I'll pay for the words of the monster that pain turns me into. Today, I squeeze my eyes shut, willing the ache to lighten up. Without meaning to, I fall asleep right there, on the middle of my bed, without a pillow.

FOR THE MILLIONTH TIME, I glare down at my lock screen. Still zero notifications. The photo booth strip of me and Mel at the fair last month that makes up my wallpaper is obnoxiously empty.

I crashed after school and messaged Cleo in the morning, asking when and where we're meeting up with Olivia. Halfway through first period, there's still no response. On top of that, Cleo's desk is empty. This happens once or twice a month. She'll skip school and waltz in the next day as if it's no big deal.

Whenever I'm too depressed to get out of bed, I'm racked with guilt. I alternate between sleeping and staring at the ceiling, thinking, *I should be in fifth period right now.* Clearly Cleo doesn't have the same issue, even when we have a very important investigation to attend to.

Where the hell is she? I shoot off a message asking exactly this (with six question marks) before pulling out my calc worksheet. I wasn't able to finish my homework since yesterday's nap turned into a full-on sleep cycle yet again, but at least it isn't due until seventh period, so I can do it now. Ms. Thomas is droning on about some Supreme Court case. I'll read about it on Wikipedia during my library aide period.

It's not easy to focus on homework though. I'm distracted by

Cleo's empty desk. Yesterday, she'd been kind of, slightly tolerable. And now what, she's fallen off the face of the earth? I'm embarrassed that I believed she was actually going to put effort into this. I was fooled by the pig vandalism, when she sprang into action, those toned arms making our problem disappear. It was kind of hot.

My grip on my pencil slips. No. I'm not attracted to Cleo Chapman. *Of course* I'm not. I'm just hormonal because my period's around the corner. Or maybe it's part of my antidepressants making me hazy? Granted, I've missed a few doses this week thanks to all my naps, but I'm still foggy.

It's probably that. With one unsteady hand, I tuck my phone into my backpack, pick up my pencil, and get to work. I'm not going to spend the day staring at my screen, pathetically waiting for a message back.

This ends up being the right decision, because she doesn't get back to me until seventh period. When I spare a glance toward the time, I realize she messaged me five minutes ago:

Meet me at Ripleys after school. We can talk to Olivia there.

There's no explanation of where she is, no apology for ignoring me. Just a matter-of-fact statement and a demand that I go to *Ripley's* of all places.

Still, when the last bell rings, I hurry toward the parking lot, brushing past Mel and Logan with a quick wave. Thirty seconds later, my phone lights up with a text from Mel: Where are you rushing off to?

My stomach twists. I haven't told Mel that Cleo and I are investigating together now. I'm not sure how to explain our weird, temporary truce. I mean, *I* can barely understand it.

I rip the Band-Aid off and send a quick text, letting Mel know I'm meeting up with Cleo. I'll fill her in on the details later. If I have to go to the worst tourist trap in Florida, I don't want to get caught in traffic on the way.

Ripley's Believe It or Not is, unbelievably, in a castle—like, an *actual* castle from the late 1800s. It's this gorgeous, medieval-esque fortress that looks like it should house ornate paintings, rather than literal junk.

Once you get past the delicately carved archways, you're greeted by portraits made out of candy and tacky photo ops. At least, that's what I've heard. I've only read about it in the brochures that sit on a front table at the inn. After seventeen years of successfully avoiding it, here I am, about to fork over twenty-five dollars to see distorted wax figures with my least favorite person. Yippee.

"Hey, don't pay," a voice calls as I pull my wallet out at the ticket booth. I turn to see Cleo wearing a bright yellow T-shirt and red basketball shorts, like she's a walking McDonald's ad. "I got you." She pulls out her phone, shaking her open Apple Wallet.

"Okay . . . do you want cash?" I reach for my wallet again, but she stretches a hand out, presses it gently against my wrist. The suddenness of the touch makes my pulse quicken beneath it.

"Don't worry about it. Consider it my apology for falling off the face of the earth today."

I draw my hand away, considering. If she's not capable of saying the words *I'm sorry*, I'll accept this as an apology—only because it means I don't have to burn money on this place. "Thanks. Why exactly did you fall off the face of the earth?"

"I took the day off." She shrugs, like this is a perfectly reasonable explanation.

"All right . . . let's not waste any more time." Brushing past her, I make my way into a hallway arching off the lobby. "Where's Olivia?" I ask as we walk beneath portraits of characters from *The Walking Dead* made out of chocolate and sculptures of tortoises punctured with rhino tusks. Yeah, my decision to never come here was definitely the right one.

"That's the question."

"What do you mean? Didn't she ask to meet us here?"

"Not exactly? I may have just seen on her Instagram story that she's here with her cousins."

"What?!" Typical. I should have questioned why any local would want to meet up at Ripley's. "So we followed her? That's so creepy. You said you'd message her."

"I know, but I figured it'd be better to spring it on her, ya know? Make it seem like a coincidence that we ran into her, that way she doesn't know anything's up. Genius, right? I've been watching *Scooby-Doo* episodes for research."

"Wow, great strategy that's definitely not you trying to make up for the fact that you forgot to message her. Well done, Shaggy."

"I didn't forget, it's a good plan! And I'm more of a Scooby, actually. Blend in, act like your average museum guest. We'll bump into her. After you, Velma." She gestures toward the entrance of a "shrinking" hallway, the type that uses optical illusion to make you feel like you're huge, or the world is small.

I huff, ambling my way down the progressively narrow stretch. The farther I walk, the more suffocated I feel. Logically, I understand it's only a perspective trick. The portraits, the tiles, the wall coloring, they're all adjusted at the exact angle to make you feel like the building is constricting around you.

I know this. So why do I feel the urge to run back to my car and take a small white pill until my heart slows to a semi-reasonable pace? I need to get better about keeping my meds on me.

When the hallway ends, I try to be subtle about taking deep breaths, coughing into my arm to hide it. "You claustrophobic?" Of course Cleo noticed. This is the same girl who noticed my two crooked teeth. She's infuriatingly perceptive.

"No. It's just not natural. There's a reason I've never been to this place."

"Wait, never? Not even when you were a kid? I loved this place when I was little. It's so cheesy and weird and *fun*. Like, look at this! It's a spaceship made out of computer keys. Pretty cool, right?"

"I guess. But half of this stuff seems pointless." I gesture to the exhibit beside the admittedly cool spaceship. "Like, why do you need to see how tall you are compared to Chewbacca?"

"Why not?" Cleo grins, standing beside the wall in an attempt to measure up to him. "Some of this stuff sucks, and a quarter of it is super offensive. But a handful of the pieces are junk repurposed as art. It's awesome."

"I guess." It's almost more interesting hearing her talk about the exhibits than actually looking at them. "You're really passionate about this stuff, aren't you?"

She puts her hands in her pockets, seeming bashful. "I just think it says a lot, that even in places full of weird stuff like this, there's glimmers of beauty. Like, you don't always have to go to high-end museums to find quality art. You can find it anywhere. One of my favorite pieces ever is at an airport."

"An airport?"

"In San Francisco. Janet Echelman's *Every Beating Second*. These giant nets, shadows, the floor, light, airflow—they all come together in perfect harmony. It's crafted to calm you down after going through TSA, make you feel more present. I've only seen it once, when I was visiting my aunt as a kid, and it stuck with me. It's amazing how art can literally settle you down, slow your heart rate. That's power."

"Wow." It's refreshing, her caring about something openly, loudly. Even if I don't totally get it, it's nice to see her be earnest for once. "And this reminds you of that?" I point to a fake rabbit with an antler lodged in its head.

Cleo laughs. "No, not exactly. But it reminds me there's potential for art in anything."

"Like hands?"

"Yeah, like hands. Now you're getting it."

I flinch, instinctively feeling like I've been hit with that good ole Cleo condescension. But she's smiling, not smirking. I open my mouth, searching for words that aren't a comeback, but I'm distracted by black, unmistakably silky hair. With one pointy elbow, I nudge Cleo in the side.

"Olivia!" Cleo squeaks out, loud enough that she turns toward us.

"Cleo?" Her mouth drops. As she walks over to us, my breaths come out more ragged than they did in the stretching hallway.

I had gym class with Olivia when I was in sixth grade and she was in seventh. We instantly bonded, which is rare for middle school, when grade lines are more rigid, and rare for me in general. I adored her. We became close, closer than I had gotten with anyone since Mel and I first met on the playground. But it was different when we got to high school.

Schoolwork piled up, and my depression got worse, along with the fear that I didn't deserve friends like her, like Mel. Slowly, I stopped texting both of them. Mel showed up at my house and told me fading away wasn't an option, that I couldn't leave her messages unread, the seat beside hers at lunch empty.

My lifelong friendship with Mel was solidified that day, but I didn't reach out to Olivia again. It felt like the damage was already done. I spent the rest of the year avoiding her and the many glares she threw in my direction. I don't blame her for them.

"And Sadie?" Olivia raises her eyebrows. "I didn't know you two were friends."

"The very best." Cleo squeezes my shoulder tight, which feels unnecessary.

"Interesting. How are you doing? You're seniors, right?" she asks, as if high school is a lifetime behind her rather than a few months. I'm so desperate to be in her shoes that I can't judge her for it.

"Yup," Cleo and I answer in sync. "Ugh, our bestie connection is ridiculous!" she adds with a laugh. It takes the strength of a professional weight lifter to not roll my eyes. "How's life after San Marcos treating ya?"

"Good. I'm taking a gap semester, helping my family out at the restaurant for a few more months, then I'm off to college." It's surprising to hear her talk about taking a semester off so casually, like it's no big deal. I've always thought it would be the end of the world to stay in St. Augustine for even an extra few months, but she makes it sound fine, normal even.

"You're going to RISD, right?" Cleo asks, her eyes wide, excited. "That's Rhode Island School of Design," she mutters to me, as if I'm too busy with my goggles and beakers to know that.

"Yes, I'm aware."

Olivia casts a wary glance between us before answering, "Yeah, I was actually just up there staying with a friend who started in the fall, I got back yesterday. It's awesome. Are you thinking of applying? You should come visit next semester, I could show you around." All of her focus stays lasered in on Cleo, like she's a beacon and I'm nothing more than a shadow. It's painful, even if it's earned.

Cleo's arm stiffens around me, before she finally drops it. "Nah, I'm not sure I'm applying to any art schools."

"Really? You should think about it, you've got real talent. Message me if you have any questions, okay?"

"Will do," Cleo says, but she sounds unenthused. I guess she was serious about not going to college.

"I gotta get going. My cousins are visiting from Jersey, so I'm showing them around all the tourist traps. I assume you're here ironically or something?"

"Yeah, it's an inside joke." Cleo winks at me, except she's awful at winking, so it comes off like it's her first time blinking.

"All right, well, it was nice seeing you!" She turns to me at the last second, like she just remembered I'm here. "You too, Sadie."

Before I can respond, she's gone. She's older now obviously, taller too, but looking at the back of her head, I see the girl I knew in middle school. The girl with the kind heart and broad paintbrush. The girl I left behind when I realized I wasn't the type of person who gets to have it all, friends and good grades.

"So it wasn't her," Cleo says. She leads me in the opposite direction, to a statue of the world's tallest man. "She wasn't even in town when the hard-boiled egg pig went up. And honestly, I doubt she would come to San Marcos to torment us. Going back there after graduating would be torturing her more than anything."

"True. Even aside from that, she seems to really like you. I doubt she'd do anything to mess with your future. Why did you think she would?"

"I beat her at a few art competitions." Cleo rubs the back of her neck. She does that so often I'm convinced it's either a nervous tic or an attempt to look cool. "Okay, more than a few. She seemed annoyed, and I get it. Contest judges are always impressed by how well I draw hands, since they're, like, the hardest thing to draw. They don't realize it just comes naturally to me."

"Uh-huh," I mutter. Does she always have to slip in a humble brag?

"What did you do, piss in her coffee?"

I move through the museum, because it's easier to talk about this while walking. "I kind of ghosted her?" I know I don't owe Cleo an explanation, especially considering how tight-lipped she's been about why she missed school, but it feels good to get it off my chest. It's easy to say it to someone who already hates me.

"Like in a . . . romantic way?"

"What? No, in a friend way. I got busy when I got to high school, and things slipped through the cracks. *She* slipped through the cracks. It's been a few years, but I don't think she ever forgave me, which is fair." Considering I'm the queen of grudges, I can't fault her for it.

"As I live and breathe." Cleo places a hand over her heart. "Is Sadie Katz admitting she was wrong?"

"I can admit when I'm wrong. I'm just not wrong often."

She laughs, and I join in, and it's kind of cathartic—until something catches my eye that makes me stop short. In our absent-minded wandering, we've stumbled on a statue of a fat man with a bulbous stomach, his head missing so visitors can slide their own above his neck and snap photos, marveling at how ridiculous they would look if they were fat.

"Sorry, I should have warned you," Cleo says apologetically. "I usually skip over this part."

"It's fine," I say, but we stand in silence, knowing it's not. Here's a body that's a little bit mine (the larger stomach, cushioned knees) and a little bit Cleo's (the thick thighs, rolling curves). In a museum of unbelievable things, our bodies are beheaded and on display for photo fun. We're everyone's worst fear and funniest punchline. It's sickening, to say the least.

"Sometimes it blows my mind that there are people who see us and think, 'God, at least I don't look like that,'" Cleo says.

I've always been jealous of Cleo's body, the way her weight's distributed into unnervingly perfect curves, unlike mine, which hangs mostly in my stomach. But looking in her eyes, I see the same pain that I feel welling up in mine. It's a feeling I've had to explain to Mel more than once, but Cleo just gets it. "Yeah. Me too."

She nudges my hand. "I know you probably have places to be, but my favorite part of the museum is in the next room. Wanna go see it? End on a high note?"

"Yeah, that sounds nice." It feels strange to linger now that we've talked to Olivia, but I'm desperate to rinse this bad taste out of my mouth.

I follow Cleo to the next room, where she points excitedly and shouts, "Ta-da!"

"It's . . . a chair? Yay?"

She flops down on the red chair adorned with gold plating. "No, it's a throne of passion." She points up to a board with a series of hearts displaying adjectives like *sexy*, *adorable*, and *wild*, light bulbs in the center of each. "I'll spot you." She pulls out her wallet.

"Wait, it costs *more* money than the twenty-five you pay to enter? So it's a tourist trap within a tourist trap?"

"It's twenty-four to enter, actually. And it's worth it, I swear."

She procures a wrinkled dollar bill, furiously smoothing it out. "This is serious stuff. When I was a kid, I swore this chair could tell the future. It gives you your love horoscope for the year. It's never failed me."

"Sounds like legitimate science."

She fumbles with the dollar, muttering a quiet *come on* under her breath when it's spit back out. After a few attempts, it's accepted. "Yes!" Her fist pumps triumphantly, before she settles in and sits up straight, as if the chair needs to get a read on her.

The light bounces around until it lands on the word *exciting*. She glances up, grinning. "Fantastic! Looks like I'll have an exciting senior year."

"I don't think that's what that means."

"Live a little." She stands, smoothing out another dollar. "Are you determined to land on *frigid*?" She points to the heart. Not all of the words are positive. Knowing my luck, I'll land on *heartbreak*.

Reluctantly, I sit down. "I want it on the record that I think this is nonsense."

"The record has been updated." Cleo gives the bill a shove, forcing it into the feeder. My eyes roll upward, watching the light dance around. When it lands in place, I struggle to read the word upside down.

"I told you it was accurate!"

I lean forward until I can read it: *passionate*. Cleo's grinning like she won a bet. "You're telling me it's always right?" I ask as I stand, and we retrace our steps back to the entrance.

"Totally. One year, I got 'heartbreak' and my girlfriend and I had a messy breakup a week later. Granted, I broke up with her, but still."

"Was that Manuela?" My voice is high with curiosity. I need

to know for the sake of the investigation, that's all. If they went through a brutal breakup, she should be at the top of the suspect list.

"Nah, our breakup wasn't heartbreaking. I just realized she wasn't my type." She averts her gaze, toward the shrinking hallway up ahead. We're already almost back to the lobby. I feel strangely . . . disappointed? Maybe because of the mountain of homework waiting for me at home. "So, uh, who should we investigate next?" Cleo asks. "Wanna see if we can find Buzz this weekend?"

"Maybe during the week? I observe Shabbat on Fridays and Saturdays, and then I always have a lot of homework to catch up on. Shabbat is when—"

"I know what it is," Cleo interjects. "I researched Jewish holidays freshman year so I wouldn't repeat the mistake of giving Ms. Blum cookies for Yom Kippur."

I laugh at the irony. "Your heart's in the right place."

She smiles, and I find myself reciprocating it. "Are you gonna be okay going down this again?" She gestures to the shrinking hallway. "We could leave another way."

"I'll be fine." As I walk down it, I find it really is fine. The stretching room doesn't scare me anymore. From the opposite direction, it's clear that it's nothing more than an illusion.

I'M IN A FANTASTIC mood. The flare-up that caused me to miss school yesterday has mostly subsided, and our afternoon at Ripley's changed things between me and Sadie. Like, I can be friendly with her and she'll actually reciprocate.

Being around her has always reminded me of going to the aquarium as a kid. You see the penguins behind that thin sheet of glass, and all you want is to reach out and pet them, to see if their feathers are soft or slimy, but you can't. Lately, though, it's like the glass is gone—or at least thinner.

I nudge her in first period when everyone's distracted by the morning announcements. "What did you get up to last night? I bet you were busy buying a season pass to Ripley's."

She laughs. "Is that a thing? How many times can one person look at bad portraits made out of candy?"

"You'd be surprised."

Sadie smiles, and the sight makes the fluorescents feel like soft, glowing candlelight. I'm smiling right back, until a throat clears from the front of the room. I shut up, expecting a scolding for talking, until I see a scrap of blue paper in Ms. Thomas's hand. Shit.

"Sadie and Cleo, Mr. Simmons needs to see you." Ms. Thomas sounds surprised at her own words.

"What do you think it is this time?" I ask once the classroom door closes behind us.

"No clue." She presses a hand to her forehead. "Maybe they found out about the pig vandalism?"

"How, though?"

"I had my head down for a while. Someone could have seen us—"

I reach out, holding her shaking arm until it stills. "It's not your fault." She's reacting like she did when we stumbled on the vandalism last time. I don't know what it is, but it's like she's folding in on herself. "I can do the talking if you want. I've been told I can be very convincing. Consider it taken care of." I flash her another smile, and she calms down enough to nod, smile back.

We make the slow, dreaded walk through the courtyard. Images of grinning sea turtles mock us along the way. The football team won some important game against the mighty Fire Ants yesterday. "It's over the top, don't you think?" I gesture to one that shows a turtle crushing a bunch of ants under his foot. Paw? Flipper? "Is the implication that we're killing them?"

"Right? I doubt they'd die anyway," she says. "They're smaller, but they can sting."

We settle into the cushy chairs outside Mr. Simmons's office, and I can't stop shaking my leg, up and down, up and down. I have no clue what's waiting for us in this meeting, but it can't be good. I'm worried about Sadie. The only thing I'm sure of here is she doesn't deserve any of this turmoil.

Ms. Adams gestures for us to enter Mr. Simmons's office with a sympathetic smile, like she's sorry to be sending us to our sentencing. God, please don't let this be an expulsion. I'm not in the mood to be murdered by my mother right now. She's already pissed at me for letting another weekend pass without applying to Tufts.

"Girls." Mr. Simmons has his feet kicked up on the desk, much more casual than last time. "I assume you know why you're here." Ah, his catchphrase.

"We're not sure, sir," I offer, which sounds strange coming out of my mouth, but I want to keep good on my promise to do most of the talking. This shouldn't be on her.

He sighs. "This again? Fine. The bubbles?"

"The what?"

"The bubbles in the fountain this morning?" What the hell is he talking about?

"Someone filled up the old fountain in the courtyard and added bubbles to it. Like, a lot of bubbles," Sadie offers, her voice wavering. "It was overflowing. You probably missed it since you were late, like always." Leave it to Sadie to sass me even in moments of distress.

"How convenient," Mr. Simmons says dryly.

"You think we put bubbles in the fountain? Why would we do that? It was probably someone on the football team celebrating the win."

"Jason and the boys have first period off today. They're having breakfast at Cracker Barrel to celebrate." Yeah, of course they are. "I did consider that it could be an excited student—until I received an anonymous tip informing me otherwise."

He pulls out a picture and slides it in front of us. It's grainy, like it was taken on a phone from a distance, so it takes a second to register that it's me. I'm holding a bucket, filled to the brim with soapy water. "This isn't from today! Look, I'm wearing a different outfit." I gesture at myself.

Except thanks to the fact that I'm a walking cartoon

character, I'm kind of not. My current muscle tee is a different color, but the photo is in black and white for some reason, so they look the same. Actually, the reason is probably so he won't know this was taken another day. I take a closer look and realize the photo was snapped when I was passing the fountain. This is diabolical—someone was watching us, plotting this.

"Do you care to explain why you were dragging a bucket of water across the courtyard?"

"Uh . . ." Shit, I've got nothing. Maybe I could say I was giving a bird a bath?

"Community service," Sadie says, her voice squeaky. "We were leaving campus cleaner than we found it, like you told us to." I nod eagerly. She's a genius, I could kiss her face off. But, like, wrong place, wrong time, I guess.

"We? It's good to know you were involved, Ms. Katz, as I suspected." Sadie's face blanches. Yet again, shit. Mr. Simmons taps a pencil against his desk, staring into the distance. My heart speeds up as I watch him ponder if he should call our parents. Or even suspend us? Expel us? I can't fathom a universe where *Sadie Katz* is expelled.

"You're lucky you caught me on a good day. Perhaps this picture alone isn't enough proof to warrant a severe punishment. But the way I see it, you have two strikes this school year alone. The lockers, now this. I'll let you both off with a lunch detention, report to an administrator at the start of your lunch period . . ." He pauses, clicking something on his computer. "Next Thursday. But if you ever have to step foot in this office again, someone is walking out suspended at the very *least*, do you understand?"

Sadie flinches like she's been slapped. "Mr. Simmons, please," I beg, looking away from Sadie because I can't bear to see her pain, "I know it's hard to believe, but someone's framing us. They're trying to make it seem like we're doing these things."

"You're right. That *is* hard to believe, but it's not the worst I've heard. Nothing will top the boy who swore he missed a week of school because he got abducted by aliens." He chuckles, like this is all some big joke. I want to rip my hair out. No, I want to invent time travel, go back ten years (or thirty), and rip his hair out before he went bald. "Do you have any proof that someone's framing you?"

"Not technically, but—"

He lets out a hefty sigh. "Get back to class." He shoos us away, picking up a newspaper that showcases the headline: SEA TURTLES SWIM INTO 34–27 VICTORY.

"Mr. Simmons," Sadie starts, but he doesn't look up. It's like we're not even in the room. She retreats slowly, her hands clenched into fists. "I can't believe this," she groans when we get to the courtyard. "Detention?! I've *never* gotten a detention."

"Me neither!"

"Really?"

"Contrary to what you may think, I'm not a delinquent. I'm subtle when I break the rules. I keep it classy."

"Well, I don't even break the rules! It's eighty degrees out, and I'm wearing this damn cardigan so I won't get dress coded. And now I have detention? No, not just detention. *Lunch* detention. It's humiliating."

"Yeah, I know. At least it'll be on an even day, so we'll be humiliated together?" It's not the end of the world—Bria's gotten lunch detention at least four times—but to Sadie? She's never so much as been late to class. A detention is practically Armageddon. "I'm sorry. This is all my fault."

"What? How?"

"I . . . I should have been more subtle carrying the bucket."

"Well, it's not your fault some weirdo was photographing you." She buries her face in her hands. "I need to go see the cows."

I laugh incredulously. "What?"

"The cows the ag class takes care of, out by the bus loop. They're, like, the only good thing at this school. Sometimes, on bad days, I visit them in the afternoon. Never during class, but we're already in trouble. I may as well earn my lunch detention."

"Is it . . . against the rules to look at cows?"

"We're briefly skipping class! Or at least I am. It's up to you if you want to join me." She heads across the courtyard at her typical fast strut. I don't bother trying to keep up, my pace slower than usual thanks to that meeting bumming me out. By the time I reach her, she's sitting in a grassy patch across from the two cows and one goat that live here.

I sit down beside her. "This makes you feel better?"

"It puts things into perspective. Like, life is simple for Moozart. All she has to do is eat grass. It seems like a nice way to live."

"You named her?" I smile. She's too cute.

"Of course. Mel and I named them freshman year. That's Moozart and her girlfriend, Milky Way. And the goat's Gertrude. She just looks like a Gertrude." Sadie lies back on the grass, sighing. "What are we gonna do? I mean, bubbles? Really? It's so random."

"I don't think it is." I lie down beside her. "I mean, it *is* random. But it was a strategic way to use that photo against us. They're playing the long game."

"That's what I'm worried about." Sadie swallows hard. "They won't actually get us expelled, will they?"

"Not if we figure out who they are first. Manuela mentioned that Buzz is hosting a haunted house next week, some sort of fundraiser. Do you wanna go? We can investigate them next."

"Ugh, a haunted house? And in *November*?"

"Haunted houses are fun year-round."

"Yeah, I love spending money to be chased by people in shitty costumes. But it'll be better than showing up at their house, I guess." She sits up, brushing the grass out of her hair. "We should head back to class."

"We just got here."

"I said we'd *briefly* skip class. You heard Mr. Simmons; one more strike and we're out. Thanks for taking this detour with me though. It's like my own *Every Beating Second*."

"What?"

"The cows. They ground me, like your art piece." She smiles softly, and in this moment, I know I'm done for. There's no getting rid of this crush, no shaking it. I just sit here, staring at her, in awe of how hard I've fallen, how incapable I am of getting back up. I only have the good sense to look away when she clears her throat and awkwardly holds her phone out. "Um, here. Put your number in and text me. We should probably move this investigation off Instagram DMs."

"Right." I send myself a text from her phone and my chest feels like it might explode. My own phone suddenly feels very heavy in my pocket with Sadie's number in it. *It's just for the investigation*, I remind myself as I stand. I hold out my hand to help Sadie to her feet, and to my surprise, she takes it without complaint.

I tell myself it's just my imagination that she holds on a second longer than she needs to, that she looks through her thick, long lashes at everyone like that. I mean, she's only giving me the time of day because of the investigation . . . right?

MY FAMILY DOESN'T ALWAYS go to temple for Shabbat. Usually, we stay home, pray, and have dinner by candlelight. This weekend though, Mom insisted that we go to prayer service. She does this sometimes when work and school take over our lives and she can feel us "separating." That's what she calls it. Separating from God, from each other.

Dad seems grumpy to be here, but I don't mind. There's a sense of peace at our synagogue that I don't feel anywhere else. Only the inn comes close. I'm happy to experience it with a full stomach. The last time we came was a month ago for Yom Kippur. By the fifth prayer service, I was struggling to stay conscious. I think people assume that hunger is the hardest part of fasting, but the sheer exhaustion has it beat.

Honestly though, atoning is harder than any of that. Sins I'm fine atoning for; I have plenty. Like when I correct someone too condescendingly, or when I'm feeling down and snap at Mel when she's only trying to help, or when I pretend not to notice a hairball in the foyer so I don't have to clean it up. In the grand scheme of sins, these are relatively small. My bigger issue is that I'm an Olympic gold medalist in holding grudges.

Every fall, when Yom Kippur rolls around, I try to let my

hatred of Cleo go, for the sake of God and my mental health. And every fall, I fail. I make it one day, maybe two, before the grudge is back, nagging at me.

It's strange, but I don't feel that nagging as strongly as I did a month ago. Going to Ripley's, visiting the cows with Cleo, was kind of . . . fun? When we were walking back to class yesterday, I thought to myself, *Okay, I get it. I get us.* Of course we were born on nearly the same day, in the same hospital. We came into this world together, and maybe the way we move through it isn't so different after all.

Maybe, all this time, I've been mistaking jealousy for hatred. It's hard for me to admit it, even to myself, but I wish I was more like her. No normal person can find beauty at *Ripley's* of all places. She has this childlike wonder that I would love to absorb even a fraction of.

"Hey," Dad whispers over the low drone of Hebrew, tugging my sleeve. "Mom's gonna hear the gears in your head turning any second; you should cut it out."

"Thanks." Mom always gets mad when she can tell I'm thinking about school when I'm supposed to be praying. I don't bother explaining to Dad that, for once, my mind's wandering elsewhere.

Mel comes over once the sun goes down, like she does most Saturdays. I'm hit by a wave of guilt, recognizing her footsteps trudging up the attic stairs. We haven't hung out in a few days, thanks to the investigation bleeding into Shabbat. In Sadie-and-Mel time, that's basically a year.

"Hey." She lies on her favorite spot of my area rug. "You didn't text me back, so . . ."

"Yeah, sorry, I didn't have the chance to before it was time to turn it off," I say sheepishly.

"No worries, I just feel like it's been forever since we've hung out. And you never told me where you and Cleo were rushing off to."

Shit, I completely forgot to fill her in. As soon as I got home from Ripley's, I had to work on a chem worksheet. And at lunch yesterday, we were preoccupied talking about the bubble prank. "I'm sorry, it's been a hectic week. We were at Ripley's, then that whole bubble nonsense happened—"

"Ripley's?"

"Believe it or not, yeah." I make a *badum tss* noise, but she doesn't laugh. "We thought maybe Olivia was the one messing with us."

"Olivia Liu?" She says it so skeptically that I feel ridiculous for ever considering it.

"Yeah. It's not her though, unsurprisingly." I slide onto the floor beside her.

"Well, I'm sorry you had to spend the afternoon with Cleo. And at Ripley's of all places. If you believed in hell, I'd think someone down there drew up that day for you."

I bark out a laugh that sounds as forced as it feels. Mel gives me a look like, *What aren't you telling me?* She doesn't need to outright ask; her eyebrows say it all. "A week ago, I'd agree with you, but I don't know. I didn't have the worst time hanging out with Cleo. She's not as bad as I thought. And some of the art at Ripley's is kind of charming."

Mel stares at me, like she's trying to figure out if I'm joking. I stare right back. "You're . . . sorry, you're serious? Sadie, she slashed your tire."

"I've done worse to her."

"Have you? I'm not sure stealing a few pencils and shooting her mean looks is worse than that. Besides, she's taking your valedictorian spot."

"It's not mine, technically." I reach out and squeeze her hand. "Believe me, I'm not saying she's the best person on earth, but, like . . . I got to thinking about forgiveness when I was at temple. Would it really be so bad to forgive her? I know you're not Jewish, but on Yom Kippur—"

"I'm Catholic. We eat forgiveness for breakfast. So *believe me* when I say she's not worth forgiving." Her eyes get soft around the edges. "I don't want to see you get hurt. All of this running around town, investigating . . . Maybe she's trying to keep your eyes off the prize so your grades will slip."

"Yeah, maybe. But she might not even go to Tufts. Did you know she didn't apply ED?" I shake my head. "Whatever. The bigger issue is trying to figure out who's framing us for these pranks. I almost wish it was Olivia so this would be over."

"I'm sure you'll figure it out soon, you're too smart not to. If only Simmons was smart enough to realize these pranks have nothing to do with you." She nudges her shoulder into mine. "In the meantime, let's focus back on the prize, yeah? Have you finished that stats worksheet that's due next week? It's killing me."

"Same. I have a page or so done." As I grab my backpack and pull out the worksheet, it stays with me, this concept of a prize. I'm starting to realize that Cleo doesn't see the valedictorian spot the same way I do, as a prize tucked into the corner of a claw machine, the one you spend your last quarters desperately trying to grasp on to. Maybe she never has.

"Did you take your meds today, by the way?" Mel asks.

"Hmm?"

"Your Zoloft. Did you take it? I know you forget sometimes during Shabbat, when you don't have the calendar reminder."

"Oh, yeah, I took it," I say on instinct. Except I didn't, did I? I'm not sure the last time I took it. Thursday, Mom reminded me, but I was so focused on my homework that I forgot. Yesterday, we were at a prayer service in the evening when I usually would have taken it. Oh well, missing another dose won't hurt.

SADIE GREETS ME WITH a huge grin when she spots me in the downtown alleyway, fiddling with my bike lock. "What the hell are you wearing? Halloween was weeks ago."

"But we're going to a haunted house! Plus, if you dress up twice, it's twice the fun." I'm wearing an impromptu costume I put together after school: a baggy orange sweatshirt over matching basketball shorts, with a tiny green glittery hat attached to my head by a string. "I'm a pumpkin, get it?"

"And here I thought you were wearing your typical costume: a non-Jewish Adam Sandler."

"Ha." Once my bike's secure and I've been properly roasted, we head over to the folding table where they're selling tickets. There's a decent turnout despite it being well past spooky season, which is great for Buzz. The last time I saw them, they were yelling at me for *desecrating Nana's oak tree*, but I still want the best for them.

Our breakup was so abrupt I still can't make sense of it. We were sitting on a bench swing, soaking in the sunset. Completely out of nowhere, they said, "I think this needs to end. You and me, I mean."

"Oh, yeah?" I replied pathetically, because what else was there to say? They sounded so certain. If someone doesn't want me, I'm not gonna beg them to change their mind. "Is there somebody else?"

"No, not for me. I just have this gut feeling that I'm not it for you. I think it's why Ms. Skittles hasn't acclimated to you. There's someone else around the corner, waiting for you, and I'm taking up their space. I'm sure you feel the same way." Hell no, I didn't feel the same way. All I felt was confused and annoyed that Ms. Skittles never got the chance to warm up to me. I swear we were making some headway.

"I'm excited for this," I say, refusing to dwell in the memory for another second. "Halloween is literally the best holiday, so I'm down for scary shenanigans any time of year. Like, all you do is dress up, eat candy, and have good ole-fashioned fun. No family nonsense like Thanksgiving." I shudder remembering how soon it is. Thanksgiving is like the devil to Halloween's angel. The only upside is that Lily comes home.

"No, the best holiday is Purim because it has the first two without people terrifying you," Sadie says. I think disagreeing with me is like blinking to her, it's second nature. But these days, it feels different—less thorny, more fun. The jabs are made of fuzzy pipe cleaners now, rather than barbed wire.

"Are you gonna be scared in there? Do you need a big, strong butch to protect you?" I flex my barely existent bicep.

"I'll manage," Sadie says, but her voice is high-pitched. "I just don't get haunted houses. Why would I pay to have someone chase me around? At least this one won't be as intense as Halloween Horror Nights. It's probably theater kid nonsense." We shuffle to the front of the table, and she plasters on a fake smile. "Two tickets, please."

I pull out my wallet and offer up a twenty before Sadie has

the chance to pay. This time, she doesn't fight me, instead muttering a quiet thanks. The ticket seller, who's covered in six facial piercings and elaborate skeleton makeup, takes the twenty. They slide two neon wristbands toward us with a deadpan stare. "There you go. Two tickets for theater kid nonsense."

I wince. Of course they overheard that. Sadie doesn't have a great sense of volume control. "Aren't you gonna put them on for us?" I ask, gesturing down to the wristbands.

"I think you can manage. NEXT!"

We awkwardly shuffle to the side. "You make enemies everywhere you go, huh?" I chuckle.

"I didn't know they could hear me!"

"I think your voice is the only thing you underestimate about yourself. Ooh, can I have this one?" I hold a neon orange wristband above a pink one. "It matches my costume."

"Yeah, that's fine. I like pink."

"I know. You wear it a lot." Sadie blushes the color of her wristband. Before she has the chance for a sarcastic retort, I grab her hand, carefully wrapping the wristband around it.

The movement reminds me of the time in fifth grade when this kid Nathan insisted that if you wrapped one hand around your other wrist and your pointer couldn't make contact with your thumb, you were "too fat." Instinctively, I had wrapped my fingers around my wrist, wondering what it meant that they barely connected.

I stopped wondering when Sadie shot back, "That's the most ridiculous thing I've ever heard." She gave me this look like, *Don't listen to him.* I was so insecure back then, about my chubby cheeks and the way my hypermobile arms twist, the crease of my elbow always upward. Sadie didn't make those feelings go away, but she did make me feel less alone—even if the next day, she replaced all my pencils with ones with dull erasers.

"I've been keeping an eye on Buzz's Instagram," Sadie says, once I've reluctantly let go of her hand. "They're dressed as Armageddon, but they haven't actually posted pictures of the costume, so I have no clue what to expect."

"Wait, is this a weird, artistic statement haunted house?! Why am I dressed like a pumpkin then?"

"I've been asking the same question."

"I figured it was still autumnal-themed." I pull at the string around my chin. I could take it off and just be wearing an aggressively orange outfit, but at this point, I feel like I should lean into it.

"You haven't seen Buzz's posts about it?" she asks. "Do they have you blocked?"

"Nah, I just don't go on Instagram."

Sadie looks up from where she's beginning to put my wristband on, her jaw slack. "Are you serious? You post three times a day."

"More like three times a week, if that. And I don't scroll. I have other shit to do." I shrug, rubbing my neck. "So, what's this avant-garde haunted house about?"

"Your biggest fears. The post said something about how the creators are being vulnerable by putting their fears on display, and they ask the audience to do the same."

"Ah, hence Buzz dressing up as Armageddon. That scares the shit out of them. We should have dressed as ours." With our wristbands in place, we head over to the short line at the entrance. A black drape hangs over the front of the alley so you can't see what's to come—just darkness and an orange light projected onto the top of the coquina. “Let me guess, you would dress as a Tufts rejection letter. No, a C on a test.”

“Yeah, if only that was all I had to be afraid of.” Before I can ask what she means, she adds, “And you would dress as a broken hand.”

“You can do better than that.”

“Hard denim?”

“Better.”

“Having to take notes in class?”

“That would be pretty abstract, but sure.” I got so caught up in our back-and-forth I didn’t realize we’re now first in line. Before I can blink, the tapestry is brushed aside and we’re grabbed by two people with sheets over their heads, dressed as ghosts.

“Is this the kind of haunted house where they touch you?” Sadie squeals. “I didn’t sign a waiver!”

“Don’t worry, boo, I’ll protect you. Get it? Boo? Because they’re ghosts?”

“WE ARE THE GHOSTS OF YOUR PAST, YOUR PRESENT, YOUR FUTURE,” the ghosts shout in down-to-the-syllable unison. They release us, leaving Sadie and me shoulder to shoulder again. “WE WILL EXPOSE YOU AND YOUR FEARS (FEARS, FEARS).”

“Are they simulating an echo?” I laugh.

“COME FORTH AND YOU SHALL SEE (SEE, SEE).” They grab us again, pulling us into a dimly lit area. Finally, they drop us, retreating to grab their next victims.

“That was weird.” I cast a glance to Sadie, who’s catching her breath. That really scared her, huh? She must have claustrophobia or something. “You okay?”

“Fine. Let’s get this over with,” she mutters, facing forward.

The rest of the haunted house is set up like a museum. Living exhibits, separated by walls made of cardboard, are illuminated by projectors. There are signs encouraging guests to peruse slowly, to *look upon the artists' deepest fears and bear witness*.

At the beginning, it's common fears—ghosts, spiders, a man in a nondescript mask. The farther we walk, the more abstract they become. A woman falling out of bed, picking herself up, and falling out again. The text above her reads, "BAD DREAM." A boy in a grocery store set, the cashier scanning his food on the belt, his eyes darting around nervously. The text above him reads, "MOM RAN TO GRAB OLIVES REAL QUICK."

"This is ridiculous," Sadie whispers. "Is this supposed to be art?" We both laugh, but she stops short when we reach the next exhibit. It's a woman strapped to a hospital bed, wearing a light blue gown. Periodically, she shakes, tremors taking over her whole body. Empty orange pill bottles lie beside her, askew. Sadie starts trembling too.

"Are you okay?" I ask.

"I'm—"

"BOO!" a voice yells, making Sadie shriek. Not scream—a full-on, horror movie, final girl shriek.

I reach out, wrapping my arm around her. "DUDE, CAN'T YOU SEE WE NEED A MINUTE HERE?" I shout. It takes a lot to make me actually yell, but Sadie's clearly messed up over this.

"THE END OF THE WORLD BEARS NO WARNING," the voice shouts back. They're around my size, wearing a black mask and a onesie that resembles the earth, only with each continent drooping, like they're melting. "YOU WILL BE GONE BEFORE YOU KNOW TO FEAR IT."

"Buzz?" I drop my voice to its normal volume. They're unrecognizable in their costume—but I recognize them by their fear. Buzz is basically a psychic. They always know what's coming, so it scares them that one day, the world may end before they have the chance to grieve it.

A gloved hand slowly pushes the mask up. "Cleo? I'm so glad you came! And with . . . Sadie Katz. Are you okay?"

"I'm fine." She pulls away from my grasp frantically, as if we've been caught in an intimate moment.

"You should put your red stickers on," Buzz says, "the ones they gave you when you got your ticket, for if you don't want the performers to interact with you."

"What? We didn't get any," Sadie says. "And that's my fault for pissing off the skeleton, isn't it? Great."

"Ugh, this is exactly why I didn't want Louise running the booth. She always shows up drunk. Or high. Or both. Either way, she's awful at her job." Buzz reaches into their pocket (I have to admit, I'm impressed the costume has pockets) and pulls out two red stickers, placing them on our wristbands. "I'm sorry that happened, but at least now, no one will bother you. The exit's at the end of the alley, past the otter in the oil spill. You can't miss it. Thanks for coming."

Sadie shoots me an expression, like, *Do something before they walk away.* Or at least that's how I interpret it. "Could we catch up?" I ask. "We'd love to chat about the inspiration behind this, it's so cool."

"Sure?" I can tell Buzz is suspicious. "But I have another three hours on duty. Are you up for waiting? I wouldn't wanna keep you, especially if the show rattled you."

"I'm fine," Sadie says. "We can wait."

I shoot Sadie my own look, like, *Are you sure?* She throws me one that says, *Positive.* Or it could mean, *I'm hungry, let's get a snack*, for all I know. Having entirely silent conversations is pretty new for us.

“All right, we’ll meet you at the exit in three hours.” I wave. Buzz waves back before lowering their mask and yelling at another passerby.

We keep walking, quicker this time. When we get to a man wearing an otter costume that looks more like a bear, Sadie rushes past me, spilling onto the street. I race to catch up with her. “We can go home if you want. Or you can and I can talk to them alone,” I say.

“No,” she huffs. “I don’t want all of that absurdity to be for nothing. I’m good to wait.”

“Okay . . . are you sure you’re all right? What happened back there?”

“Nothing. I’m fine. What are we gonna do for the next three hours, though? Should we find a coffee shop or something? Or we could wait in the inn, it’s not too far away.”

“Actually, if you’re really fine to wait . . .”

“I am.”

“Then I have an idea. It’s something I like to do when I’m having a bad day. Keep an open mind, okay?”

THE HORSE-DRAWN CARRIAGE IS white with worn-in, red velvety seats. Cleo chats with the coachman wearing a comically large top hat, before stepping into the carriage and reaching a hand out for me.

I shouldn't do this. There are fifty index cards for my next AP Art History test burning a hole in my backpack. I should go home and use these three hours to make a dent in my homework.

"C'mon, don't leave me hanging," Cleo says, hand still outstretched. I almost don't take it. But . . . when I was younger, I was obsessed with the movie *Enchanted*. I watched it a thousand times and dreamed of growing up and having a moment just like this. Obviously, I didn't dream of it being with Cleo, but her signature smirk and swoopy hair does fit the Disney prince look—ridiculous costume aside. I can afford to take three measly hours off, right?

As soon as I'm on, the carriage jolts forward and I jolt with it. "Don't tell me you haven't been on one of these either," Cleo says as the horse takes to the streets at a slow trot.

"Only once, when I was little, during Nights of Lights. That's the one holiday activity I voluntarily participate in."

I usually hate how repetitive the holiday season is. The obnoxious tunes about reindeer playing on a loop, the strangers acting like they're doing me the ultimate kindness by wishing me a Merry Christmas in that singsong voice. But string lights are different, especially Nights of Lights, when the historic district is lit up with three million white bulbs. There's something special about walking through a city and feeling it glow.

"Me too. If you haven't gathered by now, I love all the touristy shit."

"I did gather, but I don't get why."

Cleo reaches up, presses her fingers into her neck in that slow, agonizing rhythm. "When you live somewhere—anywhere—long enough, it's easy to get bored, take it all for granted. But these tourists . . . their faces light up on every street corner. Pun intended. And it makes mine light up too, watching them take it all in for the first time."

"That's sweet," I can't help but say as the carriage stops at a traffic light. Basked in red, Cleo looks at me with an expression I've only seen from her when she's drawing—like nothing else in the world exists. She's right, I think, as I avert my gaze to the road. It's a beautiful city when I look at it through different eyes, not my own that are so focused on getting out of here. It won't be decked out in lights for another week or two, but it's beautiful now.

One side of the road hosts endless rows of kitschy shops selling ice cream, postcards, tacky T-shirts, and more ice cream. Many of the stores are newer, but the buildings are old, as foundational to the city as the streets the horse walks us down. On the other side is the intercoastal, barely visible at this time of night, but as grounding as ever. I can still make out the water, thanks to the distant glow of headlights over the Bridge of Lions.

Cleo and I sit side by side in comfortable silence, arms

brushing as we take it all in. I don't realize how long it's been until we pass the alleyway where people are spilling out of the haunted house, looking vaguely disturbed. We've done a full loop. My hips shift as I angle to get off, but Cleo holds a hand out. "I paid him to go around for three hours. Get comfortable."

"What?! That must have cost a fortune." Thanks to the special horse-drawn carriage package we offer at the inn, I know the prices are gouged way up. Three hours would cost at least three hundred dollars, probably more. "What's your Venmo?"

"N-u-n-y-a." Cleo enunciates every letter.

Embarrassingly, I type half of them before it clicks. "Wait . . ."

"Nunya business. I got it. Let me be chivalrous. Don't bruise a butch's ego."

That makes, what, three times she's paid? This isn't a date, is it? My fingers anxiously tuck a loose curl behind my ear. No, no way. I couldn't be on a date without knowing it. This must just be a butch thing, like she said. She's super into chivalry, that's all. She simultaneously has no social decorum and the etiquette of a twelfth-century knight.

"Since we have time to kill," Cleo says, nudging me to get my attention, "can I ask what happened back there? The person in the hospital exhibit seemed to really get to you—and not because of their bad acting."

I flinch like she's poured rubbing alcohol on a fresh cut—or, rather, an old one that still stings. There's that lack of social decorum, though I can't blame her for wondering. "Nunya."

"Touché. But if you want to talk about it, I'm here."

Admitting I'm depressed always feels like admitting weakness, despite my doctors and parents insisting that it's not. I've spent hours poring over the science behind it; I know it's just a chemical imbalance in my brain. But that's the thing—it's *my brain*. It's hard not to feel like it's my fault, when every bitter thought is mine and mine alone.

The antianxiety pill I snuck when we escaped the haunted house has kicked in though, and the horse's gait is soothing me. I understand why Cleo does this on bad days, in spite of the absurd price. Maybe it's my meds or the sway of the carriage, but I feel comfortable sharing a portion of the truth. "I have some, uh, health issues. I don't want to go into detail, but I had to spend some time in the hospital for it a few years ago. So, yeah, that brought back some memories I'd like to forget."

I don't like thinking about my time in inpatient care, let alone talking about it. Three years later, it's a blur of endless group therapy sessions and vague promises that "better" was on the horizon. Most of my time there was spent playing back my mom's face on the drive over. The way it contorted, like she was doing everything in her power to hold back tears, to let me be the only one crying.

"That sucks. Is that why you were absent freshman year? In December?"

"You remember that?" I like to think no one noticed. Without me having to ask, Mel spread around an excuse that I was at a funeral for a distant relative. It seemed dark, but more fitting than saying I was on vacation, I guess.

Cleo shrugs. "You were never absent, so it was surprising. And I took notes for you."

"What?"

"You know how your teachers gave you notes on what you missed? I volunteered to take them in the classes we had together."

The horse speeds up slightly, as if trying to keep pace with my heartbeat. "But you don't take notes."

"Yeah, but I knew no one would take notes thorough enough for you."

The notes certainly were thorough; everything my teachers said was typed and organized perfectly. I had no clue she was behind them. Deep in the haze of my first trial of antidepressants, it hadn't occurred to me to find out who wrote them, to thank them.

I really should have, considering I still appreciate them to this day. Along with being intensely detailed, there were mentions of the social dynamics I missed, marked with tiny asterisks *Isaac said the Civil War wasn't about slavery & Madi lost it on him (as she should!) *Paul S got caught vaping in the bathroom (again).

There was one in particular that got me. When I thought I had cried every possible tear, I was proven wrong by the last line of my Honors World History notes. I don't remember a lot from that terrible year, but I do remember those words: *Half the time when Mrs. Samuel asks a question, no one answers. The silence is awkward and it's because of you. Because you're not here.

Those three sentences meant so much to me. I took them as evidence that my absence was felt, that if my thoughts of hurting myself ever manifested into reality, I would leave a gap behind.

"Thank you." I blink rapidly, willing myself not to cry. Nothing spills over, but the streetlamps are bright enough that I'm sure Cleo can see my eyes brimming. "I appreciated that more than you could know."

"Of course." She shrugs again, as if it's no big deal, and I wonder a question so obvious I'm not sure how it hasn't crossed my mind before: Is Cleo . . . good? Not pretending to be for social media, not tricking everyone with charming words and sugarcoated smiles—is she simply a good person?

Maybe I can't fathom that because I'm, well, not. It's easier to think that someone couldn't possibly be so unflinchingly kind, because if she is, then why am I not? And maybe my brain is doing what it's hardwired to: assuming the worst.

"I have this thing with my neck," Cleo says, shaking me loose from my revelation.

"What?"

"My neck." She reaches a hand up to it. "I know everyone jokes about me falling out of that tree, but I never fully recovered. The fall itself wasn't that bad, but I was born with generalized joint hypermobility. I'm super stretchy." She holds her hands out, using one finger to push another back, back, back. I've seen this before, an old playground trick kids always begged her to show off.

"I thought it was a quirk," she says, "that it didn't matter much. But apparently it means that my body can't always heal right. When I fell out of that tree, my neck turned so quickly that I basically experienced whiplash. It never went away. For three years, it's hurt almost as badly as it did that day."

"So is that why you're always rubbing your neck?"

"Yeah."

"That makes sense. I thought it was like a cool, butch pose."

Cleo laughs this adorable half snort, half giggle. I feel like I'm hearing it for the first time. "I guess it is. But I'm also rubbing the tension out. It's funny, everyone thinks I was high when I climbed that tree, but I wasn't. I didn't smoke at all back then. I just wanted to get a better view of the sunset, and I lost my footing. Kinda wish I'd stayed on the ground, but what's done is done, I guess."

In an instant, guilt consumes me. I joked about Cleo falling out of the tree with Mel because I assumed she was fine. She *looks* fine. But then again, so do I. Shit. I've been a colossal asshole. "Is that why you get high? Like, for the pain?"

"It's also fun, but yeah. I didn't really have any interest in it, even though my friends smoked, but I tried it sophomore year to see if it would help with the pain. And it did. Almost too much. I started smoking every day, sometimes twice a day." She shakes her head, looking as embarrassed as I feel. "My grades were slipping. Everything was slipping. So I quit cold turkey. I started getting high again junior year, but way less often. Like, once or twice a month, if that. When the pain gets really bad, or when I need to blow off steam from school or . . . other shit."

I remember that phase when Cleo was high and nothing but it. To be honest, I didn't know that phase ever ended. She's so laid-back, but I guess some people are just . . . like that? And she smells like weed, but Bria's always smoking and they're always with each other.

My mind can't stop reeling. The more I piece together, the more my idea of her falls apart. Just the other day, I was hell-bent on forgiving her—but maybe *I'm* the one who needs to be forgiven.

"It's not that different from alcohol, if you think about it," she says. "There are healthy and unhealthy ways to use it, ya know? Don't think I didn't see you at Josh Sanderson's party."

"Oh my gosh." I bury my face in my hands. "That was a one-time thing."

"That much was clear." Cleo grins. I nudge my shoulder into hers, and she nudges back. There's something in that brief contact that's . . . different. Here I am, looking at a girl dressed like a pumpkin, and seeing her. Not angrily watching or enviously observing, but really, truly seeing her—maybe for the first time ever. Now that I can see her for who she is, not as a jealousy-induced mirage, I want to kiss her.

The thought is so sudden it's like a dam breaking. Every time

I watched her from across the cafeteria or a classroom is playing on a loop, completely and utterly differently. Looking at her back then, and looking at her now, I want to kiss her.

I want to, so I will. I'm going to do it. Adrenaline from this long, maddening night makes my heart pump even faster. A literal horse is pulling us through a moonlit city, and I'm going to kiss Cleo Chapman, dammit. If the whole world explodes, I'll pick up the pieces tomorrow.

As I begin to lean in, ever so slightly, Cleo opens her gorgeous mouth and says, "Ivandalizedyourlocker."

"*What?*"

She said it so fast it feels like a verbal five-second rule applies. She can pick the words back up and clarify that she's joking. She'll tell me it's not true, and this moment will be salvaged, right?

"I was angry at you. You were being so rude to me, and I was dealing with some of my own shit, so I did it. You deserve to know the truth, I shouldn't have kept it from you in the first place. But I swear, *I swear* to you, Sadie, I didn't do any of the other—"

"STOP!" I cry out. "Stop the carriage. I need to get out!" This open carriage is now as constricting as the alleyway.

She actually did it. She fooled me, like she fools everyone. With that quick wit and soft smile and those lips I should have known better than to believe, let alone almost *kiss*. How could I let a horse and some moonlight convince me she isn't exactly who I've always known her to be?

The man in a top hat that now seems way less charming pulls the reins, bringing the horse to a halt. "Sadie, if you let me explain—"

"No. Absolutely not. To think I almost . . ." I don't say it, I can't. It's too humiliating. I stumble out of the carriage without help from Cleo. Now, more than ever, it's clear that I don't need any. "To think I almost trusted you," I spit over my shoulder.

And then, as if every angry, anxious inch of me depends on it, I run without looking back.

WELL, SHIT.

Once Sadie's running away like she's being chased by a bear, the horse takes back off. "HEY!" I call out, scooching to the edge of the seat. "Can you stop again?"

"No can do." The coachman shakes his head. His top hat that's definitely from Party City shakes with him. "That unexpected stop was one too many. Tennessee needs to stay on course."

"Tennessee? Is that the horse? Ugh, never mind. It doesn't matter." I slump down. Why did I say anything? This is exactly why I didn't tell Sadie to begin with.

I only vandalized her locker, that's it. Not my own, not the tires, not the egg-eating pig, not the bubbles, not whatever that weirdo's probably scheming up next. But who would believe me? Not Sadie, that's for sure. Hell, some days *I* can't believe I did something so immature. I barely let myself think about it because it makes me so queasy.

Another horse passes by, pulling along a couple snuggling and sharing a scarf. I close my eyes to avoid the sight. Sadie leaned in. Sadie maybe, almost kissed me. And I had to open my big mouth and ruin it.

"Wow. You look like shit," a voice calls out. At last,

Tennessee comes to a stop. Buzz, now wearing a tank top and jean shorts, waves. I clamber down and into their arms. They've always given the type of hugs you never want to end. I'm desperate for one right now. "Where'd your girl go?"

"What?" My voice is muffled by their shoulder.

"Sadie?"

A thrill shoots through me at the thought of it. Sadie Katz, *my girl*. It doesn't last long. I'll be lucky if Sadie ever looks me in the eyes again after tonight. "I messed up big-time," I say. Buzz pulls back, forcing me to detach. My shoulders strain, the knots tenser than ever.

"Yeah, you tend to do that with people you like." Buzz has this uncanny ability of looking through people like they're sliding glass doors. I'm not surprised that they sensed my crush on Sadie.

"I didn't with you," I say defensively.

"Fair enough." We walk a few steps before sitting on a bench. Here we are again, except this time, the bench is rooted to the ground and I've lost someone else. "What's going on? I know you didn't come for the art. I can sense urgency from you. Guilt. Loss too."

Damn. Buzz proves time and time again that they really are an empath and a witch and every word in between. There's no sense in hiding it, since I swear they can read my mind. So I tell them everything, not sparing a detail. I tell them how spending time with Sadie outside school felt special. How I didn't confess my small role in the vandalism because I knew it would mean the end of our co-investigation. And the end of the investigation would mean the end of us.

I knew I would have to watch her run off, exactly like she just did, her ringlets flying behind her. Worst of all, I knew that the next day, she would go back to being the pretty girl who gives me dirty looks. Nothing more.

"So you're here because you think I did it?" Buzz asks once I've said my piece. "You think I went to a school I haven't stepped foot in in two years and . . . committed petty crimes?"

"No, not really. That's why Sadie's here, but I mostly wanted to spend time with her. It's pathetic, but I really like her."

"That much is clear. Have you considered, ya know, telling her how you feel?"

I nearly laugh out loud. That's not happening. She'll never forgive me now that she knows the truth. As much as I regret telling her, I regret actually doing it tenfold. I regretted it right away. I was having that record-breakingly terrible day, and all roads led back to Sadie slashing my tire. In a rash, angry moment, I texted Bria and asked her to help me mess with Sadie's locker early the next morning.

Once we were done, I looked at the blobs (I'm used to charcoal, not spray paint, so it came out thicker than I expected) and realized it was something a bully in a bad school-sponsored PSA would do. I wanted to clean it off, take it back, but it was too late. People were starting to file in. Bria got one last spray in and pulled me by the arm until I fled the scene. If I could invent time travel and undo it, I would. I even tried to sneak back during first period to clean it off, but some janitor had beat me to it.

"Wow, you're thinking ten million more thoughts than you usually do. Need a hit?" Buzz asks. I glance their way, making eye contact with the joint now dangling between their fingers. When the hell did they light that?

"Nah. I'm good." I want to get high, but I want a clear head more. I need to figure out who we're really up against. Maybe if I figure out who did this—the rest of this—Sadie will see the truth and forgive me. Maybe we can make that almost-kiss a reality. God, that would be awesome. I stand up, eager to go home for once, so I can take another look at the suspect list. "I gotta head out. It was nice seeing you though. I've missed you—as a friend, I mean. I really am sorry about your grandma's tree."

"It's okay, bud. Water under the bridge." Buzz reaches their hand out for a fist bump. I pull them in for another hug instead. I'm making my way back to my bike when they call after me, "They're close to home."

"What?"

"Whoever you're dealing with, they're a friend, maybe a family member. Of yours or Sadie's, I'm not sure. But I get the sense that you're trusting the wrong people. Be careful, yeah?"

Bria. My mind goes straight to her, sinks its teeth into her name. When I asked her to vandalize Sadie's locker, she said yes, no questions asked. "That's all ya got for me?" I call back, my heart racing.

"I'm not all-knowing. If I was, I wouldn't have just told you there was someone else waiting for you when we broke up. I would have known it was Sadie."

Sadie

AS I RUN BACK to my car, all I can think of is my stack of homework that's basically gathering dust at this point. That stack that Cleo's been trying to keep me away from. No, not just trying—succeeding. How did I let her stand between me and school? And why the hell is this even on my mind right now?

Tears well up as I start my car, taking a hard left when I should take a right. On instinct, I head to Mel's. Back before my parents renovated the guest house, when we lived smack in the middle of the inn and couldn't escape the sounds of guests coming and going, I always ran to her place for peace and quiet. Tonight isn't any different. Four words are on a loop in my head as loud as a siren: *I almost kissed her. I almost kissed her. I almost kissed her.*

When I get to Mel's house, I pull out my phone and text her, telling her I'm here. I swipe out of a text from Dad reminding me to take my meds and a series of messages from Cleo begging me to hear her out. *As if.* I've heard more than enough.

Thirty seconds after I've texted Mel, the front door bursts open. "What's wrong?" Mel asks, donning her comfiest T-shirt that I know she only wears on relaxing, homework-free nights. I spare a second to feel guilty before collapsing in her arms. "What happened?"

"I . . ." *I almost kissed her.* I want to say it, but it's the type of secret that you don't even put in your diaries at risk of your grandkids finding out after your death. "I don't think I can go to Tufts," I blurt out.

"What?" Mel blinks. The words seem to shock her as much as they shock me. They feel heavy coming out of my mouth, strange—but they take a weight with them too. Maybe that's why I said it, to get *something* off my chest. "Where is this coming from?"

I stumble inside and sink into her couch. "I feel weird lately. Worse. My depression—"

"Your depression shouldn't get in the way of you going to Tufts," Mel says, plopping down next to me. "What's really going on?"

"I'm just wondering if this is all worth it. School, I mean." I'm being vague, because I can't tell her the whole truth. That after nearly putting my heart on the line for Cleo and having it smashed to pieces, my first thought was *homework*. It wasn't my pursed lips or the way she blurted out the words like she was terrified of them.

Sure, I'm playing all that back now and likely will be for years to come. But immediately after? I was thinking about the 94 I got on an English essay last week that may have been a 98 if I hadn't been playing detective with Cleo. And that's not how it should be, right? My grades shouldn't be so much a part of me that I nurse them before my heart.

"Of course it's worth it," Mel says. "You're just burnt out, trust me."

"I'm always burnt out." I laugh through my tears. "That's kind of the problem."

"Okay, so you take more breaks. We could plan something worth looking forward to after graduation, like our trip to the

Keys." She smiles fondly at the memory. I can't help but follow suit. That one week we spent at her uncle's time-share was heavenly. It was the only time in recent memory I wasn't worrying about my grades.

For once, I was present. I was looking at the ocean, and I wasn't thinking back to last year's classes or ahead to Tufts. I was just *looking*. "I'd like that," I say softly, "and I'd like a recommendation for a good hitman. It turns out Cleo *did* vandalize my locker. She told me tonight."

Even if I can't tell her about the kiss, I can tell her this much. There's no sense delaying the truth any longer. Saying it, hearing Mel gasp, makes it painfully real. "Seriously?"

"You're sweet to act surprised. I really trusted her . . . It's so embarrassing."

"There's nothing embarrassing about being a trusting person. She's the one who should be embarrassed. Did she admit to anything else?"

I shake my head. "No. She says it was just the locker, but her word's as strong as one-ply toilet paper apparently. So, I don't know. Maybe she did do all of it." I squeeze my eyes shut. "I really thought . . . I thought that maybe I'd been wrong about her."

"Some people are exactly who they seem to be," Mel sighs.

"Yeah, but some people aren't. I mean, remember when you first met Logan? You thought he was an airheaded jock."

"He *is* an airheaded jock. But he's kind too." Jealousy flares in my chest. I wish I had been wrong about Cleo. For once, I'm not happy to be right. "I can't believe she wasted all of your time, running you around town like that."

"I can't believe I let her." I groan. "Well, I'm sorry I interrupted your movie."

When she quirks her head in confusion, I gesture at her shirt.

"Oh! Yeah, I rewatched *The Incredibles* earlier—still solid—but then I started working on the stats packet. I wasn't going to, but I seriously can't procrastinate any longer."

"Shit, that's due next week, isn't it?" Fifteen pages and I only have two done, maybe. Mission accomplished, Cleo.

"Do you wanna work on it together? I was about to take a break and start *Incredibles 2*, but—"

"*Incredibles 2* sounds great." After the night I had, there's no way I'll be able to focus. At least now, I'll be with someone who's actually worth ignoring homework for.

Mel gets me a blanket, makes some popcorn, and pulls up the movie. Before she hits play, she says, "If you want Tufts, you can have it. Don't let Cleo get in your head. She never deserved to be there."

"Thanks. I know that now." I nod. Satisfied, Mel hits play—but the dialogue in the opening sequence is like jumbled background noise to me. *Is* Tufts what I want? Or have I wanted it for so long that I don't remember how to hope for anything else? Ugh, I can't go there right now. Tonight's been hard enough without an existential crisis.

I grab a handful of popcorn, turning my attention to the screen. When I take a bite, I feel a zap in my head. A literal zap, like a full-on electric current skating across my brain. *What the fuck?* I grab on to the couch for dear life.

"You okay?" Mel asks.

As quickly as it came, it's gone. The tingling makes way for lightheadedness and then . . . nothing at all. "Fine," I say distantly. "I'm fine."

I KEEP MULLING OVER what to say and coming up short. In the end, I approach Sadie in the courtyard before first period with two words: "I'm sorry."

"If you're so sorry, why have you been lying to me for weeks?" she snaps back. Mel sits beside her, looking up at me like I'm a monster. Assuming Sadie filled her in, I can't blame her.

"I shouldn't have. I was just so afraid you wouldn't believe me. Like, yeah, I did vandalize your locker." I rub my neck. It's not in any more pain than usual, but I know now that Sadie apparently finds the move *cool*. It certainly wouldn't hurt to add the power of butch suggestion to my apology, would it?

The answer comes in Sadie's eyes traveling upward. Hook, line, and sinker. "But I didn't vandalize my own locker," I add. Now that I've got her attention, I can only hope that she sees I'm being honest. "I didn't slash any tires, and you *know* I didn't make that pig mural. I was with you when it went up, and if I made it, don't you think it would look better? I'm telling you the truth. The *whole* truth this time."

Slowly, Sadie's lips part. My chest's tight from holding my breath. I can see an exhale on the horizon though. Forgiveness is inching its way into her eyes, little by little.

"Why would she ever believe you?" Mel scoffs. "Just leave us alone."

The bell rings, signaling the start of the day. I look down at Sadie, giving her one last chance, but she's dropped her gaze completely. My heart drops alongside it. "If you change your mind, you know where to find me—like, in all of our classes. And at lunch detention today. I'll be around." I head to the bathroom before first period so we don't have to awkwardly walk together.

When I reach my desk, my head hung low, I pull out my phone. I can't sit here wallowing. I need to get back to work. After leaving Buzz last night, I had a solo brainstorming session, and I've landed on two primary suspects: Matthew and Bria.

I hate that Bria's half of my options, but I can't rule her out solely because she's my best friend, especially after what Buzz said. I scroll through our texts, looking for hints of resentment. My breath catches when I reach one particular exchange.

CLEO: Wanna vandalize Sadie's locker
with me tomorrow?

BRIA: I thought you'd never ask lol
Need me to bring spray paint?

CLEO: Yeah, thanks
You aren't gonna ask why?

BRIA: It's sadie
Enough said lmao

CLEO: True

Except, no, bitter past Cleo, not true. We've pranked Sadie before, but never anything big enough to be called to the principal's office. And I hadn't pulled a prank in months. Why wouldn't Bria ask why? She didn't even know about my slashed tire yet. Or *did she know* because she's the one who slashed it?

I don't know what to make of any of this, but I do know I can't go straight to Bria, not with evidence this flimsy. In the meantime, I'll have to look into Matthew. He's on the other end of the spectrum: no history of pranks (as far as I know), but he has a clear motive. He's been hovering right below me and Sadie in the class rank for years. I'm sure he'd love to weasel his way into the valedictorian spot.

I need to talk to him, gauge how desperate he is—but that isn't an easy task. He always acts like it's a privilege to speak to him, like his air is so valuable that no one else should breathe it.

The only person harder to talk to than him right now is, well . . . I look to where Sadie's settling into her desk, neatly unpacking her backpack. I will her to turn and blink those big brown eyes at me, even if they're furrowed in anger.

She keeps her gaze firmly planted ahead for the rest of class.

As the day goes on, Sadie's quietness starts to feel . . . weird. Of course it makes sense that she's ignoring me, but she's being quiet with *everyone*. On a typical day, she answers so many questions that our teachers have to beg her to give someone else a chance. To some, it's probably annoying, but I love hearing what she has to say. Now there are long stretches of silence after questions.

She's had the occasional day like this before, but this one feels different somehow. I have this nagging feeling that it's not me or the horse-drawn carriage, that there's something else going on. When she gets to lunch detention, she doesn't suck up to the administrator babysitting us. She doesn't throw a snarky remark in my direction. She sits there, staring out at the cafeteria blankly. It's unsettling.

"What are ya in for?" a freshman asks Sadie. He's probably trying to flirt, poor thing. She doesn't respond—not even sarcastically.

"We're both in for bubble-related crimes," I say.

"Like the fountain? Cool. I rode a cow," he says proudly, like he's telling us he made the honor roll.

"Nooo, not Moozart!" I look at Sadie, but she still won't meet my eyes. She doesn't look the least bit amused or concerned. If this kid riding one of her precious cows won't get her attention, I'm not sure what will.

"I made it a few feet before Mr. Perry pulled me off. I would have gotten further with a saddle, I swear."

"And you got off with a lunch detention?"

"I didn't hurt it or anything."

This is why we'll never stand a chance against Mr. Simmons. Why does (allegedly) pouring bubbles in a fountain earn the same punishment as animal abuse? The fact that Sadie can't even spare an eye roll is concerning. "Okay, what's going on with you?" I ask.

"Hmm?" She turns toward me, but her gaze doesn't focus.

"Are you okay? You're acting weird."

"I don't exactly want to be at lunch detention." I'm relieved to hear a quip, but once she's said it, she's gone again. It's like her body's still here but her mind's far away.

For the rest of lunch, I watch her. She either doesn't notice or doesn't care. She doesn't eat either. When Mel waves at her from their usual table, she doesn't wave back. Weird, weird, weird. I expected her to be angry today, maybe sad, but not gone entirely.

I try to distract myself by going on my phone under the table, but that only makes me feel worse. My mom's custom mask for the gala may not get here until January 2, and she's in shambles. Like, sending-the-family-group-chat-ten-panicked-texts-in-a-row shambles.

I reply with supportive words, since I know Lily won't. But that backfires, because then Lily knows I'm on my phone and she starts spamming me with texts about college applications *yet again.*

When I finally give up and stuff my phone in my backpack, it's time for the most humiliating part of lunch detention: cleaning the tables of the "good kids." How this is a legal form of punishment, I have no clue. Some dude shouts out an awful joke about how Sadie's a cat in the dog house. She doesn't shout back or even flinch. When I yell at them to shut up, she doesn't tell me that she can handle herself, thank you very much.

"Seriously, are you okay?" I ask again, wiping my rag haphazardly on the table. "Sadie?" She doesn't respond. "Come on. One word. I know you're pissed at me, but give me one."

"Fine."

I laugh. "That's what you always say when you're lying."

Now, she does flinch. "You don't know me as well as you think you do."

"Well, you don't know me as well as you think you do if you believe I really slashed your tire and painted that ugly mural." She ignores me, staring at the same spot of table she's been cleaning for a minute. "Speaking of, I'm continuing the investigation. Well, I'm attempting to. Matthew doesn't exactly want to talk to me." I tried after first period and he brushed past me.

"I can relate," Sadie mutters. Ouch.

"Fine. You don't have to talk to me, but think about talking *with* me—to Matthew, that is. A good cop, bad cop approach could work well with him, don't you think?"

"What I *think* is I'd be wasting my time talking to him when I already know who the culprit is."

"But—"

She grabs her rag and descends deeper into the cafeteria, disappearing into the crowd. At least she's annoyed at me. That's a good sign, right?

I HAVEN'T GOOGLED IT yet. I haven't told my parents. I can't bring myself to do either. I can't quite feel fear—or much of anything—right now, but I still know this electricity in my brain is something to be afraid of. Google will almost definitely tell me I'm dying or already half dead.

I was hoping the zaps would go away on their own, but they've only gotten worse the past two days. On top of that, I'm starting to feel . . . sick, kind of. I'm more exhausted than usual, which is saying something. Chills are taking up camp under my skin. Sometimes when the zaps pass, intense bouts of dizziness follow.

It's getting harder to go through the motions, to convince everyone I'm fine. I told my parents I ate something funky to excuse how quiet I am. That's the easiest way to be right now—silent. Somehow, I never realized how much energy speaking takes.

I feel nothing but exhaustion—and I do mean nothing. I don't know how to explain it. It's like . . . the world is closing in around me, crushing me, but I don't care. If I'm on my way to becoming rubble, I'm not concerned with how my heart will look when it's ground to dust.

I sit at my desk with a big gov essay I've been procrastinating drafting. I'm a paragraph in, and I'm struggling to write any more. I can't remember why it matters so much, getting As. Will failing one assignment really be the death of me? I don't see how it would be. Ms. Thomas can go ahead and be disappointed, or however teachers feel when their students turn in subpar work.

I lay my head on top of my textbook, like I'll absorb the information somehow. Liesl climbs on top of me, nestles into my hair. She's been around more the past few days, like she knows I need her. Before I have the chance to pet her, another jolt comes. It takes a hold of me, grabs me, shakes me. It's like my brain's a toaster submerged in water.

When it passes, I push Liesl off, lift my head, and grab my phone. My thumbs hover over the Google search bar. I know that once I find an answer, I can't turn back. But the sun's about to set; Mom will be calling me down for Shabbat dinner soon. This is my last chance to look it up before I turn my phone off for the weekend.

I inhale, exhale, and finally type the words. For perhaps the first time in internet history, the results are pretty conclusive. Brain zaps, six different medical journals tell me, are a side effect of antidepressant withdrawal syndrome. Along with changes in sleep, flu-like symptoms, nausea, fatigue, and more. Apparently if you stop taking antidepressants suddenly, your body and brain revolt against you.

I eye the bottle of Zoloft sitting on my desk, untouched, unopened since . . . I don't know when. Has it been days since the last time I took it? Weeks?

Shit. I'd be freaking out right now—if only I could recall how to care.

Cleo

A FEW DAYS BEFORE Thanksgiving, I get a gift from God. Or, rather, from Ms. Tucker, our AP Art History teacher. "Group projects." She slaps her hands together. "Get into groups of three . . ." She starts walking through the rubric, but after I heard "groups of three," she sounds like an adult in a Charlie Brown special.

Matthew and Sadie are in this class. This is the perfect opportunity to pummel two birds with one stone. I wad up a piece of paper and lob it at the back of Matthew's head. His neck swivels, searching for the source.

I wave until his bewildered gaze lands on me. "Me, you, Sadie," I mouth.

His eyebrows knit together and he mouths back, "I. Can't. Read. Lips."

I repeat myself, whispering this time. More accurately, I shout quietly.

Ms. Tucker laughs. "It looks like our first group is Sadie, Cleo, and Matthew."

If death has a stare, it's pointed at me right now. I've been on the receiving end of many different Sadie looks over the years. There's the *I can't believe you did that* look, the *you got a 99 on this test and I got a 96 and that's somehow worth resenting you over* look.

But this look? I've only been the subject of one this lethal three times: at the Fountain of Youth all those years ago, on the horse-drawn carriage, and now. Matthew shoots me a similar one as he reluctantly scooches his desk over.

"We're spots one, two, and three in the class." I gesture at each of us in turn. "We'll make a great group."

"Actually," Matthew says with a menacing smile, "your pointing needs redirection. Sadie slipped a spot. I'm second now."

"You did?" I ask at the same time that Sadie says, "I did?"

Two words and the concern I've had the past few days increases tenfold. Sadie slipping a spot is worrying enough, but the fact that she didn't know? That she hadn't been refreshing the virtual grade book every day, agonizing over losing her salutatorian status? It's so unlike her that I can't help but wonder if she's been replaced by a clone.

Is it my fault? Did what happened between us throw her off course? Or could it be the fear of the next prank pulling her focus? Maybe that's the point of this whole convoluted scheme—for them to swoop in while we're distracted and snatch up the valedictorian spot. Now I'm even more suspicious of Matthew.

I set out to watch him for the rest of class, but Sadie keeps distracting me. As we dissect the rubric, she doesn't contribute to our brainstorming much, which is odd enough. When she does contribute, her voice is thin, like a murmur. Seeing her up close, I notice some things that I wasn't able to from a few desks away. Like how her typically shiny ringlets are dull, some of them matted together. How her skin has lost its olive tone and is abnormally pale.

"You're sick," I blurt out, interrupting a mansplaining rant from Matthew.

It takes Sadie a moment to realize I'm addressing her. "I'm

not," she says passively. Out of everything, this is the most distressing. It's not that her voice has changed; she doesn't sound hoarse like she has the flu. She just doesn't have any fight in her.

"You're sick?" Matthew's eyes go wide. "Get away from me. I *cannot* afford to get sick right now."

"I'm not sick."

"My family's going to Disney for Thanksgiving. All four parks *and* both water parks. If you're sick, you should go home." He whips out a small bottle of hand sanitizer from his backpack and rubs his hands together vigorously, as if this will protect him somehow. I never pegged Matthew as a Disney fan. It almost humanizes him.

"I'm not contagious," Sadie says.

"What's wrong with you then? Is it that *time of the month*?" Jesus Christ, the nerve of this guy. When the only answer he gets is blank stares, he has the audacity to add, "Ya know . . . shark week?" Yeah, emphasis on *almost* humanizes him.

"Whether you're contagious or not, I should take you home," I say. "You need to rest."

"What are you gonna do?" Sadie breathes out a laugh. "Put me in the basket of your bike?"

"Give me your keys, I'll drive you."

"No way." This time, her laugh's louder than a breath and takes over her whole body. I can't let it get to me. She's sick, after all. In what way, I have no clue. But it's clear she needs to be in bed, not sitting on a hard chair getting pestered by Matthew.

"Come on, I can drive, I just bike because it's easier. And it's fun." And because my parents expected Lily to pass her car on to me, but she took it to New York with her like a weirdo.

"There's an hour left in the day," Sadie says, laying her head on her desk. "I'm fine. I just need a nap."

Okay, I really need to get her out of here. Across years of early mornings and long afternoons, I've never seen Sadie sleep in class. Not once. I stand up, tugging her arm. Miraculously, she follows me, as if in a daze. It's easy to get permission from Ms. Tucker to take Sadie to the nurse's office, considering her current state.

I grab both of our backpacks and head straight for the parking lot. Sadie follows quietly, letting me carry her backpack across my chest. She doesn't keep insisting that she's able to stay in class. Instead, she goes willingly. She's scaring me shitless.

When we get to the parking lot, I dig through her backpack in search of car keys. My fingers graze over a small case shaped like a daisy. It must hold pills. I have a similar one that's shaped like a corgi and stocked with Advil. I consider offering it to her, but would medication help? I wish I hadn't opened my mouth and ruined our heart-to-heart. Maybe if I hadn't, we'd be close enough that I'd know what's going on with her.

As I reluctantly let go of the pill case, Sadie gasps. "Where are you taking me? You told Ms. Tucker we were going to the nurse's office . . . didn't you?" she asks like she can't quite remember herself.

"I'm taking you home."

"But you said—"

"I know what I said. It was a lie. I've done the whole nurse's office thing." *Aha.* I pull out a pink lanyard attached to her keys. "They'll give you an ice pack and send you back to class. It's easier to leave."

"I don't cut school."

"There's a first time for everything." I fumble with the button, unlocking the car and sliding into the driver's seat. Sadie makes a show of stomping to the passenger side, but she gets in, buckles up, and lets me take over.

The farther we drive, the more she seems to fade. It takes a lot of self-restraint to not speed to her house. It also takes a lot of self-restraint to not take the exit to the hospital. Should I? No, definitely not. If this is because of an existing health condition, they'll give her nothing but a huge bill. At least her parents work at home. They'll be at the inn, and they can help her. *She'll be okay*, I tell myself, ignoring my abnormally high heart rate insisting otherwise.

I try to put all my focus into driving. I haven't driven in a few months. My mom threw a fit about Lily not passing the car on to me, but I didn't totally mind. Sure, it's annoying having to borrow one of my parents' cars when I need to drive, but driving in St. Augustine traffic is hellish. Merging now, with cars honking angrily behind me, just affirms my decision. Granted, it's scarier on a bike, but at least I can access the historic side streets that cars can't.

"Hands," Sadie says, making me break eye contact with the rearview mirror.

"What?"

"You have pretty hands. No, handsome. I hate how handsome you are. How are you as handsome as you are annoying?" she drawls. Instantly, my cheeks burn as red as the traffic light hovering above us.

"Let's be quiet." I swallow hard. "I need to, uh, concentrate on driving."

In truth, I want to hear every thought in her head. I want to write them down and save them for tomorrow, when she inevitably isn't interested in speaking to me anymore. But engaging with her blurted-out words seems like an invasion of privacy. I'm sure she doesn't mean to say them, so it doesn't feel right to hear them.

We're a few blocks away from the inn when she speaks again. "You don't need to grip so tight."

"What?"

"The steering wheel. You can let go. You're good." She turns her head, looking at me head-on before closing her eyes. "You're doing a good job."

Instinctively, my fingers flex, then relax. I keep my hands loose for the remainder of the drive. After two more excruciating minutes, I clumsily parallel park out front and exhale hard. We did it. I got her home in one piece. Leaning over the center console, I nudge her shoulder. "We're here."

She lifts her head, looking out the window and groaning at the sight of the cat sign swaying in the breeze. "You really should take me back to school."

"You need to be home," I insist. "I don't know if this is your health issues or the flu—"

She shakes her head. "Flu-like symptoms."

"What?"

"It's not the flu. It's flu. Like. Symptoms. Did you know that antidepressants change the chemistry of your brain? It's fascinating stuff. I didn't mean to stop taking them. It wasn't some grand plan I had to feel like this. I just . . . stopped. Then the zapping started. And now I'm, well, this. I'm this."

"Oh," I say, searching desperately for the right words. This explains her breakdown when we saw the pig mural, the few times I've seen her squeeze her eyes tight, like she's holding back tears. But knowing why she's feeling like this doesn't make much of a difference. It doesn't make it any easier to watch the most put-together person I know fall apart.

"Yup." She pops the P. She's still rooted to the passenger seat, her feet now kicked up on the dashboard. I have to get her out of the car and into her house, but I need to be tactful about it. No matter how out of it she is, it's still a big deal, her opening up like this. "That's right, I have de-pression. Bet you didn't know I was . . . you know . . ." She circles a finger around her ear in a *cuckoo* gesture.

"You're not—"

"Bet it all makes sense now, doesn't it?"

"I didn't say that," I lie, feeling guilty for thinking exactly that. I get out of the car, walking to the other side to open the door for her.

She stays sitting, staring up at me. I figure maybe she needs space, so I look up too, toward the sky. Clouds are forming overhead. I didn't notice them on the drive. Maybe I was too preoccupied, or maybe they weren't there a few short minutes ago. Storms come on so suddenly in the afternoon. Blue skies can switch to gray in an instant.

"Sadie's so uptight," she drawls, bringing my focus down to earth. "Sadie's such a bitch. No, I'm broken. Well, I'm a bitch too. But I'm also broken. You know that now." She pulls herself to her feet finally. It looks like the movement took every bit of strength she had left. "You know my big secret. I'm a shell. I'm a shell of who I'm supposed to be. Of who I could be."

My heart, no longer racing, crumbles at the words. "You're not a shell," I say firmly. I know firsthand what it's like to disappoint people because you're not reaching your "full potential." And Sadie? She does more than reach her potential—she exceeds it.

She's the type of girl who barely knows what a dream is, because she makes every single one a reality. The way she approaches life is similar to how she stepped out of the car a moment ago. She puts everything into it. *Everything*. I don't think she's a shell at all. But if she is, she's coquina. Gritty and gorgeous and strong enough to fend off a whole army.

"You're not a shell," I say again, hoping she'll find it in herself to believe me. "You're the most whole person I've ever met."

"I *am* a shell." She closes the passenger side door behind her so weakly it barely shuts. Thunder rumbles, loud and too close for comfort. "I'm a seashell. Put me to your ear, you'll hear the ocean. Listen."

She comes closer, pressing her face against my chest. Then, she begins to cry. Loud sobs, the type that come from deep inside you. The type you cry in your bedroom, never letting anyone overhear. Yet here I am, hearing them. "It's okay," I say pathetically, knowing that it isn't.

"You know now," she whispers, barely audible. "You know I'm a fucking mess." The rain starts falling in droplets, slowly at first. "Don't use it against me, will you?"

My throat constricts, unnervingly tight. Sadie's pain soaks through my T-shirt along with the rain. Seeing her like this is a hurt on par with my worst pain days—the days when my neck hurts so badly I can barely form words. I force a few out now, for her sake. I know she's hurting ten times as much. "How in the world would I use it against you?"

"I don't know." I barely have an inch on her, but she looks up at me, her eyelashes wet from tears and rain. It's coming down harder now. "But I really hope you won't."

"I won't. Sadie, I know I've made mistakes. I've made plenty. But I wouldn't do anything to hurt you, at least not again. I . . ." *I care about you too much*, I want to say. But would she believe me? *Could* she believe me?

"Honey?" a voice calls, loud and frantic. I'm unsure which

one of us pulls away first, but suddenly, we're separated. Sadie runs toward the front door, toward her mom. I stay put, watching them hug in the dim light of the entryway, barely registering that the rain has transformed into a full-on downpour.

MOM RUNS ME A hot bath, lathers my hair in shampoo and conditioner, and brushes out the mats. It hurts like hell, but at least it's a feeling.

I WAS UP ALL night, playing the day back on an excruciating loop. After hours of picturing Sadie's crumpled face, I gave up on sleep and headed to school early. I'd rather not sit through breakfast with my mom today—not after seeing Sadie's mom hold her so gently. I can't remember the last time my mom hugged me like that without an audience.

Donning my comfiest, baggiest outfit, I make the trek to the art room, savoring how deserted the halls are since school doesn't start for another two hours. Along the way, I only cross paths with a lone janitor and two miserable-looking freshmen. The sun hasn't risen yet, so it's cool out, by Florida standards at least. The fourteen-year-olds are huddled together for warmth, poor things.

Luckily, I'm headed inside. Ms. Blum's pretty scatterbrained and never remembers to lock the second door that leads from her classroom to the courtyard. Though sometimes I think she "forgets" on purpose, to give kids a safe haven before she turns up.

I wiggle the knob and it opens, thank God. When I walk in and flick on the lights, I'm more than ready to be greeted by tables splattered in years' worth of paint stains and make myself comfortable.

Instead, all I see are hands.

Images of hands cover every inch of the room. They paper the walls, tables, floor, ceiling, Ms. Blum's desk. There must be hundreds of them. Or thousands? A lot of them are layered on top of one another.

The images are grainy, but they're definitely my drawings. It seems like they're screenshots from my Instagram, blown up and printed out. The majority of them are from a series I did sophomore year. I went through an "edgy" phase—drawing hands holding joints, flashing a middle finger, two suggestive fingers upright. I've debated deleting them, but I kept them up to showcase my growth. Now, here they are. My most obscene, adolescent artwork, on display as a wallpaper. "Shit," I whisper into the empty space—but it won't be empty for long.

Ms. Blum's an early riser. I have twenty minutes to clear all this out of here, maybe less. What will she think if she sees it? I can picture the headlines now. LOCAL ART TEACHER GETS A HANDFUL, SUFFERS HEART ATTACK AFTER HORRIFIC DISPLAY OF OBSCENITIES

I pull my phone out, frantically snapping pictures so I can show Sadie later. Then, I grab a trash bag from under Ms. Blum's desk and get to work filling it up. I tear ferociously, snatching images off the floor, brushing handfuls (pun unintended) off tables.

It's not easy considering my own hands won't stop shaking. I can't believe they've done it again. Seriously, what the hell is their problem? Who is this desperate to make me look like a cartoon villain? It's the cruelest prank yet.

Sure, having "lazy" spray-painted on my locker stung—but making it look like I've gone after Ms. Blum? This is the woman who once stayed with me after school for two hours when the thought of going back to my cold, empty house was too daunting. She wrote Olivia Liu a glowing recommendation that helped her get into every art school she applied to. She promised to do the same for me, if I apply like she keeps pushing me to.

Ms. Blum sees me—and more than that, she sees who I could be. The fact that someone would try to make it look like I'm out to get her is . . . well, it's genius. But evil genius. Very, very evil. I crawl on top of a table knees first, stumbling to my feet so I can rip pictures off the ceiling. Whoever did this was *dedicated*.

"Cleo. What are you doing to my ceiling?"

Immediately, I stop ripping, but I keep my hands in the air, as if I've been caught by the cops and not an art teacher wearing a dress embroidered with chameleons. "I'm . . . taking hands off of it?"

"Hands off," Ms. Blum quips. "Hmm, why does that phrase sound familiar?"

I tear off the last picture from this section of the ceiling before sitting on the table, my legs hanging over it. I somehow managed to rip most of them off, so it doesn't look totally deranged, but there's still at least fifty littering the classroom.

"What are you doing?" she repeats, tapping an emerald ring against her coffee cup. She doesn't sound angry, but it's clear she's running out of patience. The tone she's using is similar to the one she employs when freshmen purposefully don't smooth out the air bubbles in their clay, hoping their pieces will explode in the kiln.

I can't tell her the truth. Yet again, it's too absurd. She'll think I'm messing with her. "I welcome you," I blurt out, "to a farewell to arms. Get it? Because I'm saying goodbye to drawing hands and hello to . . . art school?"

"Really?" Ms. Blum's eyes go wide. "You'll apply?"

I scramble off the table. "Maybe. I'd like to hear where you recommend." It's not a total lie. The last few times she's lectured me on art school, I've zoned out. After everything she's done for me, I should at least hear her out.

"SCAD," she says immediately. "There are a lot of options, but I think you'd like SCAD best. This is great, Cleo. But this"—she waves her hand around the classroom—"is not."

"Exactly why you saw me ripping them down," I practically shout. "I thought it would be a cool metaphor, like making way for my future art, but then I realized it's a bad idea. Horrendous, actually!"

"Yes, very. Take the rest off, will you? Especially the ones on the ceiling. Talk about a fire hazard."

"Right, of course." Finally able to breathe again, I climb onto the next table over, reaching up to rip some more off. I got lucky. If it was any other teacher, I wouldn't have been granted the chance to explain myself. And what would have happened if I hadn't stumbled in so early? If the whole room had been covered in obscene drawings, would I have gotten off so easily?

I keep ripping, ignoring the paper cuts stinging my palms. This is war. We won a few battles, but we can't always play defense, as that weird bubble incident proved. If there's one more prank we can't intervene on, just *one*, we're screwed.

At least it's almost fall break. I just need to get through the rest of the week, then we can regroup after Thanksgiving. I'll tell Sadie what happened soon, but not now, no way. Mel messaged me last night to let me know that Sadie's taking school off for the next week and a half, until break's over.

Taking an absence is huge for her. She didn't even miss that much time freshman year. She needs to rest, recover—not be dragged down by this. For now, I'll take care of it. I dust off my hands, gather the trash bags, and take the long, winding walk to the recycling bin.

For the rest of the morning, the mental image of the hands gnaws at me, along with the memory of Sadie's sobs. When I get to lunch, I know what I need to do. I pull up a picture of the art room and slide my phone to Bria, staring intently at her face for a reaction.

She barely blinks. "What is this?"

"Whoaaa." Zeke grabs the phone from her. "Is this an art installation? It's sick, Cleo."

In spite of myself, I smile. "Thanks—but, no. It's another prank. Can you believe it?" My eyes don't leave Bria's.

"What's Sadie think of this?" she asks.

"She's absent today. Why?"

"Hmm. It's kinda convenient that she's out the same day this happens, don't you think?"

I bite the inside of my cheek. The more suspicious she gets of Sadie, the more suspicious I get that she's using her as a scapegoat. "She's sick, trust me. How are you so sure she would do this anyway?" I ask. In response, Bria pushes back the tip of her nose with her middle finger. "What's that supposed to mean?"

"That she's a pig. You know, because she's greedy," she says, like this is obvious. "That's why I drew one on her locker, I thought you got that. Did you think it was a reference to *Animal Farm* or something?"

Wait . . . what? "You drew a pig?"

"Well, your circles weren't exactly sending a clear message, so I improvised."

"Are you serious? You can't draw a *pig* on a fat girl's locker. That's so fucked up." The thought makes me physically recoil. Bria's never been fatphobic to me. In fact, she's told fatphobic assholes to leave me alone more than once. I never thought she'd be capable of stooping so low as to draw a pig on a locker . . . or two lockers? And a wall? Oh my God, it could really be her.

"Come on, you know I didn't mean it like that. Don't twist this into something it's not."

"Seriously? You're calling a fat Jewish girl greedy and comparing her to a pig, yet *I'm* the one in the wrong here?" I stand up, grabbing my backpack.

"Cleo," Manuela says gently, "sit back down, let's talk this out."

"I'm good. I have nothing left to say."

GOING TO DR. MILONAS'S OFFICE is like going to Mr. Simmons's office, but with even more scolding. "You can't stop taking your medication cold turkey, Sadie." She presses her pen hard against a pad of paper. "That's incredibly dangerous."

"I know."

"It could have been very, very bad."

"It was bad," I mutter. "It was a mistake. I didn't mean to do it. I just . . . missed a few doses. I got busy." I hang my head. The fog has cleared a bit over the past week, now that I'm back on Zoloft. I'm not doing well by any means, but the brain zaps are minimal. And I'm *feeling* again—which would be good, if I had anything to feel besides shame.

"Are you sure it was an accident?" Dr. Milonas asks. "A missed dose or two is one thing, but the amount you missed . . ."

"What are you getting at?" Dad asks, narrowing his eyebrows. Usually, he runs the inn during appointments, but this one was important enough to warrant a family affair.

"I think you need to figure out what led you to make such a drastic decision," Dr. Milonas says.

"But it wasn't a drastic decision. I didn't wake up one day and decide to stop taking it." I'm starting to feel something else I haven't in a while: annoyance.

"Maybe not. But you made a series of small decisions that led to big consequences. This isn't the first time I've seen this. Patients feel embarrassed about needing medication, so they stop. Or maybe you thought you were doing better, that you didn't need it anymore—but that's not how antidepressants work." I open my mouth to protest, but she continues, "Think about those moments you opted not to take it. Was it really just forgetfulness?"

My mom gives me a pointed look, and that's enough for me to comply. Begrudgingly, I think back to all the ignored texts reminding me to take my medication. All the times Mel asked, my parents, and I lied to their faces without hesitation. I didn't stop to ask myself why. I just did it, because . . .

"I didn't like the way it made me feel." I don't fully realize it until saying it out loud. "The Zoloft. It made me tired. No, exhausted. I was struggling to get my homework done. I was barely scraping by. I didn't want to feel that way anymore, I think."

Dr. Milonas presses a finger to her temple, letting out a frustrated sigh. "Why didn't you tell me that the Zoloft wasn't working for you?"

"I was scared to try anything new," I admit. "I *am* scared. What if the next one I try makes me feel worse?"

"What if it makes you feel better?"

A lump the size of a cantaloupe swells in my throat. Somehow, it never occurred to me that better was an option.

"Where do we go from here?" Mom asks, wrapping an arm around me protectively. "Should she go off the Zoloft?"

"Stay on it and we'll taper you off very slowly, whittle the dosage down over time. It's gonna be hard, but not nearly as hard as quitting cold turkey. Once you're safely off of it, we can try something new. Prozac might be a good fit for you. But, Sadie, if it doesn't work for you, you *need* to tell me. You can't do this on your own."

"I know," I say. "Actually . . . do you have any therapists you recommend? I should probably start back up again." I don't think secondhand therapy from Mel is going to cut it anymore. I need someone to help me figure out why my brain is wired to not just assume the worst, but count on it.

"I'll email you a list of names. Look into them soon, there may be a wait list." She turns to my mom. "Make sure she takes the Zoloft. Watch her swallow it." Usually, I hate how Dr. Milonas infantilizes me, but I've earned this level of supervision. And I know Mom would do it, even if she wasn't told to.

Finally, we schedule a follow-up appointment and head home. The car is shrouded in silence, until Dad caves and breaks it. "She's intense, huh? And what's up with that parrot painting?"

"It's a cockatoo." I've looked at it so many times I have its beady eyes memorized. "But, yeah, it's creepy."

"It was staring into my soul." His tone's light, but it's not long before the tense quiet creeps back.

While Dad drives us to the Bridge of Lions, Mom grips the sides of the passenger seat and turns to face me. "I'm sorry," she says.

"For what?"

"For not noticing this, not noticing *you* until it was too late. How did we miss this?"

"It's not your fault. I've gotten good at hiding it. I didn't want to worry you."

"It's my job to worry about you! You need Dr. Milonas, and you certainly need a therapist. I never should have let you quit in the first place. But you need us too, Sadie. We're here. We're your team. I want to dry your tears, but I only can if you come to me when you're crying."

"Okay." I nod, feeling some well up now.

"What your mother said. Please talk to us, we're obsessed with you," Dad jokes, his eyes flitting to the rearview mirror. "Wanna go play mini golf and tell us what keeps you up at night? We can get ice cream after."

"Honey, please, she's not eight," Mom says, turning back around.

"Actually, that sounds fun," I say, and I mean it. This is rare—my parents both having the day off work, me off school. It's been weird missing so many days in a row, but being with them has made it easier. I have to finish my gov essay, but it can wait.

Ironically, the mini golf place closest to us is run by Ripley's Believe It or Not. I know it will remind me of every messy feeling I have about Cleo, the echo of her arms holding me up. I was so out of it that I can't quite remember what she said to me, but I remember her tone, how soothing it was.

I pull out my phone, reading through texts she's sent over the past few days that I've been too hazy to read. She asked if I need soup, then immediately followed up with a long paragraph about how she understands that depression can't be treated like a cold. I smile down at the screen. It's kind of cute, watching her stumble over what to say.

I write back: Thanks for checking in. I'm doing a bit better. I just wanted to say thank you, and I'm sorry. I know that was a lot and it wasn't your problem, but I appreciate you helping me anyways

It takes barely a minute for a response to come in: Trust me when I say you have nothing to apologize for. Well, maybe you could apologize for the time you put a whoopee cushion on my chair in fourth grade and everyone laughed at me. But this? This isn't something you have to be sorry for. I'm just glad you're okay, or getting close to it.

As I read her text, then reread it, it's hard to remember why I was mad at her in the first place. Well, no, that's not true. I remember why I was mad. But it's hard to feel it—and I know that's not because of the Zoloft withdrawal. I text back: Thank you, seriously, I can't say it enough. And I'll never apologize for that whoopee cushion.

When I look up from my phone, I realize we've inched closer to the bridge. Of course, the drawbridge lifts. Mom slams a hand on the dashboard. "Every time!"

For once, I don't care. I'm in no rush.

Cleo

THE ONLY PART OF Thanksgiving I actually like is the National Dog Show. It's calming to curl up on the couch beside Lily for the first time in months, watching dogs strut across the screen. After my fight with Bria, I need this more than ever. She did text me an apology, insisting she hadn't thought that deeply about the pig comparison. Bria basically never apologizes, so that's big . . . but not big enough for me to rush to accept it.

I lean into the couch, ignoring the text burning a hole in my pocket. I'm easily distracted by the side-eye Lily keeps tossing in my direction, like she has something to say but isn't sure how. It ends up taking her five minutes to speak up.

"Are you gonna get dressed soon?" she asks. It's clear by her tone that what she's really saying is, *Get dressed now.* She's already dressed to the nines in a black turtleneck and gray checkered pants she ironed when she got in last night. Her hair's in a messy bun that looks effortless, but I'm sure she spent an hour on it.

For my part, I'm wearing a baggy toothpaste-stained T-shirt that says "*Kiss Me, I'm Irish.*" "Relax. We have an hour and a half before everyone shows up."

"You know Aunt Meryl will be early."

"Will the world end if she sees me in my pajamas?"

"No, but Mom's world will."

"I thought I shouldn't 'bend to her every whim.' " I throw her words back at her, annoyed. Since when does she care what Aunt Meryl and her overlined purple lipstick thinks?

"You know holidays have different rules. Mom's not at a ten, she's at a ten thousand."

"Yeah, Thanksgiving's tough for her. It's hard work bringing in catering and transferring it to fancy plates so no one will find out you can't cook."

Lily cracks a smile. "Exactly. She'll already be pissed you're not wearing a dress. Don't piss her off more by being in pajamas in front of her *esteemed guests*."

"Ha, okay." I nervously pick at a loose thread on my shirt, which is enough to give me away.

"You aren't wearing a dress, right?" Before I can answer, she groans. "Cleo!"

"It's like you said, she's at a ten thousand!"

"What I meant is that you shouldn't be sitting around in your pajamas at four p.m. Not that you should wear a dress and make yourself feel like shit for her benefit."

"It's easy for you to say," I mutter. Not only does she have a flight booked states away tomorrow, she can get away with pants and a messy bun. When I don't keep my hair neat and put on layers of mascara, it's different. I don't think Mom's ashamed that I'm gay, but she's embarrassed that I look the part. It's like we're all living life on her stage and I'm daring to be out of a "proper costume."

Before Lily can retort, I get distracted by a flash of orange onscreen. I gasp, slapping her arm. She recoils as if I've beat her to a pulp. "Ow!"

"Shh! It's time." As the announcer calls for the herding group, I turn the volume up a few notches. We wait with bated breath for the pièce de résistance—the Pembroke Welsh corgi. "Chester!" I squeal. His ears perk up. He trots over and whines impatiently until I hoist him onto my lap. "Look! It's your cousin."

Chester pants happily. When he was a puppy, he would bark at the other dogs, but at the ripe age of ten, he doesn't so much as whimper. Either his old age has mellowed him out or he's blind now. It's undetermined.

"You really think the corgi will win this time?" Lily asks skeptically.

"Of course I do. Look at the little guy—he's a natural." I grab a bag of Cool Ranch Doritos off the coffee table, entranced. Much to my mother's chagrin, I hate the idea that you shouldn't eat anything until Thanksgiving dinner. Why make myself sick? So I can enjoy a few extra bites of dry turkey? No thank you.

After the corgi crushes the competition, I pull out my phone with my hand that isn't dusted with cheese. The border collie is up next, total snooze. Thumbing into Instagram, I post the piece I made for Thanksgiving: a traced hand that I outlined with thick markers to resemble the kids' craft. In place of the turkey's face on the thumb is an abstract, melting drawing of my own face. all grown up, I caption it. It's corny, but I don't care.

Once I've posted it, I switch to my main feed to make sure it looks good. As I wait for it to pop up, I'm met with a sight that makes me drop my phone. Sadie posted a photo. She's wearing a red dress that hugs her stomach and chest tight, with red lipstick to match. Her curls spiral down her face, perfectly framing her rosy cheeks. She looks like a supermodel. She looks well.

I stare at the picture, transfixed, and attempt to write a comment. What should I say? *You're so gorgeous I literally dropped my phone in my lap when I saw this*? Or should I keep it simple and go with *haha, marry me pleaaaase*?

In the end, I keep it even simpler and comment a string of emojis, because words are hard to come by. I choose three: ✨ 🌟 💫 That's appropriate, right? *You're a star*, it says, without saying it outright. Perfect.

"Let's bet on it," Lily says. I nearly jump out of my skin. Even through a screen, Sadie has the ability to absorb all my attention.

"What?"

"The corgi winning. Let's bet on it."

Back when Lily lived at home, we always made bets like this. Small ones, like, *If Mom doesn't scold you for having your feet on the coffee table in the next hour, I'll make you mac and cheese* or *If Chester doesn't notice the horse in this show in three minutes, I'll do your share of the dishes tonight.*

"What are we talking here?" I sit up straighter, making Chester rustle. He squirms until I pet his head, settling him back down. "Best in show or category?"

"I'll go easy on you. Category."

"Terms? I think the loser should have to say they're thankful for Satan during grace tonight."

"What? Absolutely not, you weirdo. If the corgi doesn't win the category, you have to tell me about your new girlfriend. And you have to go get dressed."

"My what?!"

"Come on, you were just smiling at your phone. You're obviously seeing someone."

My eyes flit back to the TV. The other dogs pale in comparison to the corgi. Maybe it's my bias toward the breed thanks to a decade of growing up alongside Chester, but I swear that corgi was perfect. His run was more like a float. No part of me wants to confess my messy feelings, but the odds are on my side here. "Fine. What do I get if the corgi wins?"

"I won't hassle you about your girlfriend."

"No deal, those are awful terms." I cross my arms, appalled. She scoffs like I have no right to be. As the sheepdog's handler shows off his teeth, I say, "If the corgi wins, you have to stop hassling me about *everything*. Like standing up to Mom. And college. And how I don't floss enough. No more nagging."

"I prefer the term *advice*. But, fine, I'll stop until the end of the month."

"November is over in days! End of the year." I narrow my eyebrows. She narrows hers back.

"Till Christmas."

I tap my chin for dramatic effect. "Deal."

Lily thrusts her hand out to shake on it. I spit on my palm before pushing it forward. "EW!" she squeals, lurching back.

I still manage to rub some on her arm, cackling and taking another glance at my phone. Sadie hasn't liked my comment or replied to it. In fairness, I'm not sure what she would say. Maybe I should have gone with another angle; the stars are too vague.

I forcibly remove myself from Instagram, because, no, this is not how I'm going to spend my holiday. I need to focus on the grand finale—it's time for the winner of the herding group to be announced.

I lean forward, literally on the edge of my seat. Beside me, Lily does the same. Even Chester has his ears perked up, but that may be because he finally caught on to the fact that there's a bunch of dogs on TV. Together, the three of us hold one single breath.

And the winner is . . . the sheepdog. The damn *sheepdog* that I swear tripped over his own paws at one point.

"HELL YEAH!" Lily shouts, as enthusiastic as the dog's owner. "Tell me everything." She grins, snatching the Doritos from me.

"I don't have to because I don't have a girlfriend, ha!" I say, sounding like a twelve-year-old.

"Oh, shut up, you so do, liar." A Dorito's halfway to her mouth when she pauses, gasps. "Wait . . . do you have a *crush*?"

"What?" I look down at my phone in a fruitless attempt to hide my blush.

"You're not even dating the girl whose Instagram you spent an hour staring at?"

"It was not an hour!" She gives me this look like, *Suuure*. "But, no, we're not dating. It's complicated."

"Complicated how?"

"She doesn't like me. Okay, I guess it's not that complicated." But then again . . . *I hate how handsome you are*. Over the past week, all my attempts to forget she said that have failed miserably.

"I thought you were a ladies' man, or whatever. You have a new girlfriend every time I see you."

"Maybe that's less about me being a 'ladies' man' and more about you never seeing me." I regret it as soon as I've said it, even before Lily flinches. "I didn't mean—"

"Whatever. You should ask her out."

"I can't."

"Why? Is she straight?"

"No, she's . . ." My head presses hard against Chester's, my hair blending in with his fur. "I can't explain it, but it's different this time. That's why I didn't tell you. It feels . . . I don't know . . ."

"Aww. You *really* like her, don't you?"

I lift my head, expecting to see her laughing, but she's looking at me as serious as ever. "I do, yeah."

"Damn. Those are the worst kinds of crushes."

"Yeah. Well, there ya go. I'll go get changed, I guess." I nudge

Chester over and stand, grateful that the other half of this bet gives me the perfect excuse to leave the room.

"Hey," she calls out as I'm about to ascend the stairs. "It's not too late to *not* wear a dress."

"It's not too late to give up lecturing me," I call back. God, I wish I'd won that bet.

"Okay, but seriously . . ." I brace myself for more nagging, but she says, "This crush? Just remember it will end one of two ways. Either she likes you back or you get over her. It'll be okay, I promise."

I nod, because it's easier than explaining that it would take a lifetime to get over a girl like Sadie Katz.

Sadie

AFTER TWO WEEKS OFF, going back to school feels like going to a different planet.

The lights are harsher than I remembered. I forget about a crack in the courtyard and nearly fall face-first. The tea Mel handed me on my way in trembles in my hand. I'm off-kilter—but something in me grounds out when I walk into gov and lay eyes on Cleo.

When she sees me, her mouth stretches into a big, dopey grin. I have no control over the way my heart flutters, just like it did when she left those stars on my last Instagram post. I have no clue what they meant, but it still made me blush. "Look what the CAT dragged in," she bellows as I sit down. "It's good to see you back."

"Thanks." I take a deep breath, preparing to launch into the speech I mentally rehearsed on the drive over. "I want you to know it wasn't because of you or what happened on the carriage. I stopped taking the meds that I need. My antidepressants, I mean. I'm still sorry I put you in that position, though." I can't believe I'm admitting this to Cleo of all people. In a matter of weeks, my life has become completely unrecognizable.

"You have to stop apologizing," she says. "But thanks for telling me. I know I didn't make you depressed or anything, but I was worried I made it worse. Sadie, I swear, I *swear* I only vandalized your locker. I swear on all things holy. So my corgi Chester, my absurd amount of sketchbooks, and 3 Musketeers bars. Oh, and God! Him too. What can I do to make you trust me again?"

"Honestly? I didn't really trust you before, so I guess it doesn't matter. But I believe you." Maybe this will be the worst mistake I ever make, but I do. I see guilt in my mirror every day, and it looks a hell of a lot like what she's carrying now. If she's faking this, it's an Oscar-winning performance. "And I'm sorry too."

"Enough with the apologies! It's fine, honestly."

"No, not for that. I'm sorry I've, like, been so mean to you. I guess I can kind of understand why you vandalized my locker." Our feud has always been mutual—but I've been harsher on her, haven't I? I've assumed the worst at every turn, slipped in a jab or an insult every chance I've gotten. Hell, if I were her, I'd want revenge too. "I can be kinda a menace, huh?"

"No! Okay, well, occasionally yes. Thanks. And thanks for trusting me. That means a lot."

Her face is warm and grateful and cute and—ahh, what's happening to me? "Uh, yeah, of course. I was thinking we should get back to the investigation. I keep looking over my shoulder, wondering when they'll strike next."

"About that . . . They kind of did strike again?"

"What?!" I nearly shout. "What do you mean? Why is this the first I'm hearing this?"

"Because it happened the day after you, you know, cried in my arms for twenty minutes."

I wince, embarrassed all over again. I can't believe she's looking me in the eyes after seeing that. "It was not that long!"

"Fine, five minutes. Before I show you this, just know it's all good. I took care of it." Slowly, she hands over her phone. It's open to her camera roll, where there are pictures of printed-out hands. Like, thousands of them. Holy . . .

"Shit," I whisper. The further I scroll, the more hands there are, and the more times I say, "Shit, shit, shit." I echo it until I reach the end and swipe to a selfie of Cleo, her chin atop her corgi's head. My lips form into a smile before I can stop myself. I cover my mouth and force a cough to hide it. "How did you handle this one?"

"I got there before Ms. Blum, so I was able to take the worst ones down. She bought the terrible lie I gave about it being an artistic statement."

I exhale. "Okay, good. That's good. But if we don't beat them to the next one . . ."

"Believe me, I know." We sit in that fear, that at any moment, someone could open the door with another blue slip. At least I'm sitting in it with her again. "So, who do we investigate next?"

"Matthew. I've been trying to get him to talk to me, but he won't bite."

Right, she mentioned that during lunch detention. That whole week is so hazy to me it almost feels like a dream. "Wait, is that why you paired us up for the group project? Ooh, you genius. I thought you were just torturing me."

"Torture you? Why, I would never."

We both laugh, until Ms. Thomas clears her throat, getting our attention for a speech about how we'll get feedback on our essays after winter break. I barely register her words thanks to Cleo's laughter ringing in my ears.

When Ms. Thomas turns the other way, Cleo leans closer. "There's something else I have to tell you . . . It's hard for me to even say this, but you might be right about Bria. She admitted to drawing a pig on your locker."

"Seriously?!"

"Yeah. I had no clue she did it, and believe me, I gave her hell for it. But it's suspicious considering, ya know, all the pig motifs. Can you leave me to look into her and we'll talk to Matthew in the meantime? I don't want to rush into confronting her in case I'm wrong."

"Of course." Half of me processes this new information, while the other half can only focus on Cleo's mouth, close enough that I can practically feel her breathing. When she pulls away, I'm taken by the urge to keep her close. "I have a question," I blurt out.

"Yeah?"

"3 Musketeers? Really? Are you an old man?"

"They're an underrated candy. Oh, I almost forgot, I have a gift for you. It's not chocolate, sadly." She pulls out a red spiral notebook and places it on my desk. "Notes from the days you missed."

I raise my eyebrows, surprised. "Most of my assignments were excused, and Mel filled me in on the rest."

"Yeah, I know. They didn't ask for volunteers this time, but I figured you'd want to know everything you missed anyway."

"Oh . . . thanks." I riffle through pages of neatly written notes, even more thorough than my own. There are doodles too, mostly of cats—except, no, they're not just any cats. They're *my* cats, toying with the words like they're balls of yarn.

It hits me again, that feeling I got deep in my stomach back on the horse-drawn carriage. Only this time, there's no panicked confession to pull me away from it.

I like Cleo Chapman. I have a crush on her. What the hell has the world come to?

"All right, let's get this over with." Matthew says, drumming his fingers on his desk. I've had all day to contemplate what to ask him, but I was too caught up with my newfound feelings for Cleo. It's an adjustment, getting used to her making me feel gooey rather than pissed off.

"How was Disney?" Cleo asks brightly, like she's trying to butter him up. I doubt that that's possible.

"It was okay. Smugglers Run was down, which sucked. And my little sister cried for three hours after meeting Goofy. But it was good otherwise."

"Cool. I prefer Universal, but Disney's cool too," Cleo says. When he looks down at the rubric, not bothering to respond, she shoots me a look like, *Your turn to say something.*

"I peed my pants the first time I met Mickey Mouse," I blurt out.

"What?" He gawks. I have no idea why I said that, but at least it got his attention.

"It wasn't related to Mickey or anything. I just . . . had to pee."

"Okay? So, the project." As quickly as I got his focus, I've lost it. "Do you wanna split the PowerPoint portion fifty-fifty? Or should I handle all of it?"

I'm preoccupied trying to think of a good excuse to work bubbles and hands into the conversation, so it takes me a minute to realize not only is his math off, he's looking at Cleo. "Fifty-fifty? What about me?"

"Studies show that artistic ability directly correlates to

intelligence," he says matter-of-factly. "Cleo has her little drawings, and I play the cello. Your time spent toiling away in labs may somehow convince the rest of the world you're smart, but you don't have me fooled."

The comment gnaws at me. Thanks to the joys of middle school, I'm used to being made fun of for my weight, my sexuality, hell, even my personality. But my intelligence? That's a new one.

"Dude, seriously?" Cleo's jaw is clenched tighter than I've ever seen it. She studies me, like she's checking if I'm okay.

"You know, Matthew," I say, "I always wondered why we've never talked despite having so much in common, but it's becoming verrry clear to me now."

"What do we have in common? Good grades—well, decent in your case as of late—and an ambitious drive to get out of this town, sure. But beyond that? I have more in common with a pig wearing lipstick."

"That's it!" Cleo lunges forward, moving to slap him across the stubble that he passes off as a beard.

I reach out, grabbing her arm midair. I'm flattered that she wants to fight him in my honor, but we can't risk another trip to Mr. Simmons's office. "Cleo, stop. This asshole isn't worth getting suspended over."

She takes a deep breath, glaring at Matthew instead. He smirks, seeming unfazed by the fact that she almost hit him. Wait, is this what he wanted? For her to lose her cool, then her valedictorian status, so he could swoop in and take it? That pig comment . . . Was he dangling a carrot? Confessing *just* enough to drive us out of our minds?

"Let's get back to the assignment then, shall we?" he says, as if nothing's happened. "Cleo—"

"I am *so* not working with you, you smug asshole."

"Type your email in," I say quickly, handing him my phone. "We're gonna finish this project separately. After school, I'll email you both allotting slides to each of us." Once he's done typing, I grab Cleo's arm again and shuffle her to the back of the classroom.

"Do you think it means something?" I whisper, sitting down at an empty desk. "Pig with lipstick on? It's like he was dropping a hint."

"I don't disagree, but is *that* really what you're focused on? Not the condescending bullshit he spewed at you?"

"It's fine." I shrug. Cleo doesn't need to know about the pang in my chest. It's embarrassing, and it'll only make her more eager to beat him up. "He's a loser. I bet *he* was the one who cried after meeting Goofy and he's pretending it was his little sister. At least I was four when I peed my pants."

"Yeah, what the hell was that?"

I bite my lip, holding back a laugh. "The investigation makes me nervous! I'm not good at this detective stuff. There you have it, the two things in the world I'm terrible at. Grilling people and taking my medication. Well, three, I guess, if you count art," I say. Cleo stares at me blankly, apparently unamused by my self-deprecation. "Let's take a breather, okay?" I pull my phone out of my pocket. Luckily, Ms. Tucker's the type of teacher who can't be bothered to confiscate them.

"Okay . . . ," she says reluctantly, heading to her backpack and returning with her sketchbook. She's silent for a whopping five minutes. "He's wrong," she says. "You know that, right?"

"Hmm?"

"It doesn't matter if you're an artist or not. My sister's prelaw not because she thinks it'll make money, but because she's super passionate about it. She can't draw or act or whatever, and she doesn't need to. She's, like, the smartest person I know." She smiles fondly.

"She sounds cool."

"She is. My point is you don't *need* to be an artist. But you are one."

"Why, because science is an art form?" I scoff.

"No. The work you do in Yearbook. Laying out those photos, graphics, and texts, rearranging them until they look right . . . that's art, Sadie. And it's damn good art when you have anything to do with it."

"Thanks." I drop my gaze, hoping against hope that she can't tell how flustered I am. "Would you, uh, wanna grab a coffee after school or something? To work on the investigation, I mean. We shouldn't discuss it with Matthew in earshot."

"Yeah." Cleo clears her throat. "I'm down. For the investigation. Totally."

"YOU'RE KIDDING ME." SADIE'S laughter fills the attic.

"I'm dead serious."

"Dogs with liver cancer?"

"Small dogs, specifically, because the board member whose dog died was a Shih Tzu. I swear, the cause gets more niche every year."

Ever since Sadie asked to investigate over coffee, we've been hanging out after school most afternoons. We started in coffee shops, then upgraded to the inn's living room, until Mrs. Katz banished us here, to Sadie's room, when we laughed too loud and disturbed some guests.

Everything in here screams *Sadie*. The certificates lining the walls, the photo strips of her and Mel over the years, framed pictures of her cats, a Tufts pennant. All of it aglow thanks to warm lamps and orange bulbs strung everywhere.

Her house is everything that mine's not, I love it. Whenever I come over, I never want to leave. The company doesn't hurt either. Every time, we swear we're going to focus on the investigation—and every time, we veer wildly off course. Today we've gotten distracted by my mom's dreaded gala, now only two weeks away.

"Well, I'm excited to see what very important cause your mom will be raising money for this year," Sadie says, taking a sip of tea. "Though I'm not sure it'll beat the Shih Tzus."

"Me too. She's kept the cause so under wraps this year *I'm* not even allowed near any materials about it. All I know is it's a 'big one,' whatever that means." I roll my eyes.

"Ooh, maybe I should come then, I can't miss the big unveiling. It sounds like a riot."

"No, it's literally hell. I know you don't believe in hell, but if it was real, it would be the gala. There's only so many poorly covered Frank Sinatra songs and dry appetizers I can take."

"I actually love Frank Sinatra."

"You won't anymore if you come!" I laugh as Sadie ducks her head. I realize a moment too late that it sounds like I'm shooting her down. If she came to the gala, it might actually be bearable for once. "But, like, it'd be nice to have you there, of course," I hurry to backtrack, averting my gaze from where she's sitting cross-legged on her bed, her hair pulled into a ponytail, two loose curls hanging down her face. She's so cute that I keep staring, then awkwardly looking around the room to avoid staring.

I clear my throat. "We should get back to the investigation."

"Right. The investigation that we suck at," Sadie whines, leaning over the bed to where I'm sitting on the floor just to pout at me.

"We don't suck." I reach up, grab a pillow, and prop it behind my shoulders.

"You can sit up here if you want. I don't want you to mess your neck up. And we *do* suck. We've investigated basically everyone on our list except a teacher, and we've got nothing."

"Actually." I stand, bolting to the bed. If I move too slowly, I'll chicken out. I settle onto the mattress, careful to keep my thigh from brushing hers. "Ms. Thomas was out the day that the hand drawings went up. I was going through my texts with Bria again, and we talked about having a sub that day."

"That figures, I guess. So we're down to two suspects and we have no proof they did it. Have you found anything suspicious in your texts with Bria?"

"Not really?" My fingers fumble nervously with a tassel hanging off a pillow. Investigating my best friend feels so weird. "All I've got is she was veeery game when I asked her to help vandalize your locker. Sorry about that again."

"It's fine." Sadie opens her notebook, thumbing through it. "I just hope we can figure this out before they strike again. I'm worried the next prank will really narrow in on me, like the hand prank did to you."

"Yeah, that was a pointed one. Wait, should I add you to the suspect list?" I joke.

"I've got alibis for days. I was curled up in a ball with Liesl."

"Hmm, bring Liesl up here. I'll need to verify your whereabouts."

"Of course." She laughs, before quickly sobering up. This has happened a handful of times over the past couple weeks. We'll share a moment, then she'll cut it short, like she's scared of having fun with me. "I wish we could at least figure out their motive. Like, are they trying to teach us a lesson? Maybe they know we hated each other and they want us to get along for peace on earth or something. No, scratch that, that's absurd."

"Hate each other? You . . . you hate me?" I obviously knew she had issues with me, but I didn't know she *hated* me. It's embarrassing, but I can't hide the hurt in my voice.

"Hated! Past tense." When this does nothing to lift my crestfallen face, she adds, "It's always been me against you. Like, literally since birth. What did you think? That the pranks, the jabs, the competition over who had the higher grades, were just for fun?"

"Yeah, kinda." I feel ridiculous admitting it, even if it's the truth. My cheeks flush. I hope the lack of overhead lighting is enough to hide my humiliation. Should I leave? I should leave, right? I shouldn't stay in the bedroom of someone who apparently *hates me*.

As soon as I start pushing off the bed, Sadie pulls me back by the arm. "No, please. It's how my annoying brain works. I have this bad habit of putting people on pedestals and hoping they break. I never hated *you*. I hated the person my convoluted mind convinced me you were. Does that make any sense?"

I look over, gazing at those pleading eyes and the gentle hand pressed squarely on my shoulder. "I guess I *did* send a singing John Legend telegram to all of your classes, so I get why you thought I had it out for you."

Sadie fakes a gasp. "Wait, that was you?!" We both laugh, the tension deflating. "For what it's worth, I thought you hated me too, just a little less than I hated you. But maybe that's because it seemed like you were always intent on beating me."

"I don't *always* beat you."

"Yes you do."

"You've placed at every science fair, and I never have. And there was that spelling bee in fourth grade! I got eliminated in the first round, and you won the whole thing. I remember watching from the audience in awe, like, she sure can spell *appreciate*." She had a missing tooth back then, and every S sound came out with a whistle. It was adorable.

"I guess I never counted those because you weren't right behind me in second." Her eyes scan the wall, all the first-place awards scattered among the second, thirds, and honorable mentions. It's like she's seeing them for the first time. "Wow. I wasted a lot of time and headspace disliking you. Although, to be fair, I kind of hate most people. Me liking you is weirder than me hating you."

My face breaks out into an all-consuming grin. "You liiike me?" I know she doesn't mean it in the same way I do, but it still makes my heart practically vibrate.

"Shut up." She smacks me lightly with one of her throw pillows. "You're a surprisingly good friend."

"I'm touched." I slap a hand against my chest dramatically. I'm playing it up, but I mean it. Even if we're fated to be *just friends* forever, it's an honor to be one of the few people in this world who Sadie Katz doesn't completely despise.

"Yeah, yeah, save me the waterworks."

"I would like to thank"—I let out a fake blubber, wiping invisible tears from my face—"the academy, and my mother for giving birth to me on New Year's Day. Ow!" She hits me harder, but she's laughing harder too—and she doesn't cut it short this time.

When we're done cracking up, she thumbs open her notebook again. "Okay, but seriously, what's the next move? We've ruled out most of our suspect list, except Matthew and Bria. Well, and Kermit the Frog."

"I've never trusted him. Who's that desperate to avoid marrying Miss Piggy? She's the best."

Sadie rolls her eyes. "Save it for your fan club. There has to be something we're missing, right?"

"My money's on Matthew. At least, I hope it's Matthew and not Bria. Except . . ."

"Except what? Please tell me you're not keeping another secret from me."

"No! Not at all. I just didn't think it was worth mentioning at first. On the night of the horse-drawn carriage, Buzz said that the culprit was someone close to home. Like, a friend or a family member," I say. Sadie stares at me blankly. "Oh, Buzz is a psychic."

"Seriously?" she groans into her pillow. "We're the two smartest people at school, and all we have is a hunch from an alleged psychic?"

"They're a good psychic! They guess the winner of *The Masked Singer* correctly every season." Sadie doesn't laugh. Her anxiety's palpable, and I'm feeling it too. The fact that the prankster hasn't done anything in a few weeks is nerve-racking. It feels like the other shoe—or, rather, blue slip—is closer and closer to dropping. Like, maybe they're taking their time plotting something terrible, expulsion-worthy. So I say the last thing I want to. "We should talk to Bria."

"Are you sure?"

"No. But clearly snooping through our texts isn't getting us anywhere."

I must look as stressed as I feel, because Sadie reaches over, squeezes my hand. "It's a good idea—but there's nothing we can do about it tonight. Let's get some homework done."

"Aye, aye, Captain." I offer her a two-fingered salute.

We swap notes for the upcoming AP Art History quiz, which naturally devolves into swapping jokes and stories until long after the sun goes down. Eventually, the quiet, darkness, and absurd amount of pillows make the perfect storm to lull us into sleep, side by side.

WHEN I WAKE UP, it takes a second to process that Cleo's in my arms. The last thing I remember, I took a break from homework to rest my eyes. We were definitely a few feet apart. Now, somehow, she's nestled in my grasp, slotted in like she belongs there, her hair tickling my skin. Her right arm's tucked under mine, her left extended with the elbow jutting out, I hope because of her hypermobility and not discomfort. I look down at her, beautiful, still, and dappled in sunlight, and I'm convinced she's a figment of my imagination.

Wait, sunlight? Shit, what time is it? I search for my phone and spot it on the other side of the bed, out of reach. I have two options here: carefully remove her from my arms, or nudge her awake. Neither sounds appealing. I almost wish we could skip school, spend the day together. But I can't. We can't. For, like, a million reasons.

Before I can figure out the best course of action, I hear footsteps pounding up the stairs. Quickly, I dislodge myself from Cleo. I move to the other side of the bed just before it flies open.

Cleo jumps at the sound of the door creaking. "Wha-what happened?" she mutters, her voice raspy from sleep and absolutely adorable.

Mel's eyes widen, shifting in my direction. "Hi. You slept

through first period," she says. "I thought maybe you had a doctor's appointment, but there wasn't anything on the Google calendar, so I cut class to make sure you were all right."

I grab my phone and finally check the time: 9:15 a.m. *Shit.* "We fell asleep. Or, I fell asleep. Or . . . ahh, I gotta pee!" I hop out of bed, open my closet, and grab the first dress I see, before scurrying downstairs to the bathroom.

I've never been late to school before. My parents have left me to my own devices for years, since mornings are obviously the busiest time of day at a bed-and-breakfast. No matter how exhausted I am, I get myself up and moving. I must have been sleeping really, really deeply if I missed my alarms.

Frantically, I get dressed and pull my hair into a messy bun. Before I head back upstairs, I take a moment to collect myself. I can't believe I slept with Cleo last night. I mean, not *slept with*. I press my hands against my bright red cheeks. I'm so embarrassed that Mel walked in on us. It feels like she interrupted a private moment—but we were just tired. I'm adjusting to being back on Zoloft; of course I'm exhausted.

I take a deep breath and make my way upstairs. Mel's busy shoving folders into my backpack, but Cleo's still in bed, my knit blanket tossed over her legs. "You coming?" I ask, sliding a cardigan on.

"At this rate, I think I'll skip today." She digs a knuckle into her shoulder, and I catch her drift.

"Okay. Well, take your time," I say. "The inn serves breakfast till ten if you need to eat. You better not vandalize my room while I'm gone!" I head out the door, eager not to miss too much of second period. It feels strange, leaving her alone in my bedroom, but we're friends now. Friends have sleepovers sometimes. This is typical, platonic behavior.

Mel and I pile into her car, and for the first five minutes of the drive, the only sound is Kate Bush's crooning through the speakers and my heavy breathing. "Thanks for coming to check on me," I finally say.

"Yeah, well, when your best friend recently had a mental breakdown, you get worried when she doesn't answer your texts," Mel says.

"I'm sorry I worried you, seriously. I hope you're not mad at me."

"I'm not mad, I was just scared. And now I'm confused. Is something . . . going on with you and Cleo?"

"What? No, of course not!" I don't even consider telling her about my feelings for Cleo. She wouldn't get it, and there's no point since this crush will never go anywhere. As Mel so astutely pointed out, I just had a literal mental breakdown. Cleo not only bore witness to it, she even absorbed my snot. There's no way I'm anyone's dream girlfriend, let alone hers. "We were talking about the investigation, doing homework, and we conked out, that's all."

"All right. Are you sure it's, like, safe to leave her alone in your bedroom though? Ya know, considering what she did to your locker?"

"It's fine. What's she gonna do, spray-paint my bed? Besides, I trust her. It's weird, but we're kind of becoming friends? I was actually gonna ask, do you wanna go to her family's New Year's gala?"

Mel turns into the parking lot, sparing a second to raise her eyebrows before pulling into her spot. "But that's on your birthday, isn't it?"

"Yeah. I figure it's our last chance to see what it's all about, since next New Year's we'll be at some cool club in Boston." This makes her break out into a huge grin, like I knew it would. "Cleo's been telling me about it, and it seems like a shit show, but in a fun way?" It's not a lie; the gala does sound fun. But more than that, Cleo's been telling me how much she dreads it, and I want to be there for her.

"It sounds interesting, to say the least. I'll have to convince my mom to let me go out on New Year's, which will be an uphill battle. But I'll work on it—as long as we can make fun of all the stuffy socialites and eat too many finger sandwiches."

"Sounds like a perfect night to me. We should probably go to class now, right?"

"Oh, shit, yeah." She laughs, and I follow her to a side entrance, trailing behind as I send Cleo an apology text. I probably fell asleep first, thanks to my perpetual exhaustion. But honestly? I slept better than I have in weeks.

BEING ALONE IN SADIE'S bedroom might actually be my cause of death. A poster of Marie Curie towers above me, and I just know she's judging me for how flustered I am. I can see it in her eyes.

I seriously can't believe Sadie and I spent the whole night together. Like, *cuddling* levels of together. Ever since she pulled away from me as I was waking up, I've felt kind of cold, exposed. Already, I miss her warmth. I look past Marie Curie and find Sadie's face on the walls, smiling in photos with Mel and her family.

I can't help but wonder if there's any realm of possibility, any universe where traces of me could be on these walls. Instinctively, I search for blank spaces I could fill. *A surprisingly good friend.* Maybe I'll never know what it's like to frame Sadie's face with my hands, pull her close, and kiss her. But at least I'm a surprisingly good friend—one she snuggles with, apparently.

I kick the blanket off my legs and grab my backpack. I need to get out of here and stop soaking in the shadow of last night. My neck's in a lot of pain from sleeping without my memory foam pillow, so school isn't an option. There's no way I'll be able to focus.

Instead, I text my group chat with Bria, Zeke, and Manuela: fort, anyone? Luckily, I know Bria has a big test today and won't be able to come. I'm not sure I can face interrogating her without Sadie by my side.

Not waiting for a reply, I take off in the direction of the playground. The walk is a nice distraction. It's cool out, especially since the sun isn't at its peak. I hate that we don't get to enjoy the morning weather on weekdays, always trapped indoors. When I reach the playground, I breathe in the fresh air. In, out. In, out.

In.

Sadie's arms, wrapped around me, holding me tight.

Out.

Her chin brushing the top of my head, just for a second, before she was gone.

"Hey," Manuela's voice calls, a welcome interruption from my thoughts. She joins me, shuffling under the point where two short rock climbing walls connect.

The fort is something Bria came up with when we were younger, a clubhouse of sorts. She loves the irony that there are actual, historic forts in St. Augustine, yet this is ours: a small, tucked away spot in a playground by the water. It's guarded by rocks made of plastic and often conquered by seven-year-olds. Right now, the kids are in school, so it's empty enough that there aren't parents to chase us off, insisting we're "too old" to be here.

"I brought you a present." Manuela opens her maroon messenger bag, pulling out a Pub sub.

"Hell yeah." I take a huge bite. The piping hot buffalo chicken tenders help mask the lingering scent of Sadie's hair mousse that's driving me out of my mind. "When's the last time I told you that I love you?"

"I can't remember. Never, maybe?"

"Oh," I say around a bite, "well, I love you."

"Why aren't you in school?"

"Why aren't *you* in school?" I shoot back, sounding distinctly like I belong at this playground.

"I have family flying in for my cousin's wedding. I'm headed to the airport to pick them up later. I figured I'd stop here first since I don't have anything better to do. It didn't seem worth it to go in just for first period, ya know?"

"Makes sense. Which cousin?"

"Isa. Why aren't you in school, Cleo?" she echoes, and it's clear that she's not gonna let me weasel my way out of answering.

"I don't think I should say." I stare at the sandwich, the mulch beneath my feet, anything but her.

"So it's about Sadie?" she asks. Am I that transparent? "It's fine, you can talk to me about your crush. We broke up nearly a year ago, you can like someone else. I'm a big girl."

"But I *can't* like her, that's the problem." I set the sandwich down on the wrapper, burying my face in my hands. "I'm scared, honestly."

"Yeah, no shit. You're always scared."

"What's that supposed to mean?" I ask, half defensively, half curiously.

"It means that anytime a good thing—especially a hard, good thing—comes into your life, you push it away. You need to get past your shit and ask her out. Don't overcomplicate it." She flicks me square in the forehead, as if trying to knock sense into me.

"I'm not overcomplicating it, I'm just . . ."

"Scared. Scared enough to never date someone past the two-month mark."

"I dated Buzz for three," I say pathetically.

"Wow, someone get Ripley's on the phone, we've discovered something truly unbelievable!"

Is she right? Am I overcomplicating this? After all, Sadie held me while we slept. Maybe she was tired, thanks to her medication and mountains of homework. Maybe I was nothing more than the nearest pillow.

Or maybe she feels as safe around me as I feel around her. Maybe it means something, that she tucked in close, that she laughs at my bad jokes, that more and more often, she holds eye contact a little too long. Maybe we could be *something*—a longer-than-three-months something.

"I'm not here to lecture you," Manuela says, sounding unnervingly like Lily. "I just think it may be simpler than you realize. And I wanted to kill some time before I have to deal with my great-aunt hassling me about not having a boyfriend."

"Yikes, good luck with that."

"Thanks. Speaking of, I gotta get going. Are you gonna be okay?"

"Only if I can finish this." I hold up my half-eaten sub. She laughs and blows me an air kiss before crawling backward out of the fort. I take a big bite of the sandwich, pulling my phone out to play some music. She's given me a lot to think about—but I need *some* noise so I don't drown in my fears completely.

My thumb's primed for Spotify, but a series of texts light up my lockscreen, distracting me:

LILY: did you see mom's latest fb status bragging about my grades?

ZEKE: wait, ur skipping??

SADIE: I'm sorry about last night! I was just really tired.

My heart drops at the last one. I stare at it, unsure how to respond. The truth ("Don't be. I slept better than I have in months, maybe ever") feels too earnest, and the lie ("Haha, it's all good") is too painful.

I end up squarely in the middle, typing out a single draft: It's okay. I had a nice time with you. I hit send before locking my phone in favor of my sandwich.

Manuela's right. I'm terrified of anything that doesn't come easy. It's why hands are all I draw. Why I've never fought much to hold on to my valedictorian spot. Why I never stand up to my mom. It's just that trying means I could fail, and failing means getting that disappointed look from my mom, where her eyebrows narrow and her lips become as straight as a gender reveal party.

But I'm getting tired of living my life in fear of a *facial expression*. So tired that once I'm done with my sandwich, I pick up my phone, open my browser, and type best art schools in the US

I'm scrolling through pictures of RISD dorms when a notification flashes on the screen. My heart rises with hope that it's Sadie replying to me, and sinks when I see it's an Instagram DM. That in itself isn't weird—people are always sliding in my DMs, hitting on me or asking me to promote their art. But the first few words catch my eye.

When I click it, my heart sinks further. It's from an account that has no profile picture, no followers, and the username fessuppalready. The message is straight to the point:

I don't want to escalate this, but I will if you don't go to Mr. Simmons and tell him you're responsible for these pranks. Stop pointing fingers and start looking in a mirror.

CLEO'S AT SCHOOL THE next day, bright-eyed, bushy-tailed, and terrified.

I was too when she sent me a screenshot of that message. I'm kind of glad my Instagram is private so I wasn't the one to receive it. Seeing it secondhand was scary enough. We spent all night on FaceTime, analyzing what they could have meant by *escalate*.

One thing's for sure: sitting around talking about investigating is getting us nowhere, and interrogating Bria is more pressing than ever. "Are you ready?" I ask. Cleo inhales sharply in response. "It's not like we're gonna go up to her and say, 'Hey, we think you're a criminal.' We'll be smooth."

We're waiting by the parking lot, prepared to grab Bria on her way in, so we don't have to do this in front of Cleo's friend group. Unfortunately, that means we're skulking by the front gate like weirdos.

"What are you two up to?" Jason asks when he barrels in, half of the football team in tow. Logan waves, the only friendly face in the group.

"We're, uh, fundraising," I say when I realize he's stopped walking, expecting an actual answer. I hold up my notebook, as if it serves as proof somehow.

"For what? Weight loss surgery?" Jason says smugly, sending

a laugh through his friend group. To his credit, Logan doesn't laugh—but he doesn't stand up for us either.

"We're saving the sea turtles," Cleo says at the same time that I retort, "We're raising money to end EOED. You should donate, since it's such a personal cause to you."

He hesitates, clearly debating if he should take the bait. "What's EOED?"

"Early-onset erectile dysfunction."

His face turns comically red. His friends let out an *ohhh* before pulling him away with whispered reminders that he can't hit a girl. As Logan walks past, he gives me a dollar bill and a sympathetic smile. He's gone before I can tell him we're not actually fundraising.

"You okay?" I ask Cleo. No matter how pathetic the source, fatphobia always makes me nauseous.

"I'm fine. Should we return Logan's dollar?"

"Nah. It's his tax for being friends with assholes. Here, you take it. It can make a dent in your fund for weed. Or art supplies."

"Wow, you seriously lack street smarts if you think *a dollar* can make a dent in paying for either of those. Keep it, I don't need it. My dad gives me a ridiculous allowance to make up for the fact that he's constantly out of town."

"No, you take it! You've spent probably hundreds on me."

We're pulling it back and forth, on the verge of ripping it, when a throat clears behind us.

"What are you doing?"

"Bria!" Cleo practically shouts. "Just the girl we were looking for. I was wondering . . . why did you agree to vandalize Sadie's locker with me?"

Well, so much for being smooth. Bria's eyes go wide, cutting to me. She was obviously unaware that Cleo filled me in about that stunt. "Because you asked me to and when we were in fifth grade, we agreed to do anything for each other via a questionable spit shake. Also, your past pranks were way too juvenile."

I can't help but side-eye her for that last bit. Is she saying she wanted to up the ante? "What type of prank would you consider not juvenile?" Cleo asks, clearly having the same thought.

Bria's forehead wrinkles in confusion. "What are you . . . ? Wait, oh my God. This is for your little investigation, isn't it?" She barks out a laugh. "You think *I* did it? Seriously, Cleo?"

"No! Well, maybe. Buzz said—"

"Buzz? As in your ex of three months? You trust them over your best friend of nearly a decade? Why, because I helped you with some pranks when *you* were upset?" Bria glances at me again before taking a step closer to Cleo and lowering her voice. "Is this about the pig thing? I said I was sorry about that."

"I know, but—"

"But what? One disagreement and you assume I'm out to ruin your life? Are you fucking kidding me?" She brushes past both of us, not interested in a real answer.

"Bria—" Cleo reaches a hand out to no avail. Bria holds a middle finger high in the air and disappears into the crowd.

"That was . . . not great," I say. "I'm sorry."

"It's my own fault. I got nervous and way too accusatory." She sighs, leaning against the wall. "She's right though. She's always been on my side. It was fucked up of me to even consider her. This whole thing, it's messing with my head. That message definitely didn't help."

"It's messing with me too," I say sympathetically. "I'm sure Bria will come around. In the meantime, I'm Venmoing you a dollar."

She gasps. "You better not."

"Watch me!" I pull out my phone, ready to go through with the bit, but an email notification catches my eye. I've waited so long, but the subject line still knocks the wind out of me: Tufts University Application Status.

Heart in my throat, I click into it, scrambling to type the passcode I have memorized from all the times I've refreshed the blank admissions page, waiting for results I know won't come yet. Now they're really, actually here.

Congratulations, the first word says. My vision blurs before I can read the rest.

Here it is, the moment I've waited months for—or, more accurately, years. Whenever I played it over in my mind, I saw myself screaming at the top of my lungs. I'd rush to tell my parents and Mel, and they'd scream with me. I'd print the email out, tape it on my wall, look at it every morning, and know I'd done it.

But it doesn't feel at all like I imagined. For some reason, what should be a life-changing moment . . . isn't.

"You all right?" Cleo asks, breaking me from my thoughts. "You didn't get a message from that account, too, did you?"

"No," I say, locking my phone so she can't see it. "I'm good."

Cleo

IT'S BEEN THREE DAYS and Bria's still pissed at me. Every time I apologize, she mutters that it's fine, but I can tell it's not. She's acting like I'm not there at lunch, ignoring my texts in the group chat.

The more I think about it, the more I can't believe I suspected her. Bria's not calculating like whoever this mastermind is. That's why she drew a pig on Sadie's locker; she didn't think it through. Of course she's not the one after us. She's always been there for me, and this is how I repay her?

I miss the hell out of her. I wish I could talk to her now more than ever, and tell her that I found my dream school last night. Ms. Blum was right. When I did the virtual tour of SCAD, something clicked. I love Savannah, how it's like St. Augustine but bigger. Ten times bigger, to be exact. It's scary to think about leaving, but scary may be exactly what I need.

This morning, on the last day before winter break, I asked Ms. Blum for a letter of rec. I swear she almost cried. Now, in my final art class as a seventeen-year-old, she's playing *The Polar Express*. She does this every year before winter break, setting up a table in the back of the room with hot chocolate and all the fixings. It makes me feel more seven than seventeen in the best way possible.

I should stay here, planted to my stool, sipping peppermint

hot chocolate while an unnamed boy travels to the North Pole. Instead, I get up, fix a second cup with cinnamon, and push the art room door open with my foot. Ms. Blum's so engrossed in my recommendation letter that she doesn't notice.

I make my way to the media center, where Sadie's manning a scanner. It's not surprising that the one easy class she opted for is still surrounded by textbooks. "What's this for?" she asks, her lips quirking up. Those damn lips.

"Early Hanukkah present. Ms. Blum set up a hot chocolate bar for *Polar Express*."

"Well, thanks for bringing me some. What's up with Christians and *Polar Express*?" She takes a slow sip. "Ooh, cinnamon! Nice touch."

"I thought you may like it, since a lot of the pastries at the inn are made with cinnamon." I smile down at her. Her mouth's hidden by the cup, but I can see in her eyes that she's smiling back. "It's comforting. *The Polar Express*, I mean. Tom Hanks plays a bunch of the characters, it's great."

"That's what I don't get. Is it an artistic choice? Or did they spend their whole budget on Tom Hanks?"

"I don't know, maybe it's just for fun. It's such a good movie, it's timeless."

"Why aren't you watching it then? Why schlep a hot chocolate all this way instead of enjoying what's apparently the best movie of all time?" She lifts her chin, as if daring me to tell the truth, that I'd rather be with her than anywhere else.

So I do, more or less. I make eye contact with her padded collarbone, where a pearl drop necklace and heaven itself rests its head. "I wanted to see you."

She averts her gaze, scanning a few books in before responding, "Right, of course. We should talk about the investigation."

"Yeah." I swallow a sip of cocoa with my disappointment.

"How are things with Bria?"

"Terrible," I say, "but hopefully she'll understand that we're terrified and desperate to figure out who's doing this."

"I'm sure she will. I'm just glad whoever it is hasn't acted on that weird escalation threat. Maybe it's finally gonna work to our advantage, the way this place wears you out."

"What do you mean?"

"Like, maybe the evil mastermind doesn't have energy for another prank because of exam season. I know I'm exhausted. All you do is study, write an essay, study some more. When you finally finish, there's a whole new crop of assignments waiting for you. You tell yourself, 'I just need to get through this week,' until the next week comes, and you say it all over again. Do you ever feel that way?"

It's more of a plea, I realize, than a question. A *tell me I'm not alone in this* plea. Exam season must be getting to her. I set my cocoa down and offer her my hand. "Come with me, I wanna show you something."

"I'm not supposed to leave my post unattended."

"Your post? This isn't war, it's a library that I'm willing to bet no one has entered in the past hour. I won't take you far, I promise. Trust me." My hand stays extended until she takes it.

I walk her to the shelves of books, which are half-empty lately. Another author banned, their words picked apart and tossed aside because the characters are like me, like Sadie. It's less of a library and more of a graveyard. There are paper snowflakes lining the shelves, as if this makes up for their emptiness. I lie down, gesturing for Sadie to do the same. "I'm wearing a dress," she says shyly, picking at the sky-blue fabric.

"I won't look." I shield my eyes. "What kind of butch do you take me for?" My hand stays planted in place as I listen to her shuffling, waiting for it to settle into silence.

"Okay, I'm good."

When I lower my hand and come face-to-face with her, inches away, I swear the earth cracks open. Like, instead of this scratchy carpet, we're in a meadow, and all the snowflakes have been replaced by flowers. I forget that there's anything to see here besides her, until she says, "What did you want to show me?"

"Look." I point to the ceiling. "Sophomore year, I was sleeping off a headache when I saw it."

She tilts her head back. "Saw what?"

"If you squint, you can see some words that have been painted over." I direct the point of my finger carefully. I've always loved how hands can send so many messages, despite being so small. They can be as expressive as faces with the right movement.

"I can't see it."

"It's faded now, but it says, 'I hate it here.' Someone was so bored they pulled a chair over, stood on it, and wrote that on the ceiling. I think high school, by design, is meant to bring out the worst in us."

"It gets better though, right? Like, life?"

"Based on what I've heard from my sister, it gets different. Maybe that's enough." The carpet scratches my back, and my neck strains from the lack of support. I should sit up, but the quiet sound of Sadie's breathing is soothing enough that I stay put. I've never been so comfortable and uncomfortable at the same time.

As I'm readjusting, shifting my shoulders to a position that will hurt marginally less, Sadie blurts out, "I got into Tufts."

"What? Holy shit!" To say my heart sings would be an understatement; it's like a church choir rocking out on Christmas Eve.

I swoop her in for a hug as much as I can while lying on the floor. "Are you kidding me? That's amazing."

"Yeah. Yeah, it is." She pushes some curls behind her ear. "But it doesn't feel that way."

"What do you mean?"

"I mean, when I got the acceptance email, I was happy, but also . . . weirdly empty? And then I got mad at myself for feeling empty. I haven't even told anyone I got in. Not my parents, not Mel. Just you."

I bask in that very high honor. "Maybe telling them would help it sink in more? Make it feel real?"

"It does feel real, but it also feels . . ." She squeezes her eyes shut. "It feels like I don't know how to be happy. Because if this doesn't make me over-the-moon happy, what will?"

"Don't look at it that way. Let's break it down. Why do you want to go to Tufts?"

"Because it's Tufts?"

"Is that it?" I broach carefully, knowing that if I push too hard, she'll shut down.

"Well, no. That would be ridiculous. It's all I've ever wanted since I was ten and looked into good premed schools, found Tufts, and fell in love. This is it for me. It always has been."

"I mean, it has been almost eight years. Maybe you want something else now," I say gently. When panic springs to her eyes, I add, "Or maybe you *are* happy, but not in the way you expected. I don't know. What I do know is you shouldn't be forcing yourself to feel any sort of way. Give it a minute. Let the joy come naturally. And if weeks go by and it never comes, find something else that brings you joy."

"You make it sound so easy." She turns on her side so her whole body faces me, instead of just her head. I follow suit, a mirror image of her. "I guess it's easier to give advice from the outside, right? You can give college advice since you're not going, like how I give good relationship advice despite being perpetually single."

I resist the urge to respond with a corny *I can change that*. "Actually, I'm applying to a handful of schools—art schools, that is. I'm leaning toward SCAD."

"Oh my gosh, seriously?!" She looks as thrilled as I was for her a moment ago. It's refreshing to celebrate each other's wins, sans snark. "That's so exciting. You'll definitely get in."

"Thanks."

"Oh, that wasn't a compliment. SCAD has a super high acceptance rate." She laughs. "This is wild, though."

"What is?"

"We're not gonna go to school together anymore. That's so weird."

"Yeah," I sigh, because I've thought about that, of course. I only have a few short months left to make a move on Sadie. And if I don't? Well, I'll be in Savannah and she'll be in Boston. Our paths will only cross during breaks, when we run into each other at Publix and exchange niceties. I'll be dating some other femme who's not nearly as smart or funny as she is. I'll convince myself that I'm happy, better off even, but I'll wonder. I'll always wonder.

"How will I get good grades if I'm not trying to beat you?" she jokes.

"Please, you're gonna smoke them all. That brain of yours is too big not to." I reach a hand out, knocking her forehead lightly. I want to run my fingers through her curls, but I know her hair isn't made for that. The last thing I want is to hurt her, so I resist the urge, but let my touch linger.

She doesn't move away, keeping her eyes locked in mine. The

library's warm since the school blasts the heat once the temperature drops below seventy. Peppermint clings to my lips, and I'm desperate to know what it would taste like mixed with cinnamon.

I don't want to look back years down the line plagued with regret. But before I have the chance to lean in, Sadie begins to pull herself up. "I should get back to the desk. I'm scanning in all the textbooks for Spanish I, since they use different textbooks third quarter, remember that? It's a hassle, but someone has to do it." She stands and retreats to the desk so quickly my head spins. I stare at the ceiling for a few more moments before following her.

"I should head back to class before school's over," I say, suddenly feeling like I'm overstaying my welcome.

"Right. Of course."

"I'll, uh, see you next year."

"You'll see me sooner. I'm coming to the gala."

"You are?" I can't hide my surprise. She mentioned in passing that she wanted to come, but I didn't expect her to go through with it. I mean, it's her actual birthday. I hate having to spend even the first few hours of my birthday there.

"Yeah, I'm excited to see what it's all about. My parents donate on behalf of the inn every year anyway, so we may as well use the tickets." She says it casually, like it's a coincidence that she'll be ringing in the new year at a party hosted by *my mom*. Except, maybe it is? Is it?

"Cool. Make sure you wear a mask, my mom's making it a masquerade this year for some reason. And bring packets of your preferred sauce, the hen's always dry."

"Thanks for the heads-up. We may miss the dinner portion though, because of Hanukkah."

"Oh, shit, I'm sorry. I didn't realize. I can talk to my mom, we should move the date."

She flashes me an amused grin. "Cleo. It's a New Year's Eve gala. How could you move the date?"

The same way I'd move heaven and earth, hell and water for you. I force out a strangled laugh. "Right, yeah, of course. Well, happy early Hanukkah."

"Merry early Christmas." She waves. We watch each other for a second, the air between us thick with artificial heat. She breaks first, going back to scanning. I reach down and pick up my half-full hot cocoa, doing everything in my power to ignore the identical cup beside it, stained faintly with lipstick.

Sadie

THE BIG, MEATY ENVELOPE came in the end, so I had no choice but to tell my parents about Tufts.

My mom screamed so loudly she nearly broke a window. Dad picked up Gretl and swung her around until she meowed to be put down. And I . . . well, I stood there. I cracked a smile because it made me happy to see them happy.

"What's wrong?" Mom frowned. "Aren't you excited?"

"Of course I am. It just doesn't feel real, I guess."

"So you'll go," she said. "You'll tour the campus again. Let it sink in."

"Yeah, sure. Good idea."

I didn't realize she meant at the end of the week. She booked me the earliest ticket. It's like I blinked and suddenly I'm in my great-aunt Deb's house in the suburbs of Boston.

For some reason, I'm surprised by how cold it is here. Gray too. It's nothing like winters in Florida. I should be there now, sitting in the sun, trying to figure out who's pranking us and why they've resorted to a threatening text.

Instead, I'm here. Expecting the rush of the next four years tingling beneath my skin, but only feeling the wetness of days' old snow beneath my feet.

"Do you love it?" Aunt Deb asks after we've toured campus and settled in for the night. "You love it, don't you? It'll be so nice to have you nearby. Well, nice for me—not for your parents!"

"Right," I say around the strange, large lump in my throat. "I'm gonna go for a walk before dinner."

"In this weather? Bring your coat. You should borrow my vest too, let me get you my vest."

Once I'm properly bundled up, she reluctantly lets me stumble onto the sidewalk. It's the safest time of year to walk at night; the whole street is aglow with reds and greens and blues. I don't think Christians realize it, but Christmas has a sound to it. This buzzing emanates from all the Rudolph inflatables and vaguely sacrilegious Snoopy mangers. It's like all their televisions are set to the same movie (*Elf*), all their phones to the same playlist (Michael Bublé's greatest hits).

I wish I were home right now, in warmer weather, walking through Nights of Lights. I wish I was with Cleo, and not just because we have a mystery to solve. We've texted a bit over winter break, but only about the investigation. I'm hesitant to message about anything else, because I can't shake that afternoon in the library. When we were lying together on that scratchy carpet, I wanted to kiss her so badly. I almost did—until she told me she was going to SCAD.

Cleo's finally figuring her shit out. I'm less hazy now that I'm back on Zoloft, but I'm no less sad. I sobbed, like, six times getting through exam season. She doesn't need a long-distance girlfriend calling her crying in the middle of the night, texting her in the wee hours of the morning when she's feeling worthless.

Friends, I remind myself, pulling out my phone, *we can still be friends.*

SADIE: Hey! I hope you're not letting that weird threat get in the way of having a good break
I just wanted to say thanks. I told my parents about Tufts
Your encouragement helped 😌

She responds in thirty seconds flat. I'm not any better. I stop in the middle of the sidewalk, in the freezing cold, to read her reply.

CLEO: Omg, good! They must be so excited!!

SADIE: Yea, I'm in Boston now, actually
I'll be here for the rest of the week
They wanted me to visit campus ASAP and explore the area

CLEO: Whoa! How rya feeling about it?
R ya**

SADIE: I don't know
Cold and conflicted, I guess
But mostly cold. Holy shit, it's so cold

CLEO: It's a crisp 69 down here
actually, it's 68 but that's not as fun

SADIE: You're evil!!

CLEO:

But seriously wear a scarf, okay?
& a hat. We can't have you freezing up there.

SADIE: I won't
You stay cool, we don't want you melting like a snowman

CLEO: Heading to the beach as we speak!
So glad my top choice is in Georgia

SADIE: You're the wooorst

CLEO: Your phone autocorrected best://

I smile down at my phone and lock it, heading back to the house. It's ironic, but I kind of wish she *was* going to Tufts. I probably wouldn't have gotten in if she applied, but I can't believe she's going to be so far away. My parents too. And the cats. I've been looking ahead for years. Somehow, I never spared a second to realize what I was leaving behind.

CLEO: Okay, I'm only gonna admit this because you're probably dead from hypothermia rn
You were right
My sister put on polar express and the Tom Hanks aspect is odd

SADIE: RIGHT?!
I love Tom Hanks as woody but it's too much

CLEO: You're alive!!
& PLEASE tell me your favorite tom hanks movie isn't toy story

SADIE: No!!
It's toy story 3
What's yours?
Lemme guess!
Big
WAIT, no!
A League of Their Own

CLEO: . . . am I that predictable?

SADIE: No, you're simply a lesbian

CLEO: Very true
How's Boston?

SADIE: Cold, wet
And my flight was canceled because of
a blizzard
This place is CURSED

~~Ugh, that sucks, I miss you~~
~~Ugh, that sucks, I was hoping to see you soon~~
CLEO: Ugh, that sucks!

I shove my phone in my desk drawer, wishing I had a lock for it. It's drastic, but I need to stop rewriting texts to Sadie.

"CLEO!" my mom calls upstairs. I wince. What does she want now? My paper cuts have paper cuts; I can't fold another pamphlet.

"Yeah?" I call down anyway.

"I'm heading to Ross to return some shoes. Do you want to tag along to pick out a gala dress?"

"I'm good. I'll wear what I wore last year."

"Try it on to make sure it still fits. You've put on a few pounds."

Sometimes I think she's actively trying to make me resent her more. "I already did," I lie, scurrying to my closet and pulling it out. I shimmy out of my pajamas and into the dress, making my way to the mirror. To say I hate what stares back wouldn't be accurate. It's not that I hate how I look in it—it's that there's no *I* to be found. This girl in a champagne-colored gown is unrecognizable.

"It's a bit tight, don't you think?" Mom says.

I jump, turning to see her standing behind me. "It's fine," I mutter, like the absolute coward I am.

"Are you sure you don't want to come to Ross? Just because it technically fits doesn't mean it fits well."

"It's fine," I repeat through gritted teeth. "I don't need a new dress."

"There's some great holiday sales," she pushes. "We could find you something more . . . flattering."

"It's fine," I repeat. "I'm good." It feels weird saying no to her—but I don't want to spend my day cramped in a tiny dressing room, while she picks every inch of me apart.

"All right." She struggles to hide the surprise in her voice. "Text me if you change your mind. I can always pick up a few options and return what you don't want." At last, she retreats to her precious Ross. The second she's gone, I pull the dress off and take my phone back out. I swipe out of my pathetic texts with Sadie and into my group chat with my friends, sending off a message before I have the chance to think twice about it: Anyone free to go tux shopping?

Manuela replies in thirty seconds flat: hell yea!! I'll drive, be there in fifteen 💕

I'm pulling on my Vans when my phone lights up again, this time with a message from Bria. Just seeing her name on my screen makes me sigh with relief. The message beneath it makes the feeling spread through my whole body: For the gala? About damn time. Pick me up on the way, okay?

CLEO: Are ya surviving the blizzard?!

SADIE: Barely
I facetimed Mel earlier which helped
But mostly I'm napping my way
through it

CLEO: Sound strategy
You could facetime me too
I mean, if you need another friend, I'm
here

SADIE: Okay, yeah, gimme a sec

CLEO: 😁

[Call duration: 4 hrs, 16 mins]

SADIE: Merry Christmas!! 🎄 I hope
Santa doesn't bring you coal!

CLEO: Rude, Santa would NEVER bring
me coal
My mom gave me lipstick though
And my sister's yelling at her about
said lipstick
The joys of a Chapman Christmas

SADIE: Ew, screw her
Your mom, I mean
Is it a good shade at least? I'll accept
regifts for Hanukkah

CLEO: LMAO
She has terrible taste so it's very ugly
sadly
Also I'm too impatient to wait til
sundown . . .
HAPPY HANUKKAH!!

I hope the festivities bring you some
light in this dark storm
Literally! Because of the candles! Get it?

SADIE: Yes, I get it, thanks Cleo
It's weird to celebrate without my
parents, but at least it gives us
something to do
We're gonna play dreidel, I'm excited

CLEO: Fun! Win for meee!

SADIE: I'll be winning for me, thank you
very much
I'm gonna be sooo rich with gelt

CLEO: Yumm
Wait, should I have wished you a happy
Hanukkah today?
Or waited til the last night?
I gotta do some googling

SADIE: Any night is fine

CLEO: I'm gonna do all of them
Just to be safe

SADIE: 🙄

CLEO: Happy Hanukkah!

SADIE: You really are gonna text me every night, aren't you?

CLEO: Hell yeah
Settle in
How's this joyous night treating you?

SADIE: Pretty well, I was finally able to rebook my flight!
Flying out tomorrow 🤞
How are you?
How's gala prep?

CLEO: It's the pits, thanks for asking

SADIE: Well I'm excited for it!
~~I'm excited to see you~~

CLEO: That makes one of us
I had an idea btw

What if we hack into that instagram to see who messaged us!

SADIE: . . . do you know any hackers?

CLEO: No
Do you?

SADIE: No

CLEO: Lemme go watch a youtube tutorial

SADIE: Okay, good luck with that

CLEO: Have faith, will you?!

SADIE: I have faith in plenty of things.
Like G-d and the healing power of a good iced coffee
I just don't have faith in you hacking the mainframe

CLEO: Who said anything about a mainframe?!
Tell me you believe in me
pleaaaaase

SADIE: I do believe in you!
I believe in your ability to fail spectacularly at hacking

CLEO: **You're the worst**

SADIE: **Your phone autocorrected best**

CLEO: Happy Hanukkah! And happy
BIRTHDAY!! 🎂🎈
AKA happy anniversary of the first time
I beat you;)

SADIE: Rude!!
You're just mad that I'm older than you

CLEO: By MINUTES
You don't have to come to the gala, by the way
I mean, it'd be nice to have you here
But I know you just got back from Boston
And it's not the most fun way to spend a birthday

SADIE: I'll survive
Just promise you'll intervene if any old ladies start cooing that I should date their grandsons

CLEO: Of course
I'll jump in and rave about what a suitable bride you are

SADIE: Wow, way to let a girl down
You won't be my butch in shining armor?
Not even on my birthday?

CLEO: Oh well if it's your birthday . . .
Consider it taken care of

SADIE: Yay! 🎂
I'm gonna go eat an absurd amount of pancakes
I'll see ya tonight

CLEO: See you tonight
Jokes aside, I really do hope you have a great birthday
I can't imagine being born alongside anyone else

After sending that very risky text, I lock my phone and drop it in my lap. I'm sitting on the bathroom floor, killing time until I have to face my mom in my tux. This idea seemed a lot smarter in the Goodwill dressing room.

My phone flashes with a notification. I jump to read what Sadie said, but it's only my mom: Where are you??? The salads are about to be served, everyone's asking about you.

A second text appears from my dad: **Where are you? Your mother and I are getting worried.**

Well, it's now or never. At least if the first course is being served, it will be too late for my mom to force me to change. After securing my sparkly silver mask, I make my way through the ballroom. Every inch of it is white: the walls, the columns, the tablecloths, the people. I once suggested peppering in some color, and my mom looked at me like I said we should lace all the food with drugs.

I take slow footsteps past tables full of people enjoying their salads. Bria, Manuela, and Zeke flash me supportive thumbs-ups, and I breathe a little easier. Dad waves as I approach our table, seeming unbothered. My breathing picks up as soon as I come face-to-face with my mother.

Her jaw tightens so hard I swear a bone must break. Even hidden behind a white mask, I can see her eyes shifting, trying to figure out how to get me out of here and into a dress before anyone realizes it's me. As she raises her hand in a *walk with me* gesture, I lunge toward the older woman sitting beside her. "Ms. Constance! It's lovely to see you. It's me." I lift up my mask. "Cleo."

"How wonderful!" Ms. Constance claps her hands. I wouldn't say this about many of the attendees, but I'm excited to see her. She's the only woman in my mom's social circle who doesn't speak in passive-aggressive, coded language. "I adore your outfit. It reminds me of what my boyfriend wore to prom, you know, a century ago."

Yeah, that tracks. I couldn't go with a plain black tux, I'm not as boring as every man attending the Oscars. Instead, I'm wearing a play on the classic powder-blue prom tuxedo. I swapped the puffy, crinkled undershirt for a simple cream blouse, and left the jacket open, with blue pants to match. "A century ago? I'm sure you mean a decade." I sit in an empty seat next to her as she laughs giddily.

Unsurprisingly, my name tag has been shuffled beside hers. Mom and her friends don't take well to Ms. Constance's bluntness, but they keep her around for her absurd amount of wealth. She probably saved a million little dogs with liver cancer last year.

"Well, that's *different*," another woman pipes up. There it is. The language Ms. Constance refuses to speak, insults not so cleverly disguised as compliments. The words poke and prod despite my best efforts to ignore them.

"Isn't it? It's very progressive," my mom rushes to say, "like a feminist statement. It's wonderful how young women these days don't have to wear dresses to dress up." She smiles, proud of herself for coming up with a cover.

"I thought it was a lesbian thing." Ms. Constance takes a hefty sip of wine. God bless her. Mom's eyes bulge so hard they look at risk of popping out of her mask and into her salad.

"It *is* a lesbian thing!" I say cheerfully. "I'm what's called a butch lesbian."

"Like the type that chops wood and fixes toilets?"

Mom clears her throat so loudly it practically echoes. She shoots me a look sharp enough to cut concrete. I meet her glare head-on. I'm not backing down. I'm not skulking off to T.J. Maxx to grab a dress, or whatever she wants me to do. I'm staying put.

Mom breaks eye contact first, going back to schmoozing her guests. For the rest of the meal, it's like I'm not there. She doesn't even bring me up to brag, terrified of pulling any attention toward me. I ignore her in return, chatting with Ms. Constance and dousing the dry hen in hot sauce.

My mom doesn't get a moment of my attention until the dessert course, when it's time for her speech. She clenches and unclenches her hands as she waltzes to the podium, like she's gearing up to lift weights.

"Good evening." She presses her mouth too close to the microphone, her voice booming. "Thank you for coming. I know Chef Michael's chocolate cake is delicious, but I'm willing to fight for your attention."

The crowd laughs and applauds politely. She pulls back from the microphone, feigning surprise at their reaction. This is always my least favorite part of the night. She doesn't care about dogs with cancer, or starving kids, or this year's ever important mystery cause. All she cares about is keeping the spotlight hovering above her head.

"You may be wondering why I asked you to wear masks tonight. There's the short answer, which is that masquerade balls are good fun, aren't they?" Another laugh line, plus a rowdy cheer from Ms. Constance. "But the long answer is inspired by my eldest daughter."

She's lucky I'm wearing my mask. If I wasn't, everyone in the vicinity would see how shocked I am, beyond my subtle jaw drop. "Lily isn't here tonight because she's busy with her prelaw program at Co-lum-bia. A few months ago, when I asked her how school was going, she said, 'It could be better, Mom.' "

What the hell is she talking about? Lily always answers Mom's prying questions with one word, two max (*Fine. I'm good. No boyfriend.*). And I've never heard her say it "could be better." She loves Columbia—mostly because it's far from here. I lean in, curious to hear where this is going. "She said, it would be better if I was more than one of three women in the room. If I didn't feel like I had to wear armor—a mask, if you will—to fight to be heard as much as my male classmates."

There are lots of *mm-hmm*s from the crowd, but mine comes out sounding more like *hmm*? Lily's dealt with sexist bullshit, but there's more than three women in her program. I know because she has a study group with, like, six of them. I know because I actually talk to my sister, rather than making up stories about her.

I've been annoyed by Lily's nagging, but I can see why she's so desperate for me to go to college. She wants me to get away from this, doesn't she? Wearing a tux was a good step, but maybe the only way to truly stop bending to my mother's whims is to be out of range of them.

"So in honor of my sweet Lily, this year's fundraiser is the creation of a local scholarship: the Enhancing Women's Education Fund." She rips down a curtain, revealing a poster with the words printed in bold font. "This is our first year establishing our own fund, rather than donating to an existing charity. While it's a big undertaking, I believe it's worth it to fill our classrooms—and, ultimately, our courtrooms—with women like my daughter."

The crowd bursts into applause so loud it hurts my ears. Without a second thought, I make a run for it.

I'M ZONING OUT DURING Mrs. Chapman's speech when Cleo runs past me, a blur in a blue tuxedo. Instinctually, I chase after her. My mom yelps in confusion. Mel asks me where I'm going, shouting something about her curfew being soon. But I block it all out, following Cleo's footsteps on tile until I knock smack into her.

"Oh, sorry," she mutters.

"Cleo, it's me."

"Sadie? You're here."

"Our celebrations wrapped up early. Are you okay?"

"Yeah. Just need some air." She slumps down onto the tile floor. It's very obvious that she's lying. "How'd you recognize me?"

I clutch the bottom of my long, emerald dress, sitting down beside her. "I took a shot in the dark that you're the only other fat lesbian here. Also, these things just cover our eyes. We're not exactly unrecognizable." I pull off my mask, and I swear Cleo's eyes brighten a bit. "Are you really okay?"

A woman walks by, her footsteps echoing. Cleo waits until she's out of sight. "My mom's speech . . . it was a lot, hearing all of that shit about my sister dealing with sexism at school."

"Yeah, that must be hard for her."

"I'm sure it would be, if it was real," she says bluntly.

I turn my head frantically, before dropping my voice to a

whisper. "Is this all a scam? Does she pocket the money and put it in offshore accounts or something? Do we need to tell the FBI?"

"What? No. I'm sure she's starting a real scholarship fund, but she made up the details of the dramatic backstory. Lily—my sister—faces sexism in the classroom. I mean, who doesn't? But the specifics were all fiction. Lily barely speaks to her. And I . . . I don't know."

"What?"

"It's a dark thought."

"You can tell me. I'm the queen of dark thoughts. Like, even though they help my parents' business, I hate the tourists that come here. They're shitty drivers, and their outfits are tacky. Oh, I also follow lesbian couples on Instagram, and I get excited when they break up."

"What?" She bursts out laughing. I'm happy to serve as even a small distraction.

"It's sadistic, but sometimes it's painful, seeing people so happy. But I'm done praying for people to fail. I think I'm okay with losing—especially if you're the one who wins. I can't promise I'll stop judging those Instagram lesbians though. Some of them are *annoying*. All right, your turn. What's your deep, dark thought?"

She takes a long breath. "Sometimes, I think my mom doesn't like me, she just likes showing me off. I don't even know if my parents wanted kids. I think it was just . . . what you were supposed to do, so they did it, and they forget that we're human beings, not trophies. It's exhausting being put on display. My sister has stopped letting our mom use her, and I think I need to, too, but I'm terrified. I'm terrified of my own mom, and I'm so hot. Are you hot?" With shaking hands, she tears off her suit jacket, crumpling it into a ball. "You don't have to say anything," she adds, pressing a hand to her neck. "I know that was a lot."

"No, it's okay. I'm just sorry." Even in the time we've gotten closer, I somehow never realized that Cleo feels the same pressure I do. Hers just comes from her mom, while my impossible standards of success are self-inflicted.

Watching her now, digging at her neck, all I want is to take some of that pressure off. "Can I . . . ?" I reach a hand up and press it into her shoulder. I knead my fingers in, massaging one of her knots. "Is this okay?" She nods, and I keep doing it, ignoring the voice in my head screaming, *Holy shit, you're massaging her right now.*

As I find a new knot to tackle, my phone lights up in my lap with a text from Mel: Where'd you go? Are you in the bathroom? I need to leave soon, I was hoping for one more birthday hug before I go

I nearly laugh at the thought of her walking in on this sight: me, stroking Cleo's shoulder, her soaking in my touch like it's oxygen. Cleo lets out a shaky exhale, and I think distantly that I should stop—then press deeper.

AS SADIE MELTS MY pain away, neither of us speak. We're in some sort of trance that's convinced us it's normal for friends to massage each other until they see stars. The more she presses, the more tension releases. When she hits a particularly deep knot, she works at it harder. When it gets too intense, she lightens up without me having to ask. It's like she innately knows how to move with my body, what touches will make it hum and relax.

"What in the world is going on here?" my mom hisses. In an instant, it's over. Sadie withdraws her hands, fussing with her dress.

"My neck hurts?" It comes out like a question.

"For God's sake, pop an Advil then. Three, if you need to. Get back in the ballroom; people are wondering where you went."

"No." I'm scared to say this single syllable, but I force it out anyway.

"Excuse me?"

"I don't want to be here." I stand up, looking her dead in the eyes. "And I understand why Lily doesn't either."

She winces at the mention of Lily. "Come on." She gestures to an empty space a few feet away from Sadie.

"I'll wait here," Sadie calls after me with a reassuring nod.

Once we're distanced from our audience of one, Mom

whispers, "Sometimes you have to do things you don't want to, sweetie. That's life."

"Is part of life crafting an elaborate story to make you look good? You know Lily would hate that, right?"

"Well, she's not here, as you so astutely pointed out. Besides, it's not about her. People like a personal connection to charity, that's all. Since no one's dog was dying this year, we went the lawyer route. Maybe the details aren't true, but the scholarship will help a lot of young women. That's what matters."

"But don't you think—"

"I'm not having this conversation with you, Cleo. Not here, not now." There's a silent *not ever* tacked on at the end. She's counting on me to be the good kid I've always been and drop it.

"Okay. But can I please have a normal birthday this year? Can I leave soon and spend the morning with my friends instead of yours?"

Her eyes roll upward. I can't tell if she's annoyed or considering it. Someone walks by and calls her name, waves, and her lips curve in a smile. It's ironic, her having a mask fastened to her face, when I've never seen her without one. "Fine," she says once the woman is out of sight. "You can leave at midnight."

"Midnight," I rush to agree before she can take it back. "Deal, done."

"Fine. Now will you come back—"

"And I'm not going to Tufts," I say, because the adrenaline's already carried me this far. "I'm going to SCAD—Savannah College of Art and Design. Well, assuming I get in, which I probably will. I don't care if their eighty-five percent acceptance rate isn't brag-worthy. It's where I want to go."

She sighs and looks past me, scanning Sadie up and down, assessing if she's still within eavesdropping range. "Can we please discuss this at home? You and your girlfriend need to stop loitering in the halls. I'm going to head back, and I expect you two to be right behind me."

"Sadie's not—" I start, my cheeks aflame, but she's gone before I can finish, a flash of cream blending in with the walls. I should have known better than to think she'd humor talking about SCAD, especially in public, but I don't regret trying. Just letting the words go makes me feel lighter.

"So not that I was eavesdropping or anything, but are you sure you're okay to stay until midnight?" Sadie asks, coming up behind me.

"Yeah. I'm okay. A compromise from my mom is like winning the lottery." I can't believe it. It would be nice if she showed any remorse for that ridiculous speech, but I'm thrilled I only have to stick it out for a few more hours.

My mom *compromised*. I wish Lily was here to witness this historic moment. Although, if she had asked for the same, she'd probably be told to stay twice as long. That's why she doesn't ask at all, isn't it? She knows the best option is to not show up in the first place.

I pull my phone out and text her: I applied to SCAD, I should be hearing back soon! If I get in, can I visit to celebrate? Maybe during spring break?!

A response comes right away: OMG!! Pleaaase visit WHEN you get in!

It's not much. I'm not sure anything I do will match the grilled cheeses she made me when the fridge was stuffed with diet garbage, the compliments she gave me for every insult Mom hurled. I've always been annoyed when she acts like a mother hen—but who did that for *her*? Who sent her links to potential colleges?

Who held an umbrella over her head, even if it meant their own would get soaked?

And how has it taken me so long to ask myself this? One day, I'll find the words to thank her, or apologize, or both. But for now, I leave it at **Great! I miss you.** She knows me well enough to read between the lines.

"I should . . ." Sadie gestures vaguely behind her. "Mel and my parents are looking for me. Congrats on your freedom, Cleo-rella. I hope your pumpkin stays a coach long enough for your dramatic exit."

"Thanks. And thanks for—"

"Don't mention it. You can repay me with this." She plucks my jacket off the floor, drapes it over her shoulders. "It's cold. And I need something light to fit in, yeah? No one told me about the white-and-cream dress code." She heads down the marble hallway, meeting up with Mel at the entrance of the ballroom. I brush past them, going back in with a deep breath.

Everyone's traded tables for the dance floor, and the occasional survey of the silent auction. I hide by the crudité table to avoid being approached by people raving about how they remember when I was two feet tall.

"Hey." Manuela sidles up beside me, tossing her long brown curls over her shoulder. Maybe I have a type.

"You gonna ask her to dance?" She nods to my curly brunette crush to end all crushes, who's now swaying beside her parents. Her mom's attempting some bizarre rendition of the chicken dance, and Sadie tosses her head back, laughing. I love that her laugh is as loud as she is, how it overtakes not just her body, but everyone around her too.

"I can't. I mean, I shouldn't."

"Why not?" She makes a fair point. Sadie spent a solid half hour massaging my neck. Friends don't do that, right? And then there's that damn horse-drawn carriage, giving every St. Augustine haunt a run for its money. She was leaning in to kiss me, I swear. The more I play it back, the more convinced I become.

As if a sign from the universe or whatever higher power is out there, the band transitions into a new song: "All of Me" by John Legend. I laugh, catching Sadie's eyes from across the room. Or, at least, I think I do? It's hard to tell thanks to these masks.

Only one way to find out, I guess. I take one shaky step forward. Then another. Just as I'm brainstorming a cheeky pickup line, I hear a gasp. It's one I'm very familiar with—my mother's.

Immediately, I turn away from Sadie, heading toward the sound. I despise the instinct, but even after giving my mom a piece of my mind, I can't resist. Nearly eighteen years of tending to her every need isn't something I can just switch off. Not in a night anyway. "What's wrong?" I ask.

She puts a finger to her lips in a shushing gesture. "The bracelet," she whispers. "It's missing. I think it may have been stolen."

"Wait, you put the actual bracelet out on the table? Isn't it worth, like, *one hundred thousand dollars*?" I've always wondered if my mom is embarrassed to admit that she drove Lily away, or if she's naive enough to believe she's not to blame. I'm starting to think it's the latter.

"Ninety thousand, actually. These are good people! We've never had issues with theft before. People like to inspect before they buy, to make sure the diamonds are worth the money. And the bidder takes it home tonight." She presses her hands to her cheeks. Damn, she must really be freaking out if she'd risk messing up her makeup. "You have to keep this quiet. We need to find it before the bidders notice. I'll speak to the waitstaff, you speak to the other kids here. It has to be someone from those two groups."

I grimace. "It doesn't have to be—" Unsurprisingly, my mother doesn't care to hear the end of my sentence. Her typically light footsteps are more like aggressive stomps. She gives a two-fingered signal to the lead musician, and the slow, romantic crooning transitions into the "Cha Cha Slide." The few people lingering by the silent auction are lured to the dance floor by the white suburbanites' kryptonite.

I'm rooted to the spot as everyone cha-chas real smooth. This is just so weird. A lot has gone awry in these galas over the years, but it's always small stuff. Like flowers being delivered to the wrong spot, or a firework going off a nanosecond too late (my mom still won't let this one go, since it ruined the heart formation they were supposed to make).

It was definitely foolish to put out an expensive bracelet and expect no issues simply because these are "good people." But she's right that after all these years, nothing's been stolen before. And now I have to spend the rest of my night figuring this out, even though I don't exactly have a proven track record when it comes to solving mysteries.

Wait. Could it be . . . ? No. Absolutely not. Every prank has happened in school. There's no way this is related. I look to the snack table for Manuela, in need of a grounding voice to tell me I'm being ridiculous, but she's gone.

So I follow my feet in the direction they were leading me before all hell broke loose: Sadie. She's shimmying her heart out, not immune to the siren's song of the "Cha Cha Slide." I move aimlessly beside her, not bothering to follow the instructions. My hand brushes her arm lightly enough to get her attention.

"I need to talk to you," I say through a smile. The women

dancing around us are like bloodhounds. If I show any discomfort in my face, they'll sniff it out and spin it into gossip.

"What's up?" The smile Sadie flashes me is far more genuine, wide enough to make me lose focus and stumble over my own feet. "Do you know how to Charlie Brown?"

"Did you bring a purse with you?" I whisper. "I need you to smile and laugh so it looks like we're having a normal conversation. Speak quietly, so no one hears us, okay?"

"Okay? Whatever you say, James Bond."

"Did you bring a purse with you?" I repeat, nodding to the beat before giving the Charlie Brown a go. My interpretation of it is flailing my limbs around.

"Uh, yeah. A clutch. It's at my table."

"I need you to get it and meet me outside in five minutes. Hang a left past the bathroom and go through the double doors that lead out to a courtyard. If anyone asks, you're going to pee. Okay?"

"Okay? Why—" The rest of her question is drowned out by the band enthusiastically shouting at everybody to clap their hands.

I seize the opportunity to shuffle off the dance floor unnoticed, jogging to the courtyard. When I throw open the French doors, I'm surprised by how cold it is. My arms are feeling the lack of a jacket, but at least Sadie will be warm when she comes out.

I take a deep breath, looking up at the vines crawling above me and the string lights adorning them. This has always been my secret spot thanks to Lily. She snuck me out here when we were younger, told me that when the party got overwhelming, I could come to this courtyard to catch my breath. Every year, usually close to midnight, I find myself here, perched atop one of the black iron tables like I am now.

"I didn't know this was out here," Sadie says by way of greeting, gripping the suit jacket tight around her shoulders. She pulls her mask off, placing it on the table beside mine. "Is everything okay?"

"Can I see your purse?" I ask before she has the chance to sit down in one of the chairs across from me.

"Do you need a tampon or something?"

"Please, let me see it. I just . . . I need to be wrong." I thrust a hand out impatiently. I know I should explain, but I don't want to freak her out in case I'm overthinking this.

"Okay, weirdo." She hands over her small, seashell-shaped purse. *I'm a shell.* The words come back to me with a jolt. God, please let me be overthinking this.

My shaky hands take everything out and place the contents on the table, item by item. A tube of red lipstick, a wallet, a tampon, Altoids mints, the daisy-shaped case of medication. I open it and only find a few pills. "Whoa, slow down there, ya little raccoon," Sadie says, casting a shy glance toward the case.

I ignore her, looking into the purse. It's now empty except for a few crumbs and a loose penny. *Thank God.* Now I have to apologize for tearing through her bag, but it's better than the alternative.

I look up, prepared to explain myself to a very bewildered Sadie, but when I do, I notice the pale blue fabric draped across her shoulders. My rising heart plummets all over again. "Suit jacket. I need your—my—suit jacket. Please."

"Cleo, what's going on?" I dig into one pocket. Empty. Another. Just some lint and an old cough drop. "You're scaring me," she whispers.

I'm scaring myself. I can't explain it, but I just know. I understand Buzz's ravings about gut feelings now. I get it. I feel it. And then I literally, physically feel it. In the breast pocket, the one too small to actually be functional, my fingers graze something cold, sharp, metal.

My blood turns as cold as the air. I reach a hand out, gesturing for Sadie to move closer, closer, closer. Once she's close enough that our bodies are pushed together, shielding us from the nearby window, I pull out the diamond bracelet.

Sadie

AS CLEO EXPLAINS THE stolen bracelet, my breaths aren't just short, they're barely existent. "But you know," I force out, "you know I didn't—"

"Oh my God, of course. Sit down, sit down." She tucks the bracelet into her pants pocket and wraps the suit jacket back around me. "Sit down," she repeats, gesturing to a chair and pressing my shoulders gently until I comply. "I'll be back. I'll take care of it, and I'll be right back, okay? Stay here."

When she's gone, my anxiety increases tenfold. Who's doing this? *Why* are they doing this? I know they threatened to escalate things, but this is a whole other level. Expulsion isn't the only thing on the line anymore. I turned eighteen today. I could go to jail for stealing that bracelet—jail!

Distantly, I realize I should get my phone, text my parents, and ask them for help. But I can't. Yet again, my panic has frozen me to the spot. I stare up at the climbing ivy until tears prick my eyes, making my vision blur through my contacts.

"Hey, hey, it's okay. I handled it, all right?" Cleo's voice comes before I've noticed she's back. She sits beside me, picking up the daisy case from the table, still strewn about with all my other stuff. "Which one of these is for anxiety? This one?" She holds out a small white pill, guessing correctly.

I nod as much as I can. She places it in my hand, a cup of water in the other. Once I've swallowed it, she rubs my back in slow circles. "I left it by the auction table," she says quietly. "Everyone was too busy dancing to 'Don't Stop Believin'' to pay attention to me. The cleanup crew will find it and think someone tried it on and dropped it. It's okay. We're okay."

I wish that was enough to calm me down, but it's not. What if Cleo hadn't figured it out? Would we be spending our birthdays in a jail cell? I hadn't ever stopped to worry that we'd end up somewhere worse than Mr. Simmons's office.

Minutes stretch by before my breath deepens enough to form words. "I don't understand who's doing this. I don't understand why they're so hell-bent on framing us, torturing us. It sucks. It more than sucks," I say—or rather sob. "I'm so scared, Cleo. What if we never figure out who's behind this?"

"I'm scared too," she admits, "but at least we have each other. I can't imagine how much scarier it would be to go through this alone."

"Agreed." I sniffle. Cleo wraps her arms around me, holds me tight—tighter than a friend would. I shouldn't let her, especially since she finally told her mom about SCAD. She's not just planning her future now, she's actually going through with it. That's something I haven't even been able to commit to, despite my Tufts acceptance. The last thing I want is to drag Cleo down with me.

Against all better instincts, I sink my head into the crook of her neck. "Forget all of this, will you?" I say, resenting how whiny I sound. "I hate how many times you've seen me cry. Promise me that when it's a new day, a new year, you'll pretend you've forgotten all about tonight."

"I would never judge—"

"Cleo."

"Okay, I promise," she whispers.

I hear a *ten* shouted in the distance, followed by a *nine*. The new year's now seconds away. It's the year I'll graduate, if this asshole doesn't ruin my life first.

Eight.

I turn my head, angling it toward Cleo before I can stop myself.

Seven.

She reaches a thumb down, wiping smeared mascara off my cheekbone.

Six.

I like her against my will. The harder I try to stop the feeling, the further I fall.

Five.

She has these eyes that look at you like they're seeing the best in you—and only the best.

Four.

"Everything?" I ask. "You'll forget *everything*?"

Three.

"Of course."

Two.

Just before midnight, I kiss her.

It's too early and too quick. My heart pounds loud in my ears, and it's a mistake, I know that right away. Cleo leans in to kiss me again, but I pull back. I want to keep kissing her so badly, but I can't. One kiss was selfish enough. She deserves better than me.

"Happy birthday," I whisper pathetically, like I'm offering a measly peck as my present.

"Oh, yeah. Right. I almost forgot. Happy New Year."

I grab my phone, look at my reflection in the camera, and wipe my face clean so my parents won't have any questions. When I'm done, I quickly refill the contents of my purse. As I move methodically, Cleo sits there, mouth agape.

"My parents will be looking for me," I explain. "They're probably wondering why I keep disappearing even though I asked them to come."

"Right. Of course."

"I'll . . ."

I literally see Cleo hold her breath, as if she's waiting for another kiss, or maybe an explanation. I know I should give her one, but what would I say? Telling her the kiss was a mistake would hurt her, but kissing her again? Becoming her girlfriend? Loving me would break her down slowly over weeks, months, years. I can't bear to watch that happen.

I gesture behind me vaguely and turn around. My heels on the cobblestone are as loud as my heart in my throat. A firework streaks above me, stunning and temporary.

She'll forget all about it, I assure myself. Not just because I asked her to, and she's too chivalrous to cross a firm boundary—but because she's kissed a hundred other girls. Or, at least a handful. This is one tiny drop in the bucket.

I'm sure it meant more to me than it did to her.

I FEEL HUNGOVER THIS morning, despite not drinking a thing last night. I'm going to kill Sadie Katz, do CPR, bring her back to life, and kiss her again. Shit, I don't know CPR though. I've always regretted not taking that Red Cross class for my volunteer hours. Why did I go with the animal shelter? They had too many volunteers; everyone wants to play with puppies.

I'm drafting out a three-paragraph-long text to her that I'll never send when an email notification pops up with "Congratulations" in the subject line.

Holy shit. Holy *shit*. I got into SCAD. On my *birthday*, no less. The odds were on my side, but *still*. Holy shit!

The first thing I do is call Lily and scream with her at the top of my lungs.

The second thing I do is text my group chat with Bria, Manuela, and Zeke a screenshot of my acceptance letter along with a million exclamation marks. Manuela immediately decrees that we get two cakes for a joint birthday/acceptance celebration.

The third thing I want to do, I can't. I want to tell Sadie. But that ship sailed last night, didn't it? Are we even friends anymore? Who are we to each other now that she's kissed me and fled like I was a house fire?

I head downstairs, determined to be happy today of all days.

I pick Chester up and dance around with him until he whines to be put down. Just as I'm setting him on the couch, Mom and Dad come in, holding take-out boxes from lunch.

"Happy birthday!" Dad says, oblivious to the daggers Mom's shooting my way. Clearly, she hasn't filled him in on my confrontation.

"Thanks. I, uh, just got into SCAD."

"In Savannah?" Dad's eyes go wide. "I didn't know you applied! That's amazing. Now we just need to hear back from Tufts and you'll have a tough decision to make."

"I'm going to SCAD," I say, staring my mom down. "I like Savannah. And I want to study art. Tufts isn't right for me. It never was."

Dad goes silent, deferring to Mom as always. She purses her lips, but she doesn't tighten them, which is a good sign. "I asked Ms. Constance about it last night," she says. "Her granddaughter goes there. She says it has a beautiful campus and very impressive programs. Make sure you let me go clothes shopping with you; you can't go to college with a wardrobe full of basketball shorts."

"Okay?" I don't mean it to come out like a question, but I'm surprised to hear anything close to approval.

"And I brought home some pancakes for you, low fat. I'll leave them in the kitchen."

"Thanks. I'm, uh, gonna head to Manuela's now if that's okay," I say. I'm glad she's fine with me going to SCAD, but I want to spend my birthday around people who are *happy* for me. People who have always loved me for me, not for what I can do for them. Maybe Mom and I will get there eventually, but it's going to take time.

"Yes, yes, go celebrate with friends!" Dad says brightly, clueless, before looking to Mom. "Right?"

"Yes, that's fine. I'll put your pancakes in the fridge." She makes her way to the kitchen, before pausing and turning back around. "You'll be happy to know we found the bracelet, by the way. It was on the floor by the auction table. Can you believe it?"

I swallow. She doesn't know, right? She *can't* know. If she did, there's no way she'd be letting me leave the house right now. "That's great. Well, I'm . . . I'm gonna head out." I make a break for it, biking to Manuela's as fast as my legs can carry.

When I arrive, I'm presented with two cakes: a chocolate birthday cake and a plain vanilla Publix cake with the words "Con-SCAD-ulations" sloppily frosted on it. We settle onto Manuela's trampoline with a bunch of blankets and hefty slices.

Everyone is talking over one another, but I can't bring myself to join in.

"You good?" Manuela asks.

"I'm fine," I mutter, except I'm anything but. The adrenaline of my SCAD acceptance has worn off, and my mind's wandering back to last night. I can't believe Sadie kissed me, then ran for her life. Am I a bad kisser? Is that why she fled? I've never gotten complaints before.

"Bullshit," Bria says. "You're acting weird, I would never guess you got into your dream school today. What's up?"

I slap my hands over my face and fall back onto the trampoline. "I kissed Sadie last night. Well, actually she kissed me. And I think I'm in love with her." I've never said it like that before, never even thought it. *In love with her.* It's severe, but it's the truth. After feeling her lips on mine, even briefly, I can't deny it anymore.

When I'm met with silence, I sit back up to make sure my friends haven't run away from me too. They haven't moved an inch, but they're all clearly shocked. Well, everyone except Manuela, who's positively gleeful.

"Wow," Bria finally says.

"So are you two, like, an item?" Zeke asks. He looks vaguely queasy, but I think that may be because he's on his third slice of cake.

"No. She ran away after she kissed me. She asked me to forget all about it."

"Weird. Are you a bad kisser?" he asks.

"That's what I'm wondering!"

"You're definitely not," Manuela says, making my face flush, "and you need to talk to her. Ask her out!"

"Right. Yeah, okay." I look at Bria, who's being pretty quiet by her standards. "How do you feel about this?"

"Me? I'm kind of shocked. I thought we all hated her. Well, except Manuela, but she doesn't hate anyone."

"I never hated her," I say.

"We literally vandalized her locker."

"Yeah, but I regret that. It's like . . . I hate my mom some days. I hate Coach Graham when I'm running the mile and he tells me to 'dig deeper.' I hate my neck and the tree that twisted it up. I hate Sonic the Hedgehog, it weirds me out how fast he can run. But Sadie?" I let my smile stretch as wide as it wants to. "She gets on my nerves sometimes, but I like her. Is that a problem?"

I size Bria up, as if I'll pummel her if she says no. I don't want to fight again, but I'm tired of holding back the truth to protect everyone else's feelings. "No problem here," Bria says. "I'm just surprised, really. Are you gonna ask her out?" The words seem to physically pain her, but at least she's saying them, I guess.

"Yeah," I say, because, fuck it. Life is short, or whatever. Why should I forget when all I want is to kiss her again? "Yeah, as soon as we're back at school, I'm gonna ask her out."

"Damn," Bria says, "am I drunk? Or are we in an alternate universe or something?"

"Nah. She's always been it for me in this one."

THE FIRST DAY BACK from winter break, I spend an embarrassing amount of time styling my hair. As I finger twirl each curl, I deliberate what to say when I see Cleo.

Hi.

Hey.

Congratulations on getting into SCAD. Yes, I saw your post about it and was unfairly sad you didn't text me first.

What's up?

Have you failed miserably at keeping your promise too? Have you thought about our kiss every day like I have?

When I get to first period, I dodge Ms. Thomas's typical side-eye and make a beeline for Cleo. As soon as she's in sight, every normal greeting disappears from my mind. "I like your shirt! It's cute," I blurt out, immediately regretting it. Why am I talking to the girl I wept all over, then kissed, like she's one of my girlfriends in the most platonic sense of the word? "And, um, congrats on SCAD."

She frowns down at her tie-dyed muscle tee. "Thanks. HeyCanWeTalkAfterSchool?"

"What?"

She inhales sharply. "Can we talk after school?"

"Oh." She wants to talk about the kiss. Of course she does. It was never fair to expect otherwise. "Okay."

"Yeah?" Her eyes light up, like I said she's won a free trip to Antarctica. I know, from all these years growing up beside her, that she loves penguins. It would be easier to turn her down if I knew her less.

"My place after school," I say. Hopefully she'll be content staying friends.

I spend all of lunch trying to figure out how to do it. It's an odd day, so Cleo and I don't have lunch together, thank goodness. It's easier to brainstorm without her in my line of vision. *I'm not looking for a relationship right now*? *It's not you, it's me*? Isn't that what you're supposed to say? I've never dated anyone. I have no clue how to turn someone down.

"You okay?" Mel asks, eyeing the PB&J that I'm gripping like it has a personal vendetta against me. I nod, because it's easier than saying the lie out loud. I haven't told her anything about what happened after she left the gala. It's hard keeping secrets from her, but there's no point sharing my kiss with Cleo when there won't be another.

I've managed to get half my meal down when a voice calls my name so loudly that I drop my sandwich on the dirty cafeteria table. Great. This day gets better and better! "Sadie Katz," the administrator supervising lunch shouts, "Sadie Katz to the principal's office."

Motherfucker.

"What is it now?!" Mel asks.

"No clue," I mutter. Mel squeezes my shoulder, wishing me

luck as I grab my backpack and make my walk of shame through the courtyard.

Three times. In one school year, I've been called to the principal's office three times. And I never know what to expect. Maybe it's the bracelet—or maybe it's something new entirely, something worse. I wish we were better at investigating. Matthew was our strongest lead, but he wasn't at the gala, so that rules him out.

When I get to the office, my mind working overtime, Cleo's already slumped in one of the cushioned chairs. "Hey." I didn't expect to see her until seventh period, and I'm wholly unprepared. "You have any idea what this is about?"

"Unsurprisingly, no. Maybe he's going to tell us which one of us is valedictorian." She smiles weakly. I'm overcome by the urge to kiss her until that smile becomes bigger.

"Sadie, Cleo, Mr. Simmons will see you now." The receptionist has none of the warmth toward Cleo that she did last time. Even worse, she remembers my name. I'm a *repeat offender*. But I'm not the same person I was the first time I was in here, I remind myself as I walk through the oak doors.

I'm stronger than I was in November. I can look Mr. Simmons in the eyes, plead our case, and convince him to finally believe us. As soon as we sit down, the doors swing open again—and in walks my mom.

"Hi, honey," she whispers, standing behind me. Cleo's mom, hot on her trail, sits in a spare chair, arms folded. I can see every muscle in Cleo's body tighten. While she tenses, I crumble. I'm not sure what we're in trouble for, but whatever it is, it has to be bad.

"I assume you know what this is about," Mr. Simmons says. They should etch those words on his gravestone.

"No, actually," Mrs. Chapman bites back. "What's so urgent that I had to leave my Pilates class?" I cast Cleo a look, like, *Is she serious?* She doesn't meet my eyes.

"Yeah, and I've got a full house at the inn. What's this about?"

"With all due respect, we should probably let the girls answer that one." He looks at each of us in turn. I cast Cleo another glance, desperate this time, but she keeps her gaze squarely on the carpet.

"Enough with the theatrics. What's the issue here?" Mom scoffs.

Mrs. Chapman scoffs twice as loudly, like it's a competition. "Agreed. Please, get on with it. Unless you're here to give my daughter an award for getting into her *dream art school*, I'll be on my way."

Slowly, like a lawyer in a cable show presenting key evidence, Mr. Simmons pulls out two stacks of paper. Zeroing in on it, I see it's my final essay for AP Gov, the one I fought hard to finish when Zoloft withdrawal was kicking my ass. Beside it is a second copy of my essay—with Cleo's name at the top.

No. No way.

"I didn't . . . This isn't what I turned in!" Cleo pulls her phone out, frantically clicking into Google Docs. "I can show you what I wrote, it's completely different, someone must have—"

"Someone must have what?" Mr. Simmons interjects. "Someone must have taken your original essay and replaced it with Sadie's? Please take accountability and spare me the crazy excuses."

My stomach swoops at the word. Any faith I had moments ago that I could get him to believe us drops right with it. Thanks to my two extended absences, my mental health issues are on record with the school. If I push the truth too hard, he'll write me off as crazy. Or, worse, he'll somehow manage to convince Mom that I *am* crazy and I'll spend tonight in a paper gown.

"Now hang on, this is a huge accusation—" Mom starts.

"Cleo would never!" Mrs. Chapman interrupts with a gasp, before leaning over, grabbing Cleo's arm tight, and whisper-hissing, "What did you do?"

Cleo flinches. "We didn't—someone's out to get us—"

Mom goes around the desk, starting a heated argument with Mr. Simmons, but I drown it out, leaning in to hear Mrs. Chapman. "I'm sick of this victim complex—yours and your sister's. I let you leave the gala early, and how do you repay me? By cheating and pulling that ridiculous bracelet stunt? That's right, don't think I didn't see you bring it back. What's your endgame here? Destroying your future? Destroying our family's reputation? Destroying *me*?"

Cleo stares straight ahead, paler than I've ever seen her. She doesn't look upset, she looks . . . empty. It's like she's full-on left her body, because that's the only way to take what her mom's throwing at her.

And that's it. That sick expression on her face is the only explanation I have for what I say next. "She didn't do it," I blurt out. "I did. I was so stressed and overwhelmed with homework that I took Cleo's phone and sent her essay to myself. She had no clue I did it, I swear. I thought . . . I didn't think Ms. Thomas would actually pay attention to what we wrote. I didn't think she'd notice."

The room is cast into a stunned silence. Cleo glances my way, shell-shocked. Her eyes, large and pleading, ask, *What the hell are you doing?*

Mine, steady as ever, answer, *I'm taking care of it.*

It's my turn. Sure, Cleo vandalized my locker, but everything since? She's the one who got rid of that pig and returned the bracelet while I broke down. She's the one who spent an hour ripping down pictures of hands, who fought to figure out who plastered them up when I had no fight left to give. It's about time I return the favor. And, well . . . if I walk out of here with a lifetime worth of detentions, my mom will still look at me the same way she did yesterday. I can't say the same for Cleo.

"No, that's not true," Cleo practically shouts. "She's lying."

"So you're saying you both should be suspended, pending potential expulsion?"

"WHAT?" Cleo and Mom shout in sync. They both keep shouting, defending me with everything they've got. I catch words like *salutatorian* and *never* and *Tufts* and *future*, but it's all just noise.

"It was me," I say, loud and clear. "It was all me, not Cleo."

"Sadie." Mom turns away from Mr. Simmons, toward me. "Are you sure about this?" All I can do is nod. Lying to Mr. Simmons is a lot easier than lying to my mom.

"Well, all right then," Mr. Simmons says, ignoring Cleo's stammering. "We don't take plagiarism lightly. You'll be suspended immediately for at least two weeks, potentially longer as we determine if this is grounds for expulsion. We'll be taking your past offenses into account, of course."

Mom asks about these past offenses, Mrs. Chapman asks if she can go back to Pilates, and Cleo asks Mr. Simmons to hear her out. Every word is fuzzy around the edges, muffled, like I'm in the bathroom at a party, hearing the lull of chatter through a closed door.

I tune back in to hear my mom talking about my depression, my *unique circumstances*, she calls it. That's enough for me to make a run for it. When I get to the courtyard, I'm gasping for air. Half of me shattered into a million pieces when the words "pending potential expulsion" were uttered. But the other half . . .

School has been pushing me closer and closer to the edge for years. Now, here I am, free-falling. All I can do is hope that when I land in the water, I manage to keep my head above it.

WHAT THE HELL? *WHAT* the hell? What the *hell*?

I find Sadie sitting on a planter, pulling a granola bar out of her backpack, casual as ever. No, more casual than ever—Sadie's not usually casual. "WHAT THE HELL WAS THAT?" I shout. "And what the hell are you doing?!"

"I didn't have the chance to finish lunch," she says plainly, taking a bite of the Nature Valley bar, granola crumbling on her lap.

"Why did you say that? That was your essay, wasn't it?" I only read the first few lines, but I didn't recognize them. They sounded like her, those long, winding sentences.

"Yeah, but it's yours now, I guess. If I knew this was going to happen, I wouldn't have spent so long on it." She may be acting nonchalant, but her hands give her away. As she sets the granola bar down, they tremble.

"Sadie, please," I practically whine, "explain to me where you're coming from here."

She sighs. "Your mom would kill you. Mine won't. When your daughter has days where she thinks she's better off dead, you let a lot slide."

What kind of logic is that? She gets to blow her life up because her parents like her? "Fuck my mom."

"You don't mean that."

"Don't tell me what I mean! You don't get to do this. You don't get to absorb all the blame without asking me. We can still figure out who's been framing us. We can prove to Mr. Simmons—"

"He'll never believe us. It sounds too absurd, and honestly, I'm not sure he *wants* to believe us. I don't know if he's homophobic or on a power trip or what, but he's not exactly giving us the benefit of the doubt. It's messed up, but . . . what can ya do?"

"Excuse me? '*What can ya do*'?" I've been annoyed with Sadie in the past, both mildly and severely. I've been bothered by her being smug, pretentious. But I've never been this mad at her before. "You might never step foot in this school again. You, Sadie Katz. After nearly four years of late nights studying, hundreds of volunteer hours, and I'm sure countless panic attacks . . . are you really gonna walk away?"

"Maybe I should," she says, sounding strangely certain. "'*Countless panic attacks*' isn't exactly incentive to stay. All of these years, I've been willing to let school kill me. Literally. I need to step back and figure out who I am outside of this place. Obviously, the circumstances aren't ideal . . ."

The bell rings, sharp and piercing. Fifth period is over. Students pour out of classrooms like ants milling to sugar. Sadie stays sitting, making it really sink in that she doesn't have a class to rush off to. "So that's it? You accept a suspension, maybe an expulsion, and let this loser win? You really don't care?"

"Of course I care!" she snaps, finally with that fight I know and love. "But I care about you too." She watches a kid pass by with a giant poster board, as if searching for an excuse to break eye contact with me. "You're so excited about SCAD. You need to go."

"I don't *need* to go. I'm an artist. I was, like, born to be a high school dropout. You can't be premed without a high school degree."

"Maybe I don't want to be premed. That's my point, I don't know what I want. I have no clue! All I've ever wanted is to beat you and get into Tufts. Now I've given up on one of those things and gotten the other—and I'm still unhappy. Maybe Tufts is where I belong. Maybe I do want to be a doctor, but I need to . . . I need to figure out what I want without strings, expectations. And right now? I want to go home and pretend school doesn't exist. I want to know that this prankster weirdo didn't damage your family and future beyond repair. That you're okay."

"How can I possibly be okay?" My voice comes out low, thick with tears. "How can I be okay sitting beside your empty desks every day for two weeks, maybe more? How can I be okay knowing I could have stopped this if I wasn't such a shitty detective?"

The warning bell rings. Almost everybody's back in class except for a few stragglers joking around with their friends. They don't care if they're late to class and won't care what they learn when they get there. And they may walk across that stage in May, while Sadie watches from the crowd. God, this is all so backward.

"It's not your fault, Cleo. Go to class. There's only one period left. Put your head down and take no notes and somehow still learn everything like the annoying genius you are."

"I can't—"

"Please. For me?" She bats those big brown eyes, like she knows they're my weakness.

"Fine. But I need to know that *you're* okay." *I need to know that if you walk away now, you won't stop taking your meds again, or worse.*

"I'll be okay," she says, which isn't what I asked. "I'll manage."

"GO TO CLASS," an assistant principal yells at us.

"I'M NOT EVEN SUPPOSED TO BE HERE," Sadie yells back, before making her way to where her mom waits outside the office.

She looks back at me only once, waving vaguely in the direction of our classroom. *My* classroom. With a trembling upper lip, I walk to seventh period alone.

Five new messages from Mel 💕:

Lunch is so boring without you i stg

Come save me

& save me from this meat loaf omfg it's awful

Three new messages from Mel 💕:

I've been researching GEDs and they really can get you far

Like, my cousin has one and she's a beast in the Nashville real estate market

I just want you to know that even if you do get expelled (WHICH YOU WON'T) you'll have options

One new message from Mel 💕:

Let's hang out soon, yea? Please?

Voicemail transcript from Cleo 🖕:

Hey since you didn't respond to my ____ text I'm doing this ye old-fashioned way. Just checking in to see how you're doing. Call me back. Or text. Or send a carrier pigeon. I just ____ hear from you. Okay. Bye. ____ busy, I guess.

Voicemail transcript from Cleo 🖕:

It's been five days now and I was concerned four days ago. Call me back when you ____. I've been thinking about it more, and I'm going to reach out to Mister Simmons. I don't care ____ want frankly. What I want matters too. And I want you here. Back at school. ____ so dramatic, wow. Just know I'm here, okay? I'm here if you need anything at all. If you asked me to come over and just sit with you I would. I would listen to the sound of your breathing until it was shallow enough that I knew you were asleep. I'd stay there quietly until you woke ____. I would be there if you let me.

Voicemail transcript from Cleo 🖕:

I got a ninety six on an econ test I didn't study for at all. Please ____ back to tell me how annoyed you are by this, thanks.

Voicemail transcript from Cleo 🖕:

Hi stranger it's uh, it's me again. I don't know what to say to get you to pick up at this point. I just want you to know that I'm here. I love ______ out with you you know that right? I hope so. School is so weird without you. No one's mean to me when I get a ninety____. How am I supposed to stay humble? I don't know. I'm filling space. I'm hoping if I ____ enough, I'll say something worth listening to. I had a killer headache during an assembly on seat belt safety yesterday, and I fell asleep and got yelled at. The presenter was like. What if you fell asleep on the road? And I was like, sorry I missed the memo where the auditorium is the road? And he ____ mad. Wait is it insensitive to talk about school? I don't know. It's different without you. It's all different ____. I get what you meant about needing to be away from school. But I worry that you took the consequences because you feel like you deserve bad things. And you don't. You're not always nice but you're so kind, Sadie. I keep thinking about what you did for me. How stupid it was. How you it was. I hate you for it and I love you for it. I don't mean I love you. I just mean ____ shit. Okay, how the hell have I not run out of time ye—

SUBJ: Sadie Katz Suspension

Dear Mr. Simmons,

I'm writing to provide evidence that Sadie Katz didn't plagiarize that paper. In fact, she wrote it herself and I wrote my own. And yes, someone swapped my paper with a second copy of hers to make it look like we plagiarized.

I realize this sounds, as you said, absurd, but sometimes the truth sounds closer to a lie. HUMANS WALK ON THE MOON sounded absurd once, but it happened (unless you ask my aunt Kathy. I recommend you don't).

I don't know how to convince you that she's not at fault here. All I can do is present you with the truth and hope that you'll hear it. She was doing me a monumental favor by lying about plagiarizing because the true story didn't sound believable. That's the kind of person she is. And a person that selfless, that noble, and let's be real, with grades that killer, deserves to come back to school and graduate.

I've attached my own version of the essay, including timestamps of when it was written. If you're at all open to discussing this further, you know how to summon me.

In thanks and sincerity,
Cleo Chapman

THE FIRST STEP TO figuring out who I am outside of high school is turning my phone off. At least, that's what Michelle, my new therapist, tells me, and I'm trying to listen to her.

I've been doing a lot of reflecting, in sessions and out. I've spent the past week practically filling a journal, trying to figure out what I want and what I don't. And what I don't want is to go down any more Instagram wormholes, or for Cleo or Mel to influence what I do want. So I let my phone die days ago and tossed it into a dresser drawer.

I'm also kind of, sort of, maybe too depressed to text anyone back. I was so confident walking out of Mr. Simmons's office, but losing school has been hard. Even without my alarm, I wake up at six on the dot some days. I'll stand up and pick out my outfit—and then I remember. When I do, I crawl back into bed, wearing the same big T-shirt I've had on for five days straight.

On the morning of day six, Dad comes upstairs and says, "Get dressed. You need to fill in for your mother." Mom's busy fighting the school board to make sure I don't get expelled. She's told me to stay out of it. For once, I'm fine not picking a fight.

I pull my hair into a bun, because it's the most I can muster. When I head downstairs, Dad's waiting for me. "You have two options," he says, "pull weeds or man the front desk."

Obviously, I choose the latter. I have a sneaking suspicion that that was his plan all along. The front desk is quiet. We do check-ins through text, so it's just a guest coming by every now and then to ask for more towels or a restaurant recommendation.

They ask, I answer. They need, I provide. Kurt curls up in my lap, rubbing his head against me until I pet him. For the first time in a long time, I feel like I have purpose. Maybe tomorrow, I'll untangle the mats in my hair, no matter how excruciating it is.

A guest comes in, trailed by Dad, who's carrying a sandwich and my meds. "I was wondering," the guest says. "What do you think of the Nights of Lights? Tourist trap or worth the time?"

Immediately, my tortuous mind goes to Cleo. "Worth it," I say, pushing the feeling far, far away. "It's truly magical. They even do special horse-drawn carriage tours." I hand her a pamphlet.

She walks away, smiling, and Dad smiles even bigger. "Well, well, well," he says, "looks like I don't have to worry about who to pass the inn on to when we retire."

I could take over the inn, couldn't I? Maybe I will. Or maybe I'll go to med school after all, be top of my class at Tufts. Maybe I'll take an online certification course and start my own business in graphic design, keep the passion Yearbook ignited in me alive.

I'm not sure what tomorrow holds, and I'm trying, with everything in me, not to care. Today, I have a guest in room three who needs a shower chair and one in eight whose TV is broken. I'll start there.

IN EVERY CLASS WE have together, there's a gap. It's like this empty, Sadie-shaped hole where she once sat. Some of our teachers instinctively look to her desk when they ask questions, before remembering she's not there. After two weeks, even Ms. Thomas seems to miss her.

The people who don't miss her still can't keep her name out of their mouths. Rumors are flying so fast I can hardly keep up. I've heard people swear that Sadie was suspended because she set Mr. Simmons's car on fire—no, she drove it into the ocean, let it be consumed by kelp—no, she actually *did* start a fire, but to his house. Apparently, he's living out of a Motel 6, plotting his revenge.

No matter the details, everyone seems to agree on two things: One, the ever uptight Sadie Katz finally snapped. Two, it's pretty cool that she went out with a fire or a drowning or something dangerous in between.

I don't bother spreading the truth. No one will believe it when the lies are more interesting. Even my mom doesn't believe me. She keeps telling me that my "little girlfriend" is a bad influence and I should dump her. But the only person who needs to believe the truth is Mr. Simmons. I've had no progress on that front—and none trying to get in touch with Sadie either.

Every day, I call and text. Every day, I'm ignored. I even went over once, but her dad intervened before I could reach her. He gently asked me to leave, explaining that they were "processing as a family."

After nearly two whole weeks without her, I can't stand it anymore. I walk right past my lunch table and up to Mel. She's sitting alone, sinking down low in her hoodie, like she has been since Sadie left. That must totally suck, losing her best friend in her last semester. Like, who is she gonna attend the famed Seniors Ice Cream Sundae Social with?!

"Is this seat taken?" I gesture to the glaringly empty one where Sadie used to sit.

"I think you know it's not," Mel mutters. All right, too soon for jokes, fair enough. "Sorry, that was rude, wasn't it? I've been on edge since she left. She balances me out." She gestures for me to sit down. I do, but in the seat beside Sadie's. Maybe I'm being dramatic, but it would feel wrong to sit where she sat.

"I get that. Wanna talk about it?"

"I just keep waiting for her. I sit down at lunch, and on instinct, I wait. Then I remember and end up eating five minutes later than I need to."

"Same. Not the lunch thing, but the seat beside me in first period feels so empty. I mean, it *is* empty. But the emptiness is jarring. Is she coming back Monday?" I try to sound nonchalant, like the answer doesn't have the potential to make or break me. I honestly don't know what I'll do if she gets expelled. Chain myself to Mr. Simmons's desk until he changes his mind?

"You didn't hear? They're having a public hearing this afternoon to decide if they should end her suspension or expel her. I got my dad to ask Mr. Simmons about it, and her odds are looking okay. Mr. Simmons wouldn't say much though." She stabs a straw into a juice box far harder than necessary. After hearing this news, I wish I had a juice box of my own to puncture.

"It's public? Maybe we could show up with posters. 'Save Sadie, You Scoundrels!' I'll think of something better than that."

Mel's gaze drops. "Yeah, it's public, but I can't go. I have a track meet I can't miss. It's all such bullshit. Why did it have to happen to *her*?"

"I don't know. I still don't get who would do this to us. Like, what did they gain? And how were they not caught? Everything was right out in the open where anyone could see. The graffiti, the bubbles—"

"The bracelet," Mel adds under her breath.

"Yeah, the bracelet! Why plant it on us when they could steal it?"

"Right? I'm sure they could make a lot off of those diamonds."

"Exactly." I take a bite of lukewarm pizza as it sinks in. She might get expelled *today*. I have to see her. It's nonnegotiable at this point.

Mel takes a long sip of juice. "How does Mr. Simmons not see that she doesn't deserve this?"

"He sees what he wants to see, I guess. And we don't have much proof. I've sent him a few emails, begging him to reconsider, but he hasn't responded."

"You did? That's really nice of you."

"It's only the truth." I shrug. "I've tried to talk to him in person, but the receptionists won't let me in." I'll have to email him again today, tell him that Sadie under no circumstances deserves to be expelled. And I'll tell Sadie herself too. There's no way I'm missing that hearing.

Sadie

THE CONFERENCE ROOM OFF the front office is stuffy—or maybe it's the blazer Mom insisted I wear. After two weeks of not having to follow dress code, covering my shoulders feels weird.

"You've got this," Mom whispers from where she sits beside me at the large, wooden table. I can hear a small audience trickling in behind us, a few students and teachers likely here to witness my downfall. I do my best to ignore them, focusing ahead, where Mr. Simmons and two school board members sit. At least three people hold my fate in their hands now, instead of one.

I try to grasp on to the tiny flicker of hope that this will turn out in my favor. I could spend the rest of my life in St. Augustine, working at the inn, and maybe I'd learn to be content. But I'd like the choice to go further. I may not know what I want to do with my life yet, but I know I want a cap and gown hanging in my closet. I've earned that much.

"Ms. Katz," the woman next to Mr. Simmons says, without bothering to introduce herself, "as you know, we're here to discuss your academic standing. Is there anything you'd like to say before we proceed? Please bear in mind that the board has already conducted an extensive investigation."

So, basically, it's too late to deny anything. What's even the point of holding a hearing? "I've . . . I've worked hard," I say. "I'd like to graduate. I believe I deserve to graduate." I sound pathetic, desperate—but it's the only truthful statement they may believe. I squeeze my hands tight in my lap, sending out a quick, silent prayer.

"The board agrees," the woman says. There's an audible gasp behind me. I nearly let out one of my own. The board agrees? I didn't mishear that, did I? "Thanks to your mother's help, we uncovered proof that you were not, in fact, responsible for multiple counts of defacing school property. You can return to school on Monday."

"However," Mr. Simmons interjects. My heart stutters to a stop. I have a feeling that the other shoe I've been waiting to drop is about to plummet. "You confessed to plagiarizing another student's paper. Therefore, we'll send notice of your suspension and its reason to Tufts University. They can rescind your acceptance if they so choose." There's no *if* here. They won't let me keep my acceptance with plagiarism on my record, there's no chance.

There's more back-and-forth, Mom asking them to hold off on contacting Tufts until she can gather more proof, but I just sit here, stunned. I wasn't expelled. That's something, right? I'll graduate.

I'll probably get some Bs after missing two more weeks of school. I definitely won't be salutatorian, let alone valedictorian, but . . . I'll graduate. The thought of going back scares me, but maybe in these last few months, I can learn to be a different kind of student. Like, the kind who doesn't cry over a 91 on a test.

Mom taps my arm. I look around to see that the room has cleared out. Only her and I are left. "We can fight back," she says. "I *will* fight back. I'll do everything in my power to stop them from notifying Tufts—or to get Tufts to not rescind your acceptance. Whatever it takes, I'm not giving up on your dream."

Tears prick at my eyes. I may be conflicted now, but Mom is right—it was my dream. For years, it's all I've worked toward. And I did it. I got in. But it hardly matters now.

"Thank you," I say, choking back tears. "But . . . I'm not sure anymore if Tufts is right for me," I admit to her for the first time. It's scary, saying it out loud to her, but she doesn't look surprised.

"I had a feeling. You didn't seem very excited when the envelope came in. Why do you think I sent you up there right away? I wanted you to step on that campus and know that you deserve to be there."

"I know I deserve it," I say, "but what if it's not what I *want*? What if I have no clue what I want?"

"Then you're acting like a normal teenager for once," she laughs, "but you should know you're more than capable of going—not just going, but *thriving*."

"I think I could get there eventually. Thriving, I mean. But right now, I'm kind of focused on surviving." I look down at my hands, knowing if I see the look on her face, I won't be able to say what I need to. "It's not that I don't think I can do it. It's that I don't want to hurt myself in the process. I feel like I need more time. Time to work through things with Michelle, time to see how I'll adjust to Prozac once I'm weaned off Zoloft."

I hazard a glance up and see Mom nodding. "I understand. Let me work my magic still, okay? I'll see if I can keep Tufts on the table, and we'll talk through your options. Maybe you could defer. After a year, when you're in a more stable place, it would be waiting for you."

"Mom, there's no way they're not rescinding my acceptance." I appreciate her fighting for me, but we can't argue our way out of this one. It's as good as done.

"I'll try anyway. And if I don't succeed . . . if Tufts *does* rescind your acceptance, you'll be okay. You know that, right? Katz always land on their feet." She leans in, hugs me tight.

I let out a shaky breath that rests at the cross section of relief and distress. I'll be okay if I don't go to Tufts. I'll be okay if I don't go to college at all. I'll say it as many times as it takes to believe it. But . . . "I'm not a failure, am I?" I ask, because I can't help it.

"A failure? At what?"

"You know. Life."

"How can you fail at something you've only just begun?" Mom pulls back, tugging lightly on one of my curls so it bounces. She's the only person I let get away with touching my hair. "I'm gonna see if I can chase down one of those school board members, start pleading our case now. Meet me in the courtyard in a few. We'll get all of your favorites for dinner, I don't care if I have to order from six different places, okay?"

"Thanks." I wait for her to go so I have a minute to myself, to really breathe in the ruling. It's unreal that three people sat across from me and, in a matter of minutes, altered my future completely. And now I have to go out and live it.

Trembling, I stand, walking into the courtyard of the school that's mine again. When I step into the sunlight, the first thing I see is Cleo. Any air left in my lungs is sucked out completely.

"Hi," she says. Her baggy gray T-shirt is speckled with the rain that's now falling lightly. Her hair is messy and windswept. She's gorgeous in a stop-you-in-your-tracks kind of way.

And still, the first words out of my mouth are, "You shouldn't be here."

"Excuse me?"

"I don't want . . . I don't regret what I did. I don't need you here pitying me." The last thing I want is for her to chase the board down and tell them that she's to blame. I already lost my shot at college. She shouldn't lose hers too.

"You think I'm here because I pity you? I'm here because I'm rooting for you. I'm here because you don't get to do this, Sadie."

"Do what?" I pull off my glasses and wipe away a few drops of rain, hoping she won't notice my fingers shaking.

"You don't get to blow up your life, then disappear into the ether like you're Simba in *The Lion King*."

"That's a terrible comparison. Simba ran away because his dad died, he had every reason to run."

"I rewatched it after you corrected me last time. He actually ran away because Scar convinced him—oh, whatever, it doesn't matter! What matters is you don't get to pull away from the people who care about you. You have to know that. You have to know how much I care about you." She takes a step closer to me, reaching out to grab my hand before stopping herself. "Why did you kiss me and tell me to forget it? Why won't you let me be here for you on days like today?"

"Because . . ." I look away, up toward the light drizzle of the sun shower, around for my mom. I'm desperate for an out from this conversation. This limbo we're in is terrible, but it's better than what we have between us being completely, finitely over. Still looking anywhere but at her, I steel myself and say, "Because you have a future. You're going to college, and I refuse to hold you back. I'm a mess, and you're going to be someone."

"That's the most ridiculous thing I've ever heard," Cleo says so angrily it startles me. "What, because I'm going to art school

I'm too good for you? I call bullshit. What's actually going on here?"

Finally, I cave and look into her very sad eyes. I owe her that much. "You deserve someone less fragile. Someone who won't break every time something goes wrong. You're kind and caring and obnoxiously smart, and you deserve someone whose brain is functional. Someone who isn't me."

"Why is it up to you to decide if you're 'worthy' of me? Why don't I get a say?" She holds her hands out, palms facing the sky. "Cards on the table, Sadie. Give me all of them, and I'll decide how I want them dealt."

"Cards on the table?" I swallow hard. If this is what she wants, I'll hand her the whole, daunting truth. Even if I can't give her a stable relationship, I can at least give her closure. "Sometimes, when I'm falling asleep, I'm glad that whoever did this to us, all of the framing or torture or whatever the hell it was, chose me *and* you. Because they forced me to get to know you—and the real you is worth knowing."

"That's it?" Cleo blinks, pulling her hands back and folding her arms like a disappointed teacher.

"Don't make me say it," I whisper, the words barely audible. "Don't make me tell you that I've thought about that one-second kiss since it happened, that when I close my eyes, it's all I see—"

Cleo grabs my cheeks, holds them in her hands, and kisses me. She kisses me like I'm a trainwreck and a hero. She kisses me as if my hair isn't greasy, my lips not disgustingly chapped. She kisses me as I am.

When she pulls back, we're both panting hard. I'm torn between pushing her away, telling her to run while she still can, and pulling her back in by her damp shirt, kissing her until the rain stops and the sun sets.

She wraps her hands around my trembling wrists, holds them in place, and says, "I want this. I don't care if you're depressed. I don't care if you live in St. Augustine forever, or if you leave and get a PhD in molecular physics. I don't care if you cry more often than you don't. I want you. Can you at least give me a chance to prove that?"

I choke back a sob. Maybe, yet again, I was wrong. Maybe I can have this. I can be with her, even if it takes me a while to believe I deserve it. One thing about Cleo, she's patient. She meanders her way to class; she uses every minute during tests. It used to annoy me, but now I think it might be my favorite thing about her. Well, after her lips.

But before I say fuck it and kiss her until I run out of air, I need to make sure she understands exactly what she's in for. "I'm in therapy. I'm lowering the dosage of my medication soon and trying out a new one. But even if I find the perfect combination that makes my brain chemistry more stable . . . depression doesn't just go away. Not ever. There are always going to be days when I come to you crying and broken and scraping together the pieces of my heart."

"I'll have to carry superglue on me then," she says without missing a beat. "It's not the same, but I know a thing or two about pain that never goes away. I'm still all in."

"Okay."

"Okay?" Her jaw drops.

"Yeah. I've never been in a relationship before, so it may take me a bit to believe I'm worthy of one. But . . . it's like you're always saying. I don't have to figure it all out on my own, right?"

Cleo

KISSING SADIE TAKES OVER my whole body. Like, I feel it in my *elbows* of all places. I drop my hands to her waist and spin her around, laughing loudly, not caring who hears. I kiss her forehead, chin, nose, desperate to get my lips on all of her. Sadie laughs, giddy and breathy.

I keep my arms firm around her, refusing to let her slip out of them. I'm not letting her run away from me again, no way. "If you hold me any tighter, you're gonna squeeze my organs out," she jokes.

"Eh, I'd smush them back in." I lean in again, content to kiss her all afternoon, when a throat clears behind us.

We pull away to see Mrs. Katz smiling ear to ear. "Hi, girls," she says. Sadie's cheeks turn bright red—I'm sure mine look the same. "What did I tell you, Sadie? More in common than you think! Would you like to join us for dinner, Cleo?"

"Uh, sure," I sputter. "Great job with getting the suspension lifted, by the way." Mortifying embarrassment aside, I really am grateful for her. Watching Sadie's spot at Tufts be threatened was hard enough. If they'd expelled her, I would have lost it. "The board lady said you were able to prove it wasn't Sadie?"

Mrs. Katz rolls her eyes. "Don't get me started. They shouldn't have needed my help, but Mr. Simmons wouldn't look at the surveillance footage, something about it being a 'security risk.' Isn't that ridiculous? He caved when I threatened to lawyer up. The cameras didn't catch everything, but we could see that horrid hog vandalism, and the— What was it? Oh, the bubbles. We couldn't quite make out who it was on those grainy things, but it was clearly not you."

Wait, what? Sadie and I exchange a confused look. "But the security cameras don't work," Sadie says before I have the chance.

"I agree, they don't work well; they're black and white and fuzzy. It's like a VHS tape; you think they'd be more up to date with all this new technology."

"No, like, they're only for show. I've heard . . . we've heard they're broken and the school can't afford to replace them." Yeah, Mel said . . . no, Mel *insisted* they were broken, didn't she? She said she knew it for a fact.

Mom laughs. "You think I'd send you to a school with no security cameras? In this day and age? No, they have them, that must be a rumor. Mr. Simmons is just so stubborn he wouldn't let me get eyes on them for a week. He kept insisting on 'following protocol,' whatever that means."

Sadie's understandably speechless, so I ask the burning question, "Do you have any idea who did it?"

"Well, like I said, we couldn't identify them because of those awful cameras and because they wore a hoodie that blocked most of their face. It looked like a girl, but she clearly had a different body type than Sadie, on the thinner side. See, what did I tell you when you were younger? These curves aren't a bad thing."

Sadie, clearly having the same thought as me, glances at her lockscreen, at that photo strip of her and Mel. One long sleeve of her signature hoodie is wrapped around Sadie's shoulder. It can't be. It's not like she's the only person on earth who owns a hoodie.

Maybe Mel was mistaken about the cameras. Maybe she misspoke. She wouldn't hurt Sadie . . . would she?

"Can we have our take-out extravaganza another night?" Sadie blurts out, pulling off her blazer and tossing it to her mom. "There's, uh, something Cleo and I have to do."

"Ooh, your first date! Lemme get some pictures before you go."

"Mooom," Sadie groans. I would laugh if I wasn't so terrified.

ONCE MY MOM'S GONE, Cleo and I stare at each other for a solid thirty seconds while I work up the nerve to say it. "What if it's Mel?"

"It can't be, right?"

I wish she sounded more confident, because I just can't. I can't add *finding out my best friend's the reason I might not go to college* to the list of today's emotionally intense events. "Really? You don't think it's a possibility? Even though I spent weeks pointing the finger at Bria?"

"Well, I guess nothing's impossible," she relents. My heart drops even further, my lips trembling. Cleo spots the telltale sign that I'm about to cry and wraps me into a hug. "It's okay. There's an easy fix here. We can talk to her. I've learned that that works, you know."

"Okay. Let's go." I take off to the parking lot without a second thought.

"Oh, we're going now?" Cleo scurries after me.

We're halfway there when I stop short. "Shit! I don't have my car, I drove with my mom."

Cleo raises her eyebrows. "We can ride my bike."

I laugh. "Absolutely not."

"You can sit behind me, and I'll pedal. I've done it with my friends! It's either that or wait for an Uber."

"Ugh, fine." I don't think I can wait one more second. Mel lives close to the school, so it should at least be a short ride. I'm too busy spiraling about her maybe, possibly bulldozing over my future to concern myself too much with the logistics.

"There's still a chance it's not her," Cleo says as we continue to the parking lot. "I talked to Mel about the bracelet theft at lunch today, and she was as confused as us."

"The bracelet?" I ask, my panic rising higher. "Did you bring it up or did she?"

"I brought it up," she says after taking a second to think. "Or wait, no. I brought up all the other pranks, but she mentioned the bracelet. Then I said something about the person benefiting more from selling it, and she agreed because, ya know, diamonds."

My world starts to tilt. Holy shit.

"Sadie? Are you okay? Your face is turning really red."

"I never told her about the bracelet," I say through a grimace. "Telling her would mean telling her about the kiss, so I didn't mention it."

I practically run toward the bike rack, Cleo taking extra-wide steps to catch up with me. When we reach our lime-green ride, Cleo fiddles with the lock while I try some breathing exercises Michelle taught me. This can't be happening. Mel wouldn't. Would she? But why?

Cleo unlocks her bike, and I immediately straddle the seat. She hesitates to join me. "Maybe we should take a minute before heading over. Once you accuse her of this, it's not easy to take back, trust me. We can get coffee and plan what you're gonna say. Mel has a track meet anyway, so she's probably not even home—"

"A track meet? She does *not* have a track meet!"

"Yeah, she does. She said that's the only reason she wasn't coming to your hearing—"

I cut off Cleo again. "I practically have her schedule memorized. We have a shared Google calendar." I pull out my phone and check it just to be sure. Yup, her next meet isn't until next Tuesday. My anxiety's quickly morphing into rage. "Cleo, get on this damn bike and pedal."

"Safety first." She hands me her helmet. As I clip it over my curls, she looks me in the eye and says, "Whatever happens next, I've got you. Just hold tight and tap me once when I should turn right, twice when I should turn left, okay?"

"Okay."

She leans forward and kisses me again, firmly on the lips, like she's trying to instill confidence in me. "All right." She pulls away, climbing on board in front of me. Like she instructed, I wrap my arms around her.

The feeling of her waist comforts me as we ride through St. Augustine. I wish I could just close my eyes until we get there, but I do my job as navigator, tapping once, then twice, then once again. The rain has let up, the sun beating down on us. My heart thumps hard, as loud to me as the cars speeding by.

When we reach Mel's house, Cleo skids to a stop on the driveway and helps me off. As we make our way to the front door, I'm dangerously close to throwing up in her mom's garden. I did that once, when I was nine. We were sitting in her driveway, and I had too many boxes of apple juice and vomited my guts out. The whole time, she held my hand.

It can't be her, can it? She can't be the reason I lost two weeks of school, Tufts, and our shared dream of Boston. She wouldn't do this to me. I ring the doorbell, wait five seconds, then ring it again for good measure. She *couldn't* do this to me.

She finally opens the door, and throws her arms around me. I haven't seen her in two weeks, the longest we've been apart since I went to science camp in eighth grade. "How did the hearing go? Please tell me you're here to celebrate!" When she detaches, she spots Cleo, and her smile nose-dives. "Oh, hi."

"It went fine," I say, trying my best to keep my voice neutral. "Too bad you had that track meet. Awful timing."

"I know, right? I tried to get out of it, but you know how Coach Graham is."

I look back, casting Cleo a glance, like, *Where do I go from here?*

She shrugs, like, *It's up to you.*

Cleo's right, it's not an easy conversation. How do you accuse your best friend of attempting to ruin your life? In the end, I ask the only way it's been asked of me. "I'll give you one chance to tell me the truth up front. If you confess, I'll consider forgiving you."

This is, of course, a lie. If she's really done this—big emphasis on *if*—no amount of groveling or confessing could make me forgive her. I know this about myself, but my heart still smashes to smithereens when Mel drops her gaze and says, "I don't know what you're talking about."

This is the girl who I helped buy a whole new wardrobe when she was going through an alternative phase, who dragged me to the movies to see *Frozen 2* six times. When we laugh about those memories together, her face is shaded by the same shame she's wearing now.

"The tires. The mural. The threatening message. The bracelet. The essays. All of it. Were you involved? I need to know the truth. If you really did this, any of this, you owe me that much. Why, Mel?"

She looks back up at me, and I can see it. She's weighing her options. "Because," she says. One word and she's all but confirmed it.

She knows better than to keep pretending. She knows I'm too smart for that. She knows, because she knows me as well as I know her. I'm the girl who she held as I cried over my first cavity, who she came up with elaborate dances with to convince our parents to let us have sleepovers. And, apparently, I'm the girl she's been sabotaging for months on end. "*Why?*"

"Because of her." She points one shaky finger out, past me, toward Cleo.

"Me?" Cleo turns around, as if Mel could be pointing at someone else. "What did I do?!"

Mel ignores her. "She doesn't deserve to skate her way into the valedictorian spot while you claw your way to every A. It wasn't fair, it never has been. I was only trying to right that wrong. I didn't mean for anything bad to happen to you."

"Why frame us both then?" Cleo asks, because I'm far too speechless to form words.

"I didn't!" Mel yelps. "I didn't try to, at least. It got so out of control, I've obviously never done anything like this before, and I screwed it all up. I never, ever meant to hurt you, Sadie. I just wanted Cleo out of the way—for you! That's why I never fessed up. I wanted your hands to stay clean. Well, and I was terrified you would hate me. Please don't hate me. I really was only trying to help."

I lean against the wall to stop myself from teetering over as I play it all back. She's wrong. We were both framed, weren't we? Except . . . the bracelet was slipped into Cleo's tux jacket, even if I was the one wearing it. The art room was covered in her literal handiwork. And the essay that was copied was mine. Cleo threw the egg at me, like the one in the mural. She was the only one captured in that grainy photo, holding the bucket of water. She's the one who got the weird Instagram message. Fuck, how did I not see it? That just leaves . . .

"Why did you slash my tire?" I need to understand this in its entirety. Maybe if I do, I can find sense in it somehow.

"I didn't, Cleo did. Then I slashed her bike tire. For you, it was all for you." She says it like she offered to carpool to school, not send me to the principal's office three times over and get me suspended.

"For the last time, I didn't slash her tire," Cleo pipes up. "Why would I do that?"

"Yes, you did!" Mel's shame is gone, replaced by anger. Has she always hated Cleo this much? I knew she wasn't a fan thanks to me. There's a reason I've been nervous to tell her about my crush, the kiss. But she's the one who was always telling me not to let Cleo occupy too much space in my mind. Unless . . . Did she say that because she was "taking care of it" for me? The thought gives me full body chills.

"No, I didn't," Cleo says again.

"If you didn't, then who did? Will you stop lying already?"

It takes Mel's glare for the explanation to hit me. When it does, I burst into loud, maniacal laughter. "Oh my fucking . . . It was no one."

"What?" I don't know if the question comes from Mel or Cleo. I can barely hear them over my delirious laughter.

"Nobody slashed my tire. It was probably ripped by the

cobblestone or something. I assumed it was Cleo because I always did. Because it was easier to blame everything on her than admit that life's just not fair sometimes. And I guess it really isn't fair. I mean, I lost two weeks at school and my spot at Tufts over *nothing*."

I let out one more low, deranged chuckle as Mel's face contorts with shock. "You lost your spot? For real? I tried to convince Mr. Simmons it was all Cleo's doing, but he said he'd need more proof. I can't believe this. It was *your* essay."

"What did you think was gonna happen?" Cleo takes a step forward, standing shoulder to shoulder with me. I've only seen her like this twice: in the alley, when Buzz-as-Armageddon accosted me, and the day I took the fall for her. Oh, she's *pissed*. "You can't honestly be surprised that you messed up her future after all the convoluted shit you pulled."

"It was supposed to be *your* future," Mel says, frantic. "It was the pig *you* drew on Sadie's locker that I put on the wall. It was *your* hands flipping off Ms. Blum. Sadie, you have to believe me. I thought you would blame the plagiarism on Cleo and this would finally be settled. She's tricked you into going soft on her. Don't you see that?"

"The only person who's tricked me here is you. I thought you were my best friend." Mel is one of the only people I've ever loved. I can't . . . I can't believe she would do this. I can't believe I have to lose her. When I was sitting shotgun on Cleo's bike, I thought to myself for a split second, *Maybe she didn't do it. Maybe there's a reasonable explanation for this.* I would leave here with no more answers, but at least I would still have her.

"I *am* your best friend." With a quiet huff, she adds, "Even though lately you seem to have forgotten that." Her glare turns toward Cleo again.

"No. Absolutely not. You don't get to act wounded and jealous of Cleo. At least *she* showed up for me today. You faked a track meet to get out of it. Why? So Mr. Simmons wouldn't sniff out your guilt from across the room?"

"I was scared," she says, her lip trembling like she's the victim here. "I was scared it wouldn't go your way, and I couldn't watch that happen. I couldn't watch you get hurt. I didn't mean it to come to this, seriously. I was just looking out for you, like we always do. I know you better than you know yourself. I know what you need, what you deserve. I was only trying to get that for you. Please at least try to believe me."

"You do not know me better than I know myself. Nobody knows me better than I know myself." For years, we've joked that we've shared a brain, but my mind is mine. No matter how messed up it is, how hazy, how often it convinces me I'm unworthy—it's mine and mine alone. "Your intentions don't matter. Not after you tortured me for months when you knew my depression was getting worse. Where can we even go from here? Do you expect a thank-you or something? Yeah, thanks, Mel. Thanks for trying to get my girlfriend expelled. Silver lining, I probably can't get a college degree! Really cool."

"Girlfriend?" Mel and Cleo ask at the same time, one disgusted, the other excited. I know it's too soon for the label, but *crush* feels so elementary.

"Okay, are you sure you're not in love with her or something?" Cleo asks Mel, annoyed. "Like, I get it, she's great, but you're weirdly against us being together. You're not her wife, you know that, right?"

"She's my sister," Mel says, before turning to me with soft eyes. "Can't you see it? She's the same person you've always hated."

"I was wrong to hate her. I was wrong about a lot, clearly," I choke out. One day. In one single day, I've lost my best friend and my dream. I'll find a new dream, sure. But I'll never have another childhood best friend.

"What can I do to make this okay?" Mel asks. She hasn't actually apologized, I realize. Not a single *I'm sorry* has been uttered. Because she's not sorry, is she? She thinks this weird, convoluted scheme was justified.

"Go to Mr. Simmons's office first thing tomorrow," Cleo says. "You can tell him you're to blame, explain everything. Then maybe Sadie's suspension would be struck from the record. Tufts would never have to know."

"I—I can't. I can't give up Emerson. My parents would be so disappointed. My mom and I are going to Italy to celebrate this summer, like we've always planned, remember that, Sadie? It means too much to me, to my family. But anything else, seriously, I want to make this up to you—"

Right here, by this front door I've floated in and out of a thousand times, I punch my best friend in the face.

Cleo

"WHAT DO YOU WANT to do now?" I ask. "Do you wanna talk to Mr. Simmons?"

We're sitting in Sadie's bed, an ice pack positioned on her knuckles. Evidently, she's only ever used words as weapons before. She probably hurt herself more than she hurt Mel. Still, it was hot watching her throw a shitty punch before I dragged her away.

"Maybe? But you know he won't believe us," she says with a sigh. "It would be different if Mel confessed, but . . ."

"But she has to go eat pizza in Florence." I roll my eyes. I'm tempted to head back there for another punch. The *gall* of that girl. Hopefully Mrs. Katz can get Mr. Simmons to listen—but when we got home, Sadie told her parents she hurt her hand falling off my bike. She promised me she'll tell them the truth, but not yet. I don't think she's ready to say it out loud.

"Rome," Sadie says.

"What?"

"We haven't talked about the trip in a while, but I'm sure she's going to Rome. She's always been obsessed with the Trevi Fountain." She looks away from me, toward a picture of the two of them. My eyes catch on my own handiwork beside it: the doodles of Sadie's cats I drew on my notes when she was absent. I smile despite myself. "I don't know how to do it," Sadie says.

"Do what, baby?" The pet name rolls off my tongue for the first time, sweet and natural.

"Unknow everything about her. I don't know how to live a life without her in it."

I'm careful to keep the ice pack positioned on her knuckles as I come closer, wrapping my arm around her shoulder. "I think it'll take time. One day, then the next. Or one hour, to start."

"Yeah, I guess. I just keep thinking . . . how? How could she watch me get suspended and do nothing? How could she listen to me rant about this for months and say nothing? Do you believe her bullshit about having good intentions?"

"I do. It's inexcusable, but I believe that that was her motive or whatever. She mentioned the pig on your locker, you know, the one Bria drew. Mel must have wiped it away—which is terrible criminal mastermind scheming on her part. How is she gonna get me in trouble for something there's no evidence of? Whatever. What I'm trying to say is, she probably wiped it off because she didn't want you to see it. I think in some ridiculous way, she believes she was looking out for you."

Sadie picks up a pillow and screams into it at the top of her lungs. When she's done, she lays her cheek on it and says, "So, what's the point? What's the point of loving someone when something awful like this can happen?" Tears stream down her face. I've lost track of how many times I've seen her cry, but something new breaks in me with each sob.

"I guess to find out if something good will happen instead." A timer goes off, alerting me that Sadie's been icing her hand for twenty minutes. I gingerly lift the ice pack and press it to my aching neck before setting another timer.

For the next twenty minutes, we sit together silently, lulled by the patter of her parents downstairs, the muffled downtown traffic. It's quiet enough that I can hear my own heart, beating out two syllables that Sadie blurted in the heat of the moment: *girl-friend. Girl-friend. Girl-friend.*

I won't ask her today, all things considered. I won't ask her next week, while she's still nursing this fresh wound. But soon enough, I'll make things official. I'll assure her that, yes, I know she's depressed and, no, I don't care.

One day, she'll believe that she's worthy of my love. And in the meantime? When she presses a tearstained cheek to my shoulder, asks me to tell her again that I'm not sick of her crying? I'll just love her anyway.

I pull out my phone, angling it away from Sadie as I text Lily: I did it. I kissed Sadie. & she kissed me back !!!! With everything that's gone down in this whirlwind of a day, I haven't had the chance to celebrate.

Lily responds right away: OMG! Look at u, putting yourself out there yet again. I'm so proud of who you're becoming 💜

Her words hit me hard. Sometimes, I forget that that's something I'm doing—*becoming*, present tense. I'm becoming someone who stands up to my mom, to my future, to Sadie. Maybe in a few months when I go to SCAD, I'll become an artist who does more than draw hands. I can't wait to find out.

"What should we do tonight?" Sadie asks. "I don't know whether to celebrate or mourn, honestly."

"I know what I would do if I were you. Get high and eat a disgusting amount of rocky road ice cream, obviously."

"Wow, we are very different people." She smiles, leaning in to kiss me. I understand that phrase now, *putty in her hands*. Beneath her lips, all I can do is melt.

"What do you need? Whatever it is, I'm here."

"I want . . . I need . . ." She clenches her fists. I recognize that anger, the type that nestles deep in your chest, begging to be let out. It reminds me of the night I stood up to my mom. Sadie deserves that catharsis.

"I know *exactly* what we're gonna do." I stand up, tugging her hand. "Let's go get even."

THIS TIME, I DRIVE us over. After a quick stop at Publix, we arrive at Mel's house with a twelve-pack of toilet paper, now under the cover of nighttime. My first attempt to throw a roll trails pathetically across the grass. "How do you do this?" I whisper-hiss to Cleo.

"I've only TPed once, I'm not an expert! But, here . . ." Cleo stands behind me and wraps an arm around my waist, positioning the other on my elbow.

"Is this actually necessary?"

"Absolutely. So you're gonna wanna angle it up like that. Perfect! Now throw with everything you've got. Make Coach Graham proud." She pulls back, just an inch. I can still feel her breath on my neck, hot and intoxicating.

When I throw again, the toilet paper lands on a tree where Mel and I once tried and failed to carve our initials. We were ten years old and using a pen that was nowhere near sharp enough. Cleo cheers at my victory, but the memory freezes me in place. "Sadie?" she whispers. "Are you okay?"

"No, I'm not. But that's exactly why I need to do this."

Cleo nods and jogs ahead, ripping off the end of the roll and tossing it back to me. We repeat the motions, forming a TP assembly line. I throw, she rips, then throws it back. We're on our third roll when a light in the house turns on—Mel's room.

Cleo and I go still as Mel pulls open the blinds and looks right at me. Her eyes are sad, puffy from crying, I can tell all the way from here. Something tugs at me, the urge to hold her tight and forgive her for everything she never apologized for.

But I can't. She'll never be my friend again, not after what she did. Maybe one day, that fact won't hurt. Tonight, it definitely does, so I lock eyes with her and make a cranking motion with one hand, the other slowly hoisting a middle finger. She closes the blinds as soon as it gets to full form.

"Nice one. Do you think she'll call the cops?" Cleo asks.

"Nah. That would mean having to explain what happened to her mom. She'll probably clean this up in the morning before anyone sees." I sit down on the grass, tugging Cleo by the hand until she sits with me. "Thanks. This was a good idea."

"I'm full of good ideas." She smirks. I can't believe I used to hate the curve of those lips.

"Yeah? Like what?"

"Like . . ." She leans forward and kisses me for the fourth time. When I kiss back, I wonder if that stormy night we were born side by side was always meant to lead here. Then she kisses me some more and I lose the ability to wonder entirely.

Eventually, I pull away, smiling. One day soon, my world as I know it will splinter even more. I'll tell my mom about Mel, and maybe I'll still be able to go to Tufts. Maybe I won't. I'll start Prozac, and maybe it will make me feel better. Maybe it won't. I have no clue what the tomorrows ahead look like, and that's terrifying—but it's exhilarating too.

"So." Cleo locks her hand in mine. "What should we do for our first date?"

I look up at the endless sky above us. "I have no clue," I say. For once, I'm okay not having all the answers.

A NOTE FROM THE AUTHOR

Dear Reader,

I was diagnosed with depression when I was a year younger than Sadie. Over the course of my junior year, I contemplated dying more times than I'd like to admit. In the end, I stayed alive thanks to antidepressants, therapy, and a miniscule shred of hope for what waited for me on the other side of high school.

While I still have depression now, it crushes me when I remember how much I wanted to give up then. If I had, I wouldn't have fulfilled my childhood dream of publishing a book—and then another. I wouldn't have fallen in love with someone who sees me wholly and chooses me anyway. There are friends I never would have met, cities I never would have visited. I wouldn't have discovered my love for ginger ale, which I weirdly didn't try until I was nineteen.

This isn't me saying, "It gets better." You've likely heard that a thousand times, and I won't make it a thousand and one. What I will tell you—at the risk of sounding incredibly vain and quoting my own book—is it gets different. The people in your life grow, and new people join them. The world will keep moving and changing and expanding and you deserve to change along with it. Your heart deserves to heal enough to be broken again.

I suppose at this point, you might be thinking, *Okay, great pep talk, but why am I reading this right now and not another chapter? What happens to Sadie and Cleo?!* I could fill in the blanks for you, detail their dreams that come true and the new dreams they forge together. But the not-knowing is the point. When we're sad and scared and facing pivotal decisions, we have no clue what the outcome will be. All we can do is hold the people we love close and take the next step, then the next, together, like the world's most important three-legged race.

What I can tell you is that there's no magical, fairy-tale ending for Sadie. Depression doesn't work like that, and neither does life. She'll still have days where darkness absorbs all the light. She'll certainly have days when she retraces how the mystery unraveled, desperate to pinpoint a moment that could have changed its certain trajectory.

But she'll also have days when she's at a park basking in the sun, her head in Cleo's lap. Maybe she'll spare a thought for her past self, the version of her that thought school was all that mattered and happiness was a myth. Or maybe she'll be too busy thinking about that new gelato place she wants to check out, the book burning a hole in her bag. Maybe she'll be so busy living that she'll forget, at least momentarily, that there was ever a time she wanted to stop.

RESOURCES

If you're struggling, please reach out to someone you trust. The only way to get the help you need is to ask for it, no matter how daunting it may feel.

If you don't have a proper support system at this time, or if you need someone else to talk to, there are many organizations dedicated to helping you find support, medical assistance, and community. Here are just a few:

988 Suicide & Crisis Lifeline provides one-on-one free counseling services to discuss mental health struggles, alcohol/drug use concerns, or any other emotional distress.

- Visit 988lifeline.org for virtual counseling, or call 988.

DBSA (Depression and Bipolar Support Alliance) has a database of online and in-person support groups. Their support groups are free of charge and include identity-specific groups such as groups for LGBTQ+ individuals, people transitioning out of high school, BIPOC, and more.

- Visit dbsalliance.org to access their database and additional mental health resources.

LGBT+ National Help Center provides one-on-one counseling and moderated group chats for LGBT+ youth to safely make friends.

- Visit lgbthotline.org for hours and information or call 888-843-4564. If you're twenty-five or under, call their youth hotline at 800-246-7743.

The Trevor Project provides free support for LGBTQ+ youth 24/7. This includes safe, online communities to make friends as well as one-on-one, confidential crisis counseling.

- Visit TheTrevorProject.org for more information, or text "start" to 678-678 or call at 1-866-488-7386.

ACKNOWLEDGMENTS

It's probably a faux pas to start my acknowledgments with "first and foremost," but it feels warranted this time. So first and foremost, thank you to my editor, Alex Borbolla, for transforming this book with grace and care. Sadie, Cleo, and I are lucky to have you.

And a million thanks to:

My agent, Jemiscoe Chambers-Black, and the whole team at Andrea Brown for giving meaning to the word *champion*.

My team at Bloomsbury, including: Diane Aronson, Erica Barmash, Faye Bi, John Candell, Alex Card, Tiffany Coelho, Phoebe Dyer, Beth Eller, Kei Nakatsuka, and Briana Williams. I'm in awe of your dedication, creativity, and tenacity.

Ericka Lugo, whose gorgeous covers make me feel like I won the lottery twice.

PAULA GLEESON, whose name is in all caps because it deserves to be shouted from every rooftop. I'll always be indebted to you for the hand you lent me when I needed it most.

Laura Taylor Namey, who ensured this book was set by the water. Learning from you has been an honor.

Darianne Schramm, my fellow Floridian who sprinkled more authenticity into this book. Thank you to the rest of my wonderful crones for shouting and celebrating alongside me. (Darianne, you're not allowed to get a big head for being the only one thanked by name, I forbid it.)

CCC, for your solidarity in a world that left us behind.

Sophia Chang, who changed the trajectory of this book with a single question. And you probably don't even remember saying it, because genius comes to you that naturally.

Jenny Morris, who shares Cleo's almost-birthday and a chunk of my heart. You're like if the *Glee* cast cover of "Teenage Dream" was a person (yes, you're that wonderful).

My parents, for bringing me into this world and making sure I didn't leave it too soon. Thank you, Alison, for the same (except the bringing-me-into-this-world part. Let the record show that she wanted me to "stay in my mom's stomach forever").

Clementine, whose love for me is so unending and unconditional that fiction will never live up to it. Thank you for always choosing me, even when I want to eat popcorn for every meal.

IP, SP, and George for sitting by my side while I wrote.

The songs that served as my soundtrack: "Call Your Mom" by Noah Kahan. "imgonnagetyouback" and "New Year's Day" by Taylor Swift. "Poison Poison" by Reneé Rapp. "lacy" by Olivia Rodrigo. "doomsday" by Lizzy McAlpine. Pretty much everything by Rachel Chinouriri.

Danielle, for seeing me and supporting me sans judgment. Doctors like you give me hope. ALA and the Stonewall Book Award committee for uplifting me and other queer authors even in a world that demands the opposite.

The librarians, booksellers, authors, journalists, and readers who support me and my books. I wouldn't be able to do this without you. Thank you for taking a chance on me and my little lesbians. What an honor it is to take up space on your shelves.

Last but not least, anyone else who's still their saddest self—thank you for sticking around. I hope what's to come is messy and wonderful and nothing you dreamed of on your worst days.